ALSO BY A. J. PINE

THE MURPHYS OF MEADOW VALLEY

Holding Out for a Cowboy

Finally Found My Cowboy

The Cowboy of My Dreams

HEART OF SUMMERTOWN

The Second Chance Garden

Almost One Night Stand

A NOVEL

A. J. PINE

sourcebooks
casablanca

Published by Sourcebooks Casablanca, an imprint of Sourcebooks
1935 Brookdale RD, Naperville, IL 60563-2773
(630) 961-3900
sourcebooks.com

Cataloging-in-Publication Data is on file with the Library of Congress.

Printed and bound in the United States of America.
LB 10 9 8 7 6 5 4 3 2 1

For the Diamond Dogs

CHAPTER 1

Haddie Martin knew she could have driven all the way to Summertown and shown up a day early, but she wasn't ready yet. She wasn't ready to face her best friend, Emma, after quitting her current job, accepting a new one, burying the only living relative she knew, and leaving Chicago now that there was nothing and no one keeping her there. For good? Maybe. The only items left in her studio apartment were a broken barstool and a futon that had certainly seen better days. She didn't know if this was the end for the city that had been home for most of her life. All Haddie knew was that her mess of a life was jammed into the trunk of her car, and when you made a conscious decision to run from the only life you ever knew, even if it was a painful one, you didn't simply face it hours later. You waited until you were forced to unpack it—literally—in a new apartment in a new town where almost nobody knew your name.

Once upon a time, Haddie had life all figured out. Keep everyone at arm's length, and they'll neither disappoint nor hurt you. Simple enough. But even when you painted someone as the monster of your fairy tale, they still somehow crossed your moat of protection and entered the castle gates. So now she was in search of a new castle, this one with higher gates and maybe even an unreachable tower where she would finally be safe. But procrastination was key...along with the key card in her hand that she flipped over and over again as she tapped it on the hotel-lobby bar.

"I'll have whatever she's having," a distinctly male voice said to her right.

Haddie looked up from the card and nonexistent drink in front of her to the woman behind the bar and then to—ahem...make that, looked *way* up to—the tall, broad, dark-haired man poised next to the stool beside her. She raised her brows. "I haven't ordered yet." He shrugged, and it was only then that she realized he was wearing a tux.

"Order for both of us, then," he told her, a grin playing at his lips. "May I?" He gestured toward the stool.

Haddie glanced over his shoulder to the ballroom beyond the lobby, from which she could hear "The Cha Cha Slide" booming even though the doors were closed.

"I don't know," she answered dryly. "Shouldn't you be sliding to the left or maybe getting ready to clap your hands?"

He sighed. "I don't see in the rule books where it says signing up for best man obligates you to line dancing—or any sort of dancing for that matter. And for the record, I didn't even *sign up* for the gig. Apparently, this is a best-friend obligation you're not allowed to say no to."

Haddie winced but then did her best to paint back on her

mask of indifference. How many best-friend obligations was she violating by not even telling Emma that she left a day early but then chickened out halfway into her drive? "Pretty sure they call that being voluntold," she replied, attempting to lighten her own mood.

"Ha!" he said. "Great word. But the guy's my oldest friend. So I accepted my fate. However, I draw the line when the disco ball starts spinning and the line dancers hit the floor."

The bartender cleared her throat.

"Right," the tall, tuxedoed stranger replied, then dipped his gaze to Haddie's.

She pressed her lips together and thought for a moment, impressed that Mr. Tux had still not officially occupied the seat next to her. The decision was hers whether or not he stayed, and it was him giving her that choice that made her say, "Two old-fashioneds. An extra cherry in mine, unless you don't garnish with a cherry?" She looked at the handsome stranger, and his eyes twinkled.

"Two cherries for me too," Mr. Tux added, then finally took the seat next to her.

"Two old-fashioneds and four cherries coming up," the bartender told them, then stepped away to make their drinks.

"A fan of cherries, are you?" Haddie asked him.

He shook his head. "No, but I'm a fan of a woman who likes her bourbon. The cherries are all yours. I'm—"

Haddie held up her hand, and he stopped before saying anything else.

"Look," she started. "We both know what this is, so let's not pretend it's anything else." He seemed like a perfectly nice guy. Probably better than nice. Hell, the groom behind those ballroom doors thought Mr. Tux was the *best* guy, which was all the more reason to leave names out of it. Names equaled reality, and tonight reality was a far-off universe where her problems resided. Tonight was all about escape.

He raised a brow. "What is *this*, then?" He motioned between them, the man in the tux and the woman still wearing the simple black dress she had worn to her grandmother's funeral earlier that day.

"Do you have a room?" she asked.

"You certainly do." He nodded toward the card she still flipped between her fingers.

"You're wedding party," Haddie reminded him. "I bet you have a suite."

He grinned, but then his brows furrowed. "You trust me? Just like that?"

This time Haddie shrugged. "There's a banquet hall full of people who could probably vouch for you, but I don't need to check with them."

"Why?" he asked.

"Because you didn't sit down until you got the signal that I was okay with it. And that, Mr. Tux—which is your name for the rest of the night—means that I am okay with a whole lot more."

His dark-brown eyes crinkled at the corners, and good god, the man was attractive. Had he been that handsome the whole time? Maybe it was the tux. She didn't care. Haddie had stopped outside of Summertown to prolong her escape, and this man who was about to give her his cherries seemed like the best escape she could possibly imagine.

"Two old-fashioneds, *four* cherries." The bartender set down two cocktail napkins and then placed the drinks on top of them.

Mr. Tux immediately grabbed his skewered cherries and deposited them across the rim of Haddie's glass.

"Charge it to Room 801," Haddie's stranger said.

"See? It's a sign I chose well," she told him. "801 is my birthday."

His expression grew pensive for a moment, and then his eyes widened. "August first," he said. "That's—today."

Haddie nodded, swallowing the lump in her throat.

He smiled sweetly. Almost too sweetly, enough that it made Haddie ache for the last birthday she could remember where she felt really and truly loved. She had been five.

Mr. Tux held up his glass. "To you, Birthday Girl. I hope you get everything you want this year."

Haddie pressed her lips into a smile and held her glass up as well. "To me," she agreed, and they each took a sip. Then she set her glass down and reached across the short distance between them, tugging at his already loosened bow tie. A real one, not a clip-on. He looked like James Bond.

"I know what I want tonight." She untied the tie.

"Do you know how many tries it took me to get that right?" he teased, his voice soft and deep. Sexy. Yet the admission also added a hint of endearment to his words.

"I promise to help put it back on if you need to make a final appearance." Haddie nodded toward the ballroom where Sister Sledge's "We Are Family" now boomed.

He checked his watch, glanced over his shoulder and then back at her.

"I'm a dick if I don't say goodbye before they run off on their honeymoon, aren't I?"

The boyish sweetness to his tone now—the best friend not wanting to disappoint—was almost too much for her to take. He'd come out here for a drink and nothing else, and now he was considering disappointing his friend for *her*.

Haddie swirled the liquid in her glass. "How about this? We finish our drinks, and you head back inside for however long you need to. If I'm still here when you make your final exit, then this was meant to happen. If I'm not…" She shrugged. "Then I'm sorry about your tie."

Mr. Tux swirled his own drink. Then he produced a key card from the inside pocket of his jacket, handing it to her.

"I feel like this way I've got a better shot of you not disappearing. You can even raid the mini bar. Drinks…nuts… I think there might even be an eight-dollar Toblerone in there."

He had her at Toblerone.

She slipped both key cards into her purse, slid off her chair, and decided that her old-fashioned was now a to-go beverage.

"I'm eating that Toblerone," she told him.

"Call the front desk for a replacement and eat that one too," he countered. "As long as it means you'll be there when I get back."

She ignored the little cartwheel in her stomach and took a step toward him, their eyes not quite level even with him still sitting.

"Can I…um…do a little pre-assessment to make sure this is a good idea?"

He grinned. "Like a test? I love tests. Straight-A student here."

And without ruminating on how his charm was growing on her by the second, she simply brushed her lips against his, ready to step away just as quickly. But his hands cradled her cheeks and his lips lingered on hers, and dammit she couldn't ignore those extra cartwheels.

"I'm only using you for your Toblerones," she whispered against him, finding it hard to catch her breath.

"Happy to be used," he whispered back, and Haddie swore he sounded just as out of breath as she did. "Wait for me," he added. "Twenty minutes, tops."

I'll wait twenty hours if what comes after the kiss is even half as good.

But she didn't say that. "I can't promise you anything," she replied instead. Because that, at least, was the truth. "Other than—"

"Eating my Toblerone," Mr. Tux interrupted. "I know, Birthday Girl. See you soon."

Holy wow. When Haddie assumed Mr. Tux had a suite, she did not expect a shower *and* a Jacuzzi in the bathroom. Her room had a shower/tub combo, but her five-foot, seven-inch frame would have to sit in the fetal position in order to fit. But *this* tub…

She kicked off her heels and sat on the edge of the porcelain beauty, imagining putting away a Toblerone—triangle by triangle—as she soaked away the events of the past week.

Her brows furrowed. There probably was no Toblerone. At best, she might find a packet of regular M&M's, peanut if the place really wanted to pull out all the stops. But she was in Middle-of-Nowhere, Illinois, a far cry from Chicago. The Jacuzzi was jackpot enough. Still, she rose and padded out to the main area of the suite. "If there's a Toblerone, I'll eat it while soaking in a whirlpool. If there's not? Well, then that's my sign to head down to my room, sleep like the dead, and ready myself for facing reality tomorrow." She paused mid-step. "And the fact that you're talking out loud to yourself should also be a sign that you really need that soak."

She crossed her fingers and toes in her imagination and strode the final few steps to the television-stand-slash-dresser-slash-place-where-hotels-always-hid-the-minibar, paused, and opened the telltale cabinet door behind which she found the minifridge. And behind that, Haddie found a little slice of heaven. Because sitting on the top shelf of the fridge, framing the bags of plain *and* peanut M&M's and the cans of soda behind them was not one but *two* Toblerones.

This had to be a sign, right? The first good thing to happen in a week that had gone to complete and utter shit. Actually…she thought for a moment…

Mr. Tux was charming, painfully good-looking, had a suite with a Jacuzzi, and two Toblerones. That came to four good things.

Maybe her life really was starting to turn around, and all it took was hopping in her car and leaving Chicago behind.

She unzipped her dress and grabbed both Toblerones because who was she kidding? Of course she was going to eat both. Then, as she padded back toward the bathroom, she left a trail across the floor of first her dress, then her bra, and finally her underwear. A few minutes later, she was soaking in the oversized tub, steam rising from the bubbling water as she let her head fall back against the ceramic-tiled wall, a triangle of Swiss milk chocolate and chewy, honeyed almond pieces melting on her tongue.

Haddie closed her eyes and hummed a soft sigh, forgetting this was a stranger's room and simply luxuriating in the knowledge that the world hadn't gone to hell yet, not when Jacuzzis and chocolate existed in the same square footage.

"You waited," a deep voice uttered over the sound of the whirlpool, a hint of incredulity in his tone.

Haddie opened her eyes lazily, broke off another triangle of her first Toblerone, and popped it into her mouth.

"You didn't mention the tub."

Mr. Tux grinned. His untied bow tie still hung from beneath his collar, and he'd unbuttoned the top two buttons of his shirt.

"Didn't know I needed to," he replied.

Her eyes fluttered closed again. "You didn't. But it certainly helped make this a sure thing." Another sigh escaped her lips. "You gonna join me?"

He chuckled, and Haddie looked up at him. Then she looked him up and down, took in his broad shoulders and massive frame, and she laughed too. Because despite the size of the tub, it was still a hotel-sized tub, and Mr. Tux was *not* a hotel-sized man.

Without a word, Haddie turned off the jets and rose from the tub.

9

Mr. Tux's mouth fell open, and she reveled in the power she knew she held in this moment. She needed this. Him.

He cleared his throat. "Do you...want a towel?"

Haddie shook her head and held out her hand. "Just a little help so I don't slip."

"Wait," he told her, holding up a hand. He grabbed the bath mat that still hung over the towel rack on the tile wall above Haddie's head and placed it on the floor beside the tub. Then he took her hand in his, his rough palm holding her tight as she stepped onto the mat. Despite not even knowing his name, the gestures—both the bath mat and grabbing her with a quiet, confident strength— made her feel both safe in his presence and weak in the knees.

It was just a stupid bath mat. Anyone could perform that simplest of gestures, even her late grandmonster...not that the woman would have. Mr. Tux probably only grabbed it so that if she had fallen, he couldn't be somehow held liable or negligent or some other legal term that meant Haddie could sue the guy.

Except she knew this reasoning had more holes in it than a pasta strainer. The man standing before her was a good man. Tonight he was even someone's *best* man, and Haddie didn't dawdle with best men. But she wasn't the type of person to get her hopes up with silly things like happily ever afters.

Ugh. Why did she have to be so clearheaded even after an old-fashioned on an empty stomach? Damned Toblerone, soaking up her bad judgment.

"Are you sure about this?" Mr. Tux asked.

Right. Haddie was still standing naked and dripping in front of him, and he was rolling out a bath mat like it was a red carpet and asking for consent.

She nodded, everything inside her tightening into a coil that was ready to burst.

"But you won't tell me your name, and I can't tell you mine? Wouldn't you enjoy your birthday more if you spent it with someone who at least knew your name?"

"Au contraire, mon frere," she replied in her best high-school-level French, which was a sign she was heading into dangerous territory. Haddie Martin usually brimmed with confidence, but the second someone got under her skin, she began to spout aphorisms or pithy quips—in the language of love.

"At least you're using that absolute waste of a college minor!" her grandmonster would say if she were here. Of course, she wasn't here. Dead people couldn't judge you from the grave.

"But could you be the bestest of best men and fill the ice bucket?" she added. "Thought we might enjoy another cocktail first."

Haddie was sopping wet, naked, and goose bumps were starting to pepper her flesh. In what world would she want a drink when she could have this man's strong, dry body to warm her up?

"You want another drink?" he asked, and she could sense the hesitation in his tone, as if he knew that taking his eyes off her meant the chance that she might disappear.

Haddie nodded and batted her lashes, wondering what might have been if her life were anything other than the mess it was, if she—Haddie Grace Martin—actually had someone in her messy life who laid down bath mats for her and offered her free rein of the minibar.

But Haddie wasn't big on sharing, especially when it meant sharing the burden of her life with someone who shouldn't have to bear it.

"Do you have protection?" she asked.

He swallowed, then let out a nervous laugh of his own. "I feel like this is a damned if I do/damned if I don't sort of scenario. If I say yes, then I'm a fucking cliché, a groomsman hoping to nail a bridesmaid. If I say no, well then…I miss out on what might be a pretty spectacular night."

Haddie snorted. "You did not just say *nailed*."

He winced. "Regretted it the second it came out of my mouth."

She squeezed his hand.

"I like clichés," she whispered. "And mini bars."

"Then I'm a cliché," he whispered back.

They both released their grip, and the second his hand left hers, she felt the absence of it, like something she didn't realize she'd wanted had gone missing.

Shit.

Before he grabbed the ice bucket off the counter, he slung a towel over her shoulders and pulled it tight.

"I'll be right back with the ice," he told her.

But Haddie wouldn't be here when he returned. She already liked him too much, and she didn't even know his name. How much more would she like him—and, what…miss him?—if they actually went through with this? She was in no position to like or to miss or… Ugh. She was a self-sabotaging idiot. That was what this was. So the second the hotel-room door clicked shut, she scrambled to get back into her clothes, but her bra was nowhere to be found.

What the actual…? It wasn't like she'd tossed her undergarments all over the room. Had the bra gone rogue? Skipped town knowing she couldn't chase after it because that would mean running with the girls untethered? She didn't have time to contemplate the universe's plan for her or her bra, so she tossed the dress on sans brassiere, managed to slide back into her shoes, and slipped out the hotel-room door. With the ice machine near the elevator, she had no choice but to bolt in the other direction and take the stairs.

"Please don't let it be murder stairs," she pleaded to herself. But when she pushed the long metal bar on the door beneath the Exit sign, she was greeted with concrete walls, floors, stairs…and a flickering fluorescent light.

Murder stairs.

Haddie clutched her purse (into which she had stuffed the second Toblerone) to her chest—hoping it would do double duty as a surrogate bra—and gripped the railing tight as she raced down to the lobby. Only when she was through the door and in the presence of strangers milling about did she let herself breathe.

She glanced up toward the direction from which she'd come, where Mr. Tux had likely just found himself stood up.

"I'm sorry," she whispered, chest heavy and throat tight. "I'm really, really sorry."

There was no way she could spend the night at the hotel now, not when she might bump into him in the morning. Good thing she hadn't brought anything up to her own room yet. Haddie could simply leave.

So she did, but not before firing off a quick text.

Haddie: Hi. So... I'm about an hour outside of Summertown. Got any rooms at the inn?

Emma's response was immediate.

Emma: There's always a room for you. You okay? Thought you weren't coming until tomorrow.

Haddie sighed and opted for partial honesty.

Haddie: I will be. Once I get to see my best friend. But it's late. You don't need to wait up.

Emma: I'm waiting up.

Haddie smiled and sniffed back the threat of tears.

She never should have stopped at this hotel. She never should have put off the one thing that could help. *Emma.*

Haddie: See you soon.

Emma: Not if I see you first.

Haddie laughed and amended her previous thought. She never should have put off the one thing that could help: Emma and her dad jokes.

CHAPTER 2

"Tell me this is a joke." Levi Rourke ran a hand through his already disheveled hair.

His father held his arms up as if to say, "Ta-da!" and spun slowly, noting the drop cloths covering the furniture and the thin, see-through tarps not at all concealing a couple walls stripped down to the studs.

"Son…" Denny Rourke paused and crossed his arms. "I am a pest-control specialist by trade. Termites are nothing to joke about. I'm sure you can rent a room at the inn. That's where your brother and Emma are staying."

Levi sighed. He was happy Matteo and Emma were back together after all these years, but the last place Levi wanted to live indefinitely was an inn.

"Come on," his father said, clapping him on the shoulder. "You don't want to live with your old man and his girl anyway, do ya?"

Levi swallowed. He was happy for his father too. Somewhere deep down he knew he was. But despite having lost his mom almost a decade ago, it still hurt to see his dad move on, even if logically he knew it was ridiculous to feel that way.

Levi cleared his throat. "No," he admitted. "I suppose I don't. It was only going to be a week or two, anyway. Until I find something permanent. I can't do the inn, Dad. I've got everything I own in my truck out there…" Levi pointed absently toward the front of the house. "I need to sort it all out." He needed to sort his life out. He glanced around his childhood home that was quite literally in ruins and tried to reason with himself that he could live like this for a few days. The fumes weren't that bad.

To prove it to himself, Levi lowered his dust mask, inhaled a deep breath, and immediately began to cough.

"Shit," he muttered, sliding the mask back over his mouth and nose. "I don't suppose you have a laptop available for me to check on current Summertown real estate? Pretty sure mine is buried somewhere in my car."

Despite the mask on his father's face, Levi could tell the older man was sighing by the droop of his shoulders. "Come on over to Tilly's. I've got the whole Sunday paper spread out on the kitchen table. We'll flip right to the real estate section and find you what you need." Denny Rourke squeezed his son's shoulder again. "I know you weren't planning to come back home, but I'm still glad you're here, Son."

If his father was smiling along with his comment, he wasn't doing it with his eyes. Sure, the guy might be happy Levi was home, but everyone knew—meaning every resident in Summertown along with anyone else who followed the world of college sports—that

Levi wasn't simply back for a prolonged visit. He'd been suspended from his position as head football coach for at least a year, and thanks to legal fees and zero income, he needed a job and a place to crash. Thanks to his buddy who was now enjoying his honeymoon, Levi had the job taken care of. But he'd stupidly thought he could just crash at home until something better came along.

He followed his father out of the currently fumigating and partially gutted house and across the lawn to the home next door, pulling his mask off as soon as he hit the fresh summer air. Mrs. Higginson's home. His father's girlfriend's home. Tilly, the name Matteo had warned he'd better use to greet her since they were no longer children who referred to people of their parents' generation as if they were all classroom teachers at Summertown Elementary.

Before he had a chance to try out the name under his breath, the screen door flew open, and out flew the petite and spritely woman, arms spread wide.

"Levi! You're home! This is a wonderful surprise!"

He let out a nervous laugh because they all knew him showing up was no surprise.

The top of her head barely reached his shoulder, but that didn't keep her from throwing her arms around him and enveloping him in a surprisingly strong bear hug.

"Mrs. Higginson!" They were the only words he could produce in the moment.

She pushed herself back and playfully swatted him across the arm.

"Oh, come on now. Your father and I have been together for a little over a year now. You can call me Tilly."

Levi's eyes widened.

Over a year now? He'd been gone long enough for his father to not only start dating their neighbor but to have already celebrated an anniversary?

"Wow," was all he could muster. "Guess I've missed a lot. I'm, uh, sorry I wasn't able to come home after last summer's tornado to help clean up." He cleared his throat. "Or for your back surgery, Dad."

His father waved him off. "You're a busy man."

"Aww," Tilly added, lightly swatting him again. "You can't help being the world-famous football coach. Your father always talks about you being in such high demand. Says rival universities are always trying to poach you."

"Till..." Denny Rourke called from over Levi's shoulder, a note of caution in his tone.

Tilly's smile fell, which meant she'd caught on immediately.

"Right," she continued, answering an unasked question. "Shame what happened at that playoff game. We all have slumps, right? Life can't be one big, ole winning streak." She winced and glanced back at Levi's father, obviously looking for an assist. Levi couldn't blame her. He hadn't exactly told his father the whole story, but the man had surely seen enough of the fallout on TV to get the gist.

The referee made a bad call. Levi called him on the bad call. The ref growled something only Levi could hear, and Levi decked him.

Surprise! He was back in Summertown after a football coaching career that kept on climbing, reaching for the summit, until his harness snapped and Levi hit the ground with an unceremonious thud.

No, life was *not* one big winning streak. Levi had known that since he was in college. The game had been the one place, though, where everything felt right. Until now.

He sighed and let his father and Tilly lead him into the house where he'd peruse the real estate section of the newspaper like it was 1995. As soon as he stepped foot in the kitchen, though, Levi saw Denny Rourke's boxer briefs along with Mrs. Higginson's bras and panties hanging over a wooden drying rack—right beside the kitchen table.

"You know what?" Levi began. "It's a nice day. It's been a while since I've been home. I think I'm just gonna walk around town and—uh—see what I see. People still use For Rent signs, right? There's gotta be something."

After a beat of silence, Denny and Tilly burst into laughter.

"Oh, Den!" Tilly managed while wheezing for breath. "I was so excited to see Levi that I forgot to clean up!"

Levi slapped a hand over his eyes. It didn't matter that he was a grown man in his thirties or that he was no stranger to a woman's undergarments. He'd never be mature enough to handle this. Even if it was only laundry. But the laundry alluded to other things, and he was not in the right headspace to imagine...other things.

Oh god. Trying not to imagine other things only made him imagine other things.

He spun on his heel, eyes still covered, and felt his way back toward the door.

"Come on, Son!" his father called after him, still laughing. "You don't have to leave!"

"I'll call you later after I find a place!" Levi called back, dropping his hand a fraction of a second too late so that his face greeted the front doorframe with a smack.

"Shit!" he hissed, but kept moving even as the spot beneath his right eye began to throb. He thought he heard his father or Tilly ask if he was okay, but he didn't wait to make sure.

To use a sports metaphor other than football, the termites were definitely strike one, and his father and his girlfriend's mixed unmentionables were strike two. He'd venture to guess that a doorframe to the face counted as strike three, which meant he'd been in town for less than an hour so far and had already struck out.

It was time to turn this game around.

He felt like an asshole for what he was about to do, but Levi had no choice. So he pulled out his phone as he began walking toward town past trimmed topiaries and other lawn art that included hubcaps painted to look like daisies or calla lilies. He did a double take when he caught sight of a whole bunch of hubcaps painted and fashioned to look like a topiary of a teacup poodle.

For the second year in a row, Summertown had been the victor in the Twin Town Garden Fest, besting their rival, Middlebrook, with their combination of living and inanimate gardens.

If it went to voicemail, he would not leave a message. But if someone happened to pick up…

"Five-Oh-One! What is up, my friend? Didn't I just see you?" His buddy Tommy Crawford chuckled on the other end.

Despite his state of affairs, Levi always laughed at Tommy's nickname for him.

"Why are you answering your phone on your honeymoon?" Levi asked.

"Why are you calling me while I'm on my honeymoon?" Tommy countered. "By the way, we're in a freaking cabana right now. Someone comes by every twenty minutes to check if we need more drinks. I don't think I'm ever coming home."

Levi groaned. "I'm sorry to bother you. I really am, but…I'm desperate. I mean, I'm heading to town now to see if anyone's got an apartment to rent, but I just have this feeling based on the shit hour I've had back in town that I'm going to be shit out of luck once I get to the square."

"I'll be off in a second, Babe," he heard Tommy say, his voice slightly further away. "I'll head outside so you don't need to listen to us, but it's the Bat Signal, and I have no choice but to answer."

Levi wondered if this was enough of an emergency to interrupt Tommy and Juliana before they'd barely had a chance to get out of town, but it was too late now. The damage was already done.

"Right," Tommy continued, addressing Levi now. "Where were we?"

"I won't keep you. Just… Does your dad still have that apartment to rent?"

"You mean the one above the hardware store where you'd get to see yours truly each and every Saturday and Sunday? The one he wanted to rent to you, sight unseen, and you said thanks but no thanks? Yeah, I think Principal Crawford still has the place."

Levi groaned, slowing his pace as he neared the town square. He could see the tall, painted sunflowers on the tree stump that survived the tornado the summer before, and the new, *live* ones—heads tilting up toward the sun—framing the square.

"He already gave me a job. I thought I'd have a couple weeks before the season began to get my bearings…and maybe I wasn't ready to put my tail between my legs."

Tommy chuckled. "You know this isn't like college, right? He can't hire you to just coach. You'll have to teach too."

Levi waved him off, even though Tommy couldn't see him. "Sure, yeah. I know. P.E. How much harder can it be than what I do on the field?"

"And your license is up to date?"

Levi laughed. "Someone's sounding an awful lot like their father these days. Yes. The license is up to date. And just because I've never actually done the classroom thing doesn't mean I forgot everything I learned in college."

That might have been a slight embellishment. But, like he said, how hard could it be?

"Yeah, yeah," Tommy replied. "I've been doing it for ten years, and it still kicks my ass. Talk to me after the first week is up, and tell me if you still feel the same. Otherwise, I think the shop could use someone else behind the register during the week. Speaking of which, the man in question is filling in for me today, so if you pop over right now, I bet you can start unpacking within the hour."

Levi sighed, already feeling a weight lift from his chest.

"You're the best, Commissioner. I owe you one."

"No way, man," Tommy replied. "*You* sent the Bat Signal, and I saved your ass. I think that makes me Bruce for the foreseeable future."

"You're *not* Batman!" a female voice called somewhere in the distance on Tommy's end.

"Shit," Levi's friend added. "I gotta go. We'll celebrate when I get home."

"Didn't we celebrate last night?" Levi asked.

"We'll celebrate your new place and new job, and..." He paused. "It's a good thing," he continued, the playfulness leaving his tone. "You coming home. Try and see it that way."

And there it was again, the pressure on Levi's chest that had been there since the university let out last spring and he knew he wouldn't return in the fall.

"Yeah," he replied, trying to force a smile into his voice. "Of course it is. Thanks for the help, Bruce."

"Any time, Five-Oh-One. I better get back to the cabana."

Tommy ended the call.

Levi glanced down at his attire, a gray T-shirt—now damp with sweat—and red basketball shorts. Fine for hauling boxes, but what about appealing to your new boss for a place to live? Sure, he'd known Principal Crawford all his life, but while Tilly Higginson saw Levi as a grown-ass adult who should call her by her first name,

Principal Crawford had been Principal Crawford—presiding over the elementary, middle, and high school divisions of their tiny district—since Levi and Tommy were in sixth grade. He had been Coach while Levi went to Summertown High School and Principal Crawford the few times Levi got himself into some trouble. Those two monikers were the only options. He and his best friend's father were not and would never be on a first-name basis.

He could jog back to his truck in his father's driveway and try to fish out something else to wear, but he only had access to the formal attire he'd had on last night, and he'd look like more of an idiot walking into a hardware store in that.

So, he squared his shoulders and strode on, mustering the confidence he once had on the field during any number of games.

A bell jingled the second he pushed open the door to Crawford's Hardware and the man in question looked up from a newspaper spread across the checkout counter.

Seriously? Just like his dad, Coach obviously preferred the printed word to up-to-the-second news.

Was the universe trying to tell Levi he was too reliant on his phone, or was the fatherly vibe just permeating the air today?

"Mr. Rourke," Tommy's father crooned with a grin. "To what do I owe the pleasure?"

A muscle in Levi's jaw pulsed as he tried not to bristle at the title of *Mister* rather than being recognized as a fellow coach himself. Then again, he was a disgraced coach who was lucky to even have a job at this point, and that job was thanks to the man in front of him, so beggars couldn't be choosers, or he wouldn't bite the hand that fed, or whatever other proverb fit his current predicament, especially since he was about to ask for more.

"Coach!" Levi replied, striding forward with his hand outstretched. "It's good to see you."

The older man gave Levi's hand a firm grip and a hearty shake. His salt-and-pepper hair used to be brown, but the guy was probably more fit than others half his age. Levi wondered if he still ran drills with the teams.

Tommy's father narrowed his eyes. "You're not here to turn down that job coaching the varsity soccer team now that our Student Services Department has already printed the schedules, are you?"

Levi laughed, even as the thought of a schedule that included anything other than running football plays on the field made him a little nauseous.

"No," Levi assured him nervously. "I'm grateful for the opportunity. I just kind of have another favor to ask you."

Coach Crawford crossed his arms over his chest and smiled at Levi with bemusement. "Another favor, huh?" He scratched the white stubble on his chin like they were simply talking about the weather.

Then Levi grinned. "Wait… Tommy put you up to this, right? He texted you I was coming to ask about the apartment and told you to make me sweat it."

Levi crossed his arms too, both of them in a typical coach's stance as they eyed their team on the field. Only Coach Crawford did not return the grin. Instead he sighed.

"I hate to burst your bubble, Rourke, but I've already got someone upstairs looking at the apartment right now."

Levi swallowed. "Your place is one of the few available immediately, isn't it?"

Coach Crawford raised his brows just as the bell jingled over the door behind Levi and a woman spoke as she approached.

"I'd love to take it," she started, setting a ring of keys down on the counter. "But it's a little out of my budget. I guess—"

Holy shit.

"*Birthday* Girl," Levi said, and the woman's whole body froze, hand still on the counter, palm covering the keys.

Or maybe he should have said Birthday *Ghost*.

He hadn't been angry that she'd left. They were strangers, and maybe she'd gotten cold feet. No way in hell he'd fault her for that. But the *way* she'd done it, sending him for ice so she could disappear without a word? What if something had happened to her? What if... What if... What if he could just admit that being ghosted like that kinda stung? Levi traveled a lot as a coach and was no stranger to hotel beds and hotel guests. But despite her insistence on not disclosing names, something about their short time together had made him think last night might have been different. But he'd been the only one to feel that, right? Otherwise she would have at the very least left a note.

Levi rolled his shoulders, attempting to shake off what he was sure was nothing more than a bruised ego.

The woman finally let go of the keys and smoothed nonexistent wrinkles from a fitted pink-and-black running top and matching leggings. He recognized the Under Armour logo and couldn't keep the corner of his mouth from turning up at this tiny connection to his football world.

She pivoted slightly and finally met his eyes.

"Um, hi, Mr. Um…Tux." She bit her bottom lip and winced, then mumbled something that sounded like "Merde."

She hadn't been wearing *anything* the last time they'd seen each other. But he wouldn't remind her of that in front of Coach Crawford.

"Do you kids know each other?" the older man asked, eyeing them with raised brows.

"No!" the woman exclaimed, maybe a little too emphatically for someone who borrowed his Jacuzzi and took off with sixteen dollars' worth of Swiss chocolate. He figured this warranted acknowledgment that they had—at the very least—met.

"Oh," Coach Crawford replied. "That's a shame, seeing how the apartment is a two-bedroom, and if you needed to offset the cost, you could rent it as roommates. I mean, you will know each other eventually since you'll both be working for the Summertown School District and coaching the boys' and girls' high school soccer teams. At least for the next year, that is." He raised a brow and gave them both a knowing look. Levi wasn't exactly sure what the guy knew. "Of course, when I say 'roommates,' I mean roommates. With this next year being particularly important to both your futures, I trust none of us want any sort of…entanglements…that could get in the way."

Her eyes widened, and her mouth fell into an *O*. Then she took a giant step back as if horrified at the thought of not only being his roommate but *also* having to work with him.

"I'll take it, Coach," Levi told him. "But you're right about those entanglements. I don't think I need to split the rent." He actually could really use the help with the rent. But...no. Not with her. They were already—entangled. He shrugged, eyes still on the woman in front of him, and reached for the keys on the counter.

"Damn," Coach Crawford interrupted. "Would you look at that? I forgot to take my lunch break. I'm going to head on over to the inn for a quick bite. Go on up and take a look before signing on the dotted line if you'd like, Rourke. I'll be back in an hour."

Levi and his stranger from last night watched as Coach Crawford strode out from behind the counter and straight toward the door, flipping the sign to *Closed* as he marched out into the early-afternoon sun.

"Nice to see you again, *Dash*. I'm going to go check out my new apartment." Levi moved to step around her, but she burst into laughter.

"Oh my god!" She pressed a palm against her stomach, still laughing. "Did you just change my nickname to the speedy little kid from *The Incredibles*?"

Levi halted mid-step and scratched the back of his neck. And for a second, he didn't know which made him cringe more: letting on that he'd been at all affected by her vanishing act or that he'd somehow revealed that he was a thirty-two-year-old man who clearly recalled character names from Pixar movies.

"Wait!" she added, holding out her hand as if to stop him. "I'm sorry. I shouldn't tease, and maybe I shouldn't have snuck out on you without a word last night, but my head really wasn't in the right space for what we were... You know? But I am desperate here. My friend Emma's family owns the inn, and they offered me a room at a great rate, but I can't live there. I need my own space that I can decorate and make feel like home, and…" She squeezed her eyes shut, fisted her hands at her sides, and blew out a long breath. Then she met his gaze again. "I have nowhere else to go," she admitted, all amusement gone from her expression. "I need this apartment, but I can't afford it on my own. Please, please, please split the rent with me. I'll take the smaller room. I'll share my Netflix password. I'll—"

"Okay," Levi told her, no sign of his bruised ego in sight. Instead he found himself wanting to erase that look of worry from her hazel eyes.

"Really?" she beamed, her eyes turning glassy as she exhaled a shaky breath.

Levi sighed. "Really," he replied, knowing that if they actually did this, they'd both have to put last night behind them. No way he was messing up this job opportunity or the much-needed recommendation he'd need from Coach Crawford for reinstatement to the NCAA.

"But what almost happened last night?" she added. "That can't even get close to happening again. Like…ever. I do *not* date men I work with."

Levi sighed. Good. They were on the same page. It didn't matter that he could still picture her in that black dress she wore at the bar…or *out* of the dress as she climbed dripping out of his tub. From here on out, they were colleagues and roommates, and that was it.

"Like, *never*," he countered. "But I do have one condition." She nodded slowly, and he continued by extending his hand. "We need to introduce ourselves. I'm Levi."

Her lips parted into a soft smile as she took his hand.

"Nice to meet you, Levi. I'm Haddie."

CHAPTER 3

E mma followed Haddie into the small bedroom, dropped a box
labeled *Running Gear* on the floor, and then spun to peek out
onto the rest of the apartment from Haddie's bedroom door.

"Oh my god," Haddie whispered, grabbing Emma's elbow.
"You are the least subtle human to ever human!"

"I hear cheering," Emma whispered back. "Do you think they're
watching bachelor-party videos to plan for Matteo's? Do you think
I should worry?"

Haddie snorted. "Are they going to Vegas?"

"No. They're doing a pub crawl through town, which basically means hitting up two entire spots, including the inn," Emma
replied. "Matteo doesn't even drink. But you never know."

Haddie rolled her eyes and then popped her head out next to
Emma's to find Matteo and Levi standing at the breakfast bar in
front of Levi's laptop.

"Whatcha guys watching?" Haddie asked.

Matteo turned toward the two women and laughed, winking
at Emma.

Levi pivoted quickly to face them as well, and Haddie swallowed, telling herself that the stubble on his unshaven face was not sexy and that seeing him like that every morning from here on out would not be an issue.

"Um… Coach Crawford sent some video files of last year's team so I could get an idea of what I'm starting with."

Haddie nudged Emma with her elbow. "See? Just a coach doing what coaches do." She offered Levi a salute. "As you were, gentlemen." Then she turned around and winced at her utter lack of coolness, pulling Emma back into her bedroom.

Emma closed the door behind her and leaned against it with her arms crossed. "You took a bath and cleaned out his minibar?" Emma whispered back. "Matteo's brother? My soon-to-be brother-in-law!"

"Shh!" Haddie hissed, then grabbed her friend's wrist and pulled her away from the door as if that would keep Levi and Matteo from hearing them through the apartment's thin walls. "I didn't *know* he was Matteo's brother. And also, I did not clean out his minibar." She shrugged. "I took what I wanted and left the rest." Then she gasped, climbed around and over the boxes stacked all over the small room's floor, found her purse, and inside the purse, found her bounty. "Look!" she exclaimed. "The second one! Only the best commercially produced chocolate in the universe, and I'm about to share it with you."

The two women dropped down onto a tiny clean patch of wooden floor. Haddie tore open the long triangular package, ripped off the top half of the foil, and broke off a chunk of her prized possession, handing it over to her friend.

Emma accepted the offering eagerly, popping the whole thing into her mouth. "I know you plying me with chocolate is a redirect, so I won't belabor the fact that you're still attracted to Levi, and it's almost working," she mused. "But I might need one more bite."

Haddie popped a piece of chocolate into her own mouth and then broke off another wedge for Emma. If she had to buy her friend's silence, she'd do it. "He's my roommate and my colleague now. And you know I'd never date a guy I worked with. Again."

Haddie had tried that. Once. She thought that she and Collin, a fifth-grade teacher at her former school, were on the same, casual, let's-have-fun-until-this-runs-its-course page until he sprang a surprise meet-my-parents brunch on her on a random Sunday morning. That was when she knew she had to end it.

Emma sighed. "Poor Collin. I hear he still puts your photo on every New Year's vision board."

Haddie rolled her eyes. "He does not. I think he actually got engaged right before I left."

"Aww," Emma crooned. "Good for Collin. But Levi... I mean, how great would it be for me and Matteo if the two of you did actually hit it off?"

Haddie scoffed. "Oh, so this is all about you?"

"Absolutely," Emma admitted. "And Matteo."

"Ems, as much as my goal in life is to make all your dreams come true, I won't know if I'm hired back for year two until I make it through year one, so whether or not I find your almost brother-in-law attractive doesn't matter because our relationship now is 100 percent professional and...platonic." Emma raised her brows, but when she opened her mouth to retort, Haddie blurted out, "Moratorium! I'm instituting a moratorium on who I am or am not attracted to, and in exchange I will bestow upon you the great honor of coming furniture shopping with me." She gestured around the room.

Emma sighed. "Fine." She pursed her lips and thought for a moment. "You'll get hired back after a year. You're too good at what you do."

Haddie huffed out a mirthless laugh. "Principal Crawford said the last person in my position, who I guess wasn't born and raised in Summertown like everyone else on staff, didn't have the town's best interests at heart. Thanks to her, I have to prove that I do."

Emma snorted. "The last person in your position was a seventy-eight-year-old con artist who embezzled field trip money so she could buy an Oscar Mayer Wienermobile. So unless you start cruising around town in a giant hot dog, I think you're probably safe." Haddie shrugged, but Emma opened her mouth to continue. "So, I have one more question before we go, and I promise it has nothing to do with your pupils turning to hearts when you look at your roommate."

Haddie groaned and pushed herself back up to standing, holding an arm out for Emma. Then she pulled her friend to her feet.

"Why Toblerone?" Emma asked.

Haddie opened and closed her mouth. That wasn't the question she'd been expecting. "Because I love chocolate?" That was a perfectly acceptable response, right? "I am human," she added.

Emma raised her brows. "And those who don't like chocolate are not?"

Haddie scoffed. "Obviously."

"Okay," Emma continued. " I've never seen you eat a Toblerone. I feel like I should have seen one or two or ten whenever I came to your apartment."

When Emma still lived in the city. When Haddie felt like she still had some semblance of family, thanks to her friend.

"For example..." Emma pointed to her T-shirt, which sported the images of three potted flowers and read, *I Wet My Plants*, a pun and homage to Summertown, famous for its award-winning topiaries and gardens. "I not only love my punny tees, but I wear them almost every day."

"Yeah, we need to talk about that," Haddie replied with mock concern. She loved her friend's quirk and that she wore it on her sleeve...or at least the front of her tee.

Emma held her hand out for more chocolate, and Haddie pouted, yet ultimately obliged.

"It surprises me not that you came here with zero furniture but somehow managed to wedge your treadmill into your back seat. So why is your love of this—I don't know—airport delicacy a complete mystery to me?"

"*Ding! Ding! Ding!*" Haddie tapped her nose and grinned at her friend. But then her smile fell as the fragment of a memory settled in.

Emma's expression morphed to mirror Haddie's, as if she felt it too.

"You okay, Hads?" Emma asked.

"Yeah. It just reminds me of a trip I took with my mom once,"

Haddie told her. It was the last image of her mother that was seared into her brain, her breaking off a triangle of the Swiss chocolate treat and handing it to her as they sat next to each other on an airplane.

"Did your grandma never get it for you?"

Haddie shook her head. "My grandmonster? Nope. From the time I was six years old she pretty much ignored anything I said."

Emma gave her a sympathetic nod. "Do you...want to talk about your grandma? I still wish you would have let me come for the memorial service."

Haddie pressed her lips into what she hoped resembled a smile. "Nope," she replied again. "I want to get a bed, though."

Emma narrowed her eyes. "Oh, we'll get that bed, my friend. But mark my words. You're on my home turf now, and Summertown is a place where people talk. To each other. About their feelings. If you're going to live here, you're going to have to abide by our rules."

Then she grabbed Haddie's hand. "You know I just want to make sure you're okay, right?"

Haddie nodded. "I'm okay. I promise. But know that in my rusted Tin Man heart, I do appreciate you worrying about me."

"You do not have a rusted Tin Man heart," Emma insisted.

"For everyone but *you*. And my students. I'll miss those little six-year-old clouds of dirt, germs, and potential. But you have the same brand of first graders here, don't you?"

"Yes." Emma laughed. "Probably even dirtier if they're getting an early start on their topiary trimming skills."

Haddie smiled, and then they made their way back into the

main living area where the two brothers were still staring at Levi's laptop.

"Who's coming furniture shopping?" Emma called, and both men turned around. "Matteo, I volunteer you since we need your truck."

Matteo grabbed his fiancée's wrist as she approached, pulling her to him and kissing her on the top of the head. "I go where you go," he told her.

Haddie sighed. "You guys are so cute it's gross. I mean that as a compliment."

She tapped Levi on the shin with the toe of her flip-flop. "What about you, roomie? You gonna join us?"

Haddie looked down, suddenly not sure about making eye contact with him. *Ugh. Fine.* Emma was right. It wasn't like attraction just went "Poof!" and disappeared once you decided not to sleep with someone. Their chemistry or whatever it was would run its course soon enough.

Levi cleared his throat. "Um…no. You all go ahead."

Haddie's relief was capped off by an unexpected twinge of disappointment. She glanced into his room full of nothing but boxes, just like hers. "Not a big fan of beds, are ya?" she teased but immediately regretted the words as soon as they'd left her mouth because saying them only made her think of the hotel bed they had almost slept in.

"I'm actually a very big fan of beds," he countered. "But I ordered one of those mattress-in-a-bag things online. It should be here in a day or two." He turned his attention to his brother. "Dad said Tilly has an extra couch in her basement we can use, so I'm going to head over there and take a look, see if it will fit. But you three have fun."

Once out the door, Haddie let out a breath. Of course things would be weird until they got used to each other, until they found their stride. Focusing on all the parts and pieces of moving and quickly furnishing an apartment before school started would keep them busy enough to forget about what almost happened.

"Shit," she said before they'd even made it to the stairs. "I forgot my phone. I'll meet you at the truck." And while Emma and Matteo headed down to the street, Haddie jogged back toward her new front door and strode back through it.

Levi swore and slammed his laptop shut.

Haddie rounded the corner, brows raised and a bemused smile on her face.

"Levi Rourke, did I just interrupt something…scandalous?" She had no idea what he might have started watching once the rest of them had left, and she truly didn't care. He was a grown man. He could watch what he wanted. But something about the look of abject horror on his face made her want to poke the bear. Levi Rourke had a secret, and she wasn't leaving this apartment until he confessed.

"What's on the laptop?" she asked.

"I thought you left," he countered. "What are you doing here?"

"I forgot my phone," Haddie replied. "There. I answered you. Now you answer me." She took a step toward him, and he stood in front of the laptop on the breakfast bar, his big, broad body blocking any chance of her stealing it from him.

Haddie shrugged. "I'm not leaving here until I know you're not partaking in any illicit affairs that might be unbecoming to a new roommate."

His dark eyes blinked more than once. "I'm not even sure what the hell you just said."

She threw up her hands. "Come on, man! Just show me already. Otherwise, I'm going to walk out of here thinking the worst, and then I'm going to have to ask Emma and Matteo if they know what's going on, and next thing you know, whatever is on that laptop becomes the talk of the town, which, depending on what's actually there, will either bode very well or very badly for you. At least now it's just me, and you're not afraid of little old me, are you?"

Levi scrubbed his hand across his jaw and swore again. Then he spun toward the breakfast bar, flipped open the laptop, and the screen immediately awoke to show a still from... *Ted Lasso*?

He turned back to face her, crossing his arms and leaning against the counter, a muscle pulsing in his jaw.

Haddie's brows drew together. "Why wouldn't you want me to know you were watching *Ted Lasso*? It's a great show."

"One of the best," Levi agreed.

"Are you Team Roy or Team Jamie?" she added.

"Team Keeley gets to make her own damned choice," he countered, quicker than she'd expected.

"Good answer," Haddie mused, taking a step closer as the pieces fell quickly together. The videos of last year's team made sense. This added another layer of complexity. "But something tells me that Keeley's empowerment to choose herself over the two men who aren't quite worthy of her isn't the reason you're squeezing in a rewatch while we're out furniture shopping."

Levi groaned. "You're really going to make me say it, aren't you?"

Haddie shrugged, then closed the distance between them, picking up the laptop that was paused on Coach Lasso in the locker room with his players, probably in the middle of an epic pep talk about being a goldfish or believing in themselves as a team. She glanced from Levi to the laptop and then back at Levi again.

"You don't know a thing about soccer. Do you?" she asked.

He pulled his arms tighter, his biceps clearly straining against the sleeve of his T-shirt. A muscle pulsed in his jaw as his eyes met hers, and his lips—lips that had kissed hers and lit a fire within—forced themselves into a pained smile. "Not one goddamn thing," he admitted.

CHAPTER 4

Levi surveyed the myriad nuts, bolts, and screws, the various Allen wrenches and other parts and pieces that lay scattered across Haddie's bedroom floor after they'd finished putting her bed together.

"This can't be right," he mumbled, more to himself than as a conversation starter.

Haddie leaned back against the estate-sale dresser she, Emma, and Matteo had snagged on their day-long furniture quest. "But we followed the directions, didn't we?" she asked.

"I don't know," he replied with a groan. "My Swedish is a little rusty. I was just going by the diagram."

Haddie winced. "And I was just going by you going by the diagram." Then she paused for a beat. "Is the bed going to collapse in the middle of the night, fall through the floor, and send me plummeting into Crawford's Hardware store and to my imminent demise?"

Levi rolled his eyes. "No one's plummeting to their demise."

"Says the man who can't read Swedish. It might say right there on that paper"—she pointed to the one page of directions like it was sitting on a witness stand, perjuring itself in a court of law—"that if parts remain after assembly is complete, those parts indicate a clear sign that the sleeper will meet her demise in the middle of her slumber."

Levi shrugged. "And it might say 'I don't like pancakes.' But I guess we'll never know."

Haddie's mouth fell open. "That was just a random example, right? You don't really *not* like pancakes."

He blinked. "I don't...what?" He couldn't keep up. She was making him dizzy. But the good news was that since they'd embarked upon the Swedish furniture project, they'd been so zeroed in on the work that Haddie hadn't once asked him about the *Ted Lasso* debacle since she'd caught him red-handed earlier that day.

"That pancake thing. With the directions," she reminded him. "You were just using that as an example of what the directions might say because they could say anything. But you, Levi Rourke, do not have it in for pancakes... Do you? And before you answer, you should know that Emma's cat who loves me dearly—and the affection is mutual—is named Pancake."

Levi opened his mouth to respond, then closed it and paused for a beat. "Can I not like pancakes without it also implying that I don't like a cat I've never met?"

Haddie crossed her arms. "How can you not like pancakes? Or Pancake? What did a delicious breakfast treat or a sweet little tabby ever do to you?"

He held up his hands. "Nothing!" he replied with a laugh. "I have nothing against Emma's cat, and as for your delicious breakfast treat?" He shrugged. "It doesn't do anything for me." He laughed again, something about this ridiculous conversation lifting a weight off his chest. They could do this, the whole being roommates thing. They could build furniture together, and she could tease him and make him laugh.

"There's a why," she replied.

"A *why?*" he countered.

"A why," Haddie repeated. "And I'm going to get to the bottom of it."

He scoffed. "Can't a guy simply *not* like pancakes?"

"No." she answered.

"No?"

"*No.*"

Levi looked at his watch. "It's late." And he had his first preseason practice in the morning, which meant he had more studying to do that night. "You want to test it out and make sure you're not going to plunge to imminent death?"

Haddie sighed. "Fine. But I'm not done figuring you out."

Levi climbed to his feet and then held a hand out for his roommate. When she took it, he ignored the pulse of electricity that passed from her hand to his. It was nothing more than muscle memory following two strangers meeting in a hotel bar. Nothing more. Because they weren't really strangers anymore, and the hotel bar? If they both wanted to succeed in the new positions they hadn't officially started yet, it might as well have never existed.

"Thanks…roomie," she said, a little breathless as he pulled her up from the floor. Then she cleared her throat. "There's a story behind the pancakes," she added. "Isn't there?"

He dipped his head toward hers, their hands still clasped. "There's a story behind the Toblerone, isn't there?" he tossed back at her.

Haddie yanked her hand away and gave it a shake. "You're right," she replied, and for a second Levi thought she was about to confide in him until she added, "I should test it out." And then she flopped back onto her new mattress and frame that Levi hoped wasn't missing any crucial parts. When she didn't crash through the floor, he let out a breath until she popped back up and cried, "Wait!" She grabbed him by the wrist and gave him a swift yank, catching him off guard and causing him to stumble over his own two feet and fall over a newly sprawled Haddie, his hands braced on either side of her head as his body hovered over hers.

She stared at him, wide eyed, as the two of them froze, no one moving a muscle or so much as exhaling a breath.

Was she waiting to see if the extra weight proved her theory about imminent death? Or was she—like him—instead anticipating a much slower and more agonizing way to perish? Because Levi was pretty sure the sweet, citrusy scent of her shampoo or perfume or whatever it was that made Haddie smell like something he thought he knew but couldn't put his finger on was going to be the end of him. She smelled like…like the first day of summer vacation had always made him feel.

"We're not plunging," Haddie finally croaked. "I...um...think we've proven the efficacy of our furniture-building skills."

"You're right," he ground out, his voice rough. Then he held his breath, a momentary reprieve from the intoxication of her scent, and climbed off the bed and back to his feet.

Haddie pushed herself up to a sitting position. "Sorry about that," she said, her cheeks flushed. "Maybe next time I want you to jump in bed with me, I'll give a verbal cue instead of yanking you into the sack without warning." She let out a nervous laugh. Was she making jokes for the hell of it? Or was she fighting the same distracting thoughts he was fighting? Not that the answer mattered. Levi's professional reputation was riding on how this year played out. He couldn't afford any missteps.

"As I was saying," he began, deciding not to entertain any thoughts about what she might be thinking. His thoughts were his, and her thoughts were hers, and he needed to simply walk out of her bedroom door and clear his damned head. "It's late. I should get to bed. And by bed, I mean the air mattress in the middle of the floor in my room." He laughed.

Haddie did too, any tension that had been building between them finally on its way out. "Yeah. Me too. Thanks for your help tonight, Levi."

"Of course," he told her. "That's what roommates do, right?"

He kept rolling the word around on his tongue as he said good night and headed toward their shared bathroom to brush his teeth before collapsing onto his makeshift bed.

Roommates. Roommates. Levi hadn't had one since he was an undergrad and didn't suspect he would until he found the right person and settled down. Except Levi wasn't the settling type. He preferred to be on the move...on the go...never truly setting down roots. Because the only roots he had were here in Summertown, but so were his memories of grief and loss, which was why this... situation would only be temporary.

He was finally uncomfortably propped on his air mattress, laptop open to his next episode of *Ted Lasso*, when his phone lit up and vibrated with a text.

Birthday Girl: Asleep?

Levi found himself smiling before he even picked up his phone.

Levi: Nope
Birthday Girl: Do you think we should establish some ground rules?

Levi's brows furrowed.

Levi: For...
Birthday Girl: For being roommates
Levi: Is this something you do with all your roommates?
Birthday Girl: Never had one. Had a single my first year and then was an RA after that. New territory for me.
Levi: So... I'm your first?

He laughed and swore he could sense her roll her eyes and sigh. And then he watched the three dots appear and disappear several times before her next text came through.

Birthday Girl: There has to be a bathroom cleaning rotation. A bathroom using rotation. And there's the issue of the toilet seat. Vacuuming. Taking the garbage out. And then there's groceries. Meals. Do we eat together? Separately? Worry about ourselves and only ourselves? Are we friends now? Can we strike last night from the record and start from scratch?

First of all…whoa. That was a lot to take in. And second, there it was. That last sentence. The question he knew she really wanted to ask and the one that had been on his mind since the second they agreed to live together. Levi would never forget that night, but he could pretend. He had to, didn't he?

Levi: And you want to discuss this now? At 11:30 p.m.?
Birthday Girl: It's gonna keep me up if we don't. And since we're both still up…
Levi: What if I was busy?
Birthday Girl: Shit! Sorry! Forget I texted. We can talk tomorrow.

His pulse quickened as he fat-thumbed his response and sent it quicker than he could think.

Levi: wiat no not buay!

Three dots appeared and disappeared again. He waited for an interminable minute, finally exhaling when her text came through.

Birthday Girl: You're a terrible speller
Levi: Or just in a hurry to make sure you didn't go

Shit. What was he doing?

Levi: We're friends, Haddie
Birthday Girl: Ok
Birthday Girl: Just friends
Levi: Just friends

He typed the words quickly but making sure he spelled them correctly. And when he pressed Send, he felt something sink in his gut. Of all the hotel bars in all the world during all the weddings she could have semi-crashed, why did it have to be Tommy's?

Birthday Girl: I can teach you, you know.
Levi: Teach me what?
Birthday Girl: Everything you're trying to learn from Coach Lasso the night before your first practice. I played in high school and college. Promise I know more than the actor on the screen.

Levi groaned.

Birthday Girl: Swallow your pride, Coach. Consider it repayment for helping with my bed tonight. That's what roommates do, right?

He sighed not only because she was right but also because he was pretty sure he'd fall flat on his face without her help.

Levi: Okay. But I'm already halfway through Season 3. I can't NOT finish at this point.

He sent the text and held his thumbs above the keypad for several seconds before adding...

Levi: Wanna watch? If you can't sleep?

As soon as he hit Send, he knew it was a misstep. You didn't proposition a roommate to watch *Ted Lasso* at almost midnight, did you?

His phone rang with a FaceTime call from Birthday Girl, and Levi almost threw it across the room. But he managed to compose himself before the call rang out and pressed the green video button to answer.

"What are you doing?" he asked.

Haddie's sideways smiling face—she was lying down—looked back at him.

"We can watch together like this," she told him. Then she walked him through setting up the app so they could watch in sync because why would Levi have known how to do that? He'd never watched TV late at night with anyone before, let alone remotely with someone else.

"I love this episode," she told him with a sleepy sigh when he finally pressed Play. "Jamie teaching Roy how to ride a bike is my Roman Empire."

He laughed. "I thought you weren't Team Jamie or Roy, that neither deserved Keeley."

She hummed in response, a sweet sound that made him wonder if she was dozing off. "Doesn't mean I can't appreciate the beauty of their friendship."

They watched in silence after that, and when the episode ended, Levi also ended SharePlay. Before he could ask Haddie if she was still awake, he saw her sleeping face on the screen, and his chest seized at the sight. He was lying on his side now too, and it was like she was there on the other side of his mattress, close enough to touch. Except no one had ever been further out of his reach.

He swore softly to himself, which made her stir. Then he swore again before quickly ending the call, the image of her beautiful, peaceful, sleeping face branded in his memory.

His Roman Empire.

———

The next morning, Levi woke up early to the sound of someone moving around in the living room. It took a second to register before he remembered that he did not live alone anymore. He had a roommate…a roommate who fell asleep watching *Ted Lasso* with him on FaceTime like it was the most normal thing for her to do while he lay awake for a good hour or so after silently cursing himself for how much he enjoyed it.

He got dressed and made his way out to the kitchen, where Haddie was already brewing a pot of coffee.

"Good morning," she said with a smile.

"Good morning," Levi replied, returning her smile.

"Stayed up later than I meant to last night, so I think I'm saving my run for when I'm with my team today," she told him.

He glanced down at absolutely nothing on the floor and scratched the back of his neck. "Sorry if I… I mean, you should have said something about your morning runs if—"

"Don't be silly, roomie! Coach Lasso is always worth a little sleep deprivation," she interrupted, all cheer and zero awkwardness while Levi felt like…like what? Like they'd had some special moment watching TV?

That's what roommates do, dumbass. Hell, you coined the phrase. Now get out of your feelings and get your head in the game because you are hitting the pitch for the first time today.

"Wait…" he continued. "So, we both have practice this morning?"

Haddie nodded. "Nine to noon for me. How about you?"

"Same," Levi replied, brows furrowed. "So our camps are running at the same time? Does that mean we have to split the field?"

Haddie shrugged as the toaster dinged, and she slid out a toasted

English muffin. "Hope you don't mind," she told him, slathering peanut butter over the golden tops of the muffin. "I'm famished and have, like, zero groceries anywhere. I'll go shopping later today after I pop back home to shower."

Levi watched Haddie as she took a bite from her muffin, smearing a bit of peanut butter on the corner of her lip. He stifled a groan and shifted his weight, trying to will away the sudden urge to wipe it clean with his thumb. Or worse, with his tongue. That definitely wasn't something friends or roommates did, was it?

"What?" Haddie asked. "You're looking at me like my fly's undone. Spoiler! There are no zippers on soccer gear."

He only realized now that she was wearing a purple Muskies soccer jersey paired with fitted black running shorts. Jesus, she wasn't playing fair.

Get it together, man!

"You just..." he started. "You have some..." He rolled his eyes and pointed to the corner of his own mouth. "You have some peanut butter—"

Haddie gasped. "Oh god. I eat like a slob, don't I?" She scooped away the glob of peanut butter with her thumb and then licked her thumb clean.

"Yep," Levi said stiffly. "Total slob."

She grinned, oblivious to his inner turmoil that he *knew* was just a physiological reaction to a woman who—friend or no—was objectively attractive, and he'd just have to get used to it.

She polished off the rest of her muffin in record time and filled a travel tumbler with coffee.

"I'm gonna head out," she told him. "See you there?"

She moved toward the door as he poured himself a cup of coffee, her energy and maybe a bit of haste giving him whiplash.

"Wait!" he called after her. "Should we, like, drive together or something? I mean, we are going to the same place."

"Nah!" she called back. "It's beautiful out, so I think I'll walk." She popped her head back around the corner and into the kitchen. "But if the field is free after we're done with the kids, maybe we can scrimmage."

He coughed as he tried to swallow his first mouthful of coffee, hot liquid dribbling out of the corner of his mouth in a display he was 100 percent sure was not as sexy as the recent peanut butter incident.

Haddie covered her mouth, clearly stifling a laugh.

"Sorry!" she cried with a wince. "I know it's going to take some getting used to the fact that your peanut-butter-mooching room-mate knows more about your new job than you do, but I promise to make our time together as painless as possible."

Levi swiped his forearm across his mouth, which for sure made him look like a caveman, but he was who he was, and Haddie should probably know that from the start.

"Sounds like a plan," he told her, forcing his mouth into the best version of his postgame press conference smile. "See you there."

"See you there, roomie!" she cried, with so much pep and vigor that Levi decided she was the most morning person to ever morning. "It'll be great. I just know it!"

And with that, she was out the door before he could reply.

Would it be great? Did she really know it? Because the only thing Levi knew was that he knew *nothing* about navigating this new friendship and crossed his fingers they'd figure it out together... after he hid any future peanut butter jars.

CHAPTER 5

The sun was barely peeking over the horizon as Haddie stepped onto her half of the football (and today *soccer*) field with her clipboard in hand, a smile plastered on her face. She breathed in the crisp morning air, reveling in the excitement that filled her chest. Soccer camp had always been her favorite lead-up to the start of school when she was a teen, and now she had the opportunity to instill that same excitement in her own team.

Although it didn't escape her that her zeal this morning at the apartment might have been a tad over the top. But she wasn't sure how to act in front of Levi after what felt like a weirdly intimate evening the night before even though neither stepped foot out of their own room after the bed assembly that concluded with Levi accidentally straddling her. They just needed to find their rhythm, and if that rhythm meant Haddie skedaddling before Levi had a chance to drink his morning coffee so she wouldn't think about that accidental straddle every time she looked at him, so be it.

"All right, team!" Haddie clapped her hands together, catching the attention of her players as they ambled onto the field, not quite as bright-eyed as their coach. "I'm Coach Martin, and while I want to get to know each and every one of you today, let's start with a warm-up and show 'em what we're made of! Stretch out and gimme four laps around the track!"

Despite several yawns and a few groans at being asked to run a mile first thing in the morning, Haddie's team hit the track and did as they were asked. When she dropped her clipboard on the bench and *joined* them, she was met with a few raised brows, a few whoops and claps, and even a shout of, "Coach Martin is for *real!*"

This was a *much* better start than the whole peanut butter incident. *Ugh.* She knew they'd eventually learn the less curated sides of each other's personalities, but the key word here was *eventually*. Not morning one! She hadn't anticipated transitioning so quickly from sexy stranger at a bar who stole his Toblerone to woman who can't eat without smearing food all over her face like a toddler.

Haddie averted her eyes as they passed the boys' coach taking roll on the other end of the field. It was hard enough trying to navigate how to act around Levi now that they lived together and apparently watched late-night television together as well. But she hadn't anticipated coaching on the field beside him in addition to teaching in the same district. For all intents and purposes, they'd gone from complete and total strangers without even know each other's names to basically spending every waking minute together. And…in her case…every not-so-waking minute.

How long had she been sleeping on their video chat before he finally ended it? And was she snoring? At least Levi had been nice enough not to mention it.

Mon dieu, she thought to herself, then picked up speed. "Who's going to beat me to the finish line?" she cried, looking over at her shoulder as she pulled ahead of her entire team.

"Smoke her!" one girl cried. "We can't let some old lady show us up!"

Old? Haddie's inner voice screamed. *OLD?* If these young women thought barely thirty-one was old, they were in for a rude awakening in the not-too-distant future.

Haddie only had one choice. She *had* to win. So she broke into a sprint as they hit lap two, and from there, she thought about nothing other than her breathing, putting one foot in front of another, and making sure she maintained the lead until lap four came to a close.

She crossed the finish line at least a half a minute before anyone else and found herself greeted with applause, whistles, and whoops from the entire boys' soccer team *and* their coach.

Haddie slowed to a backward jog as she watched her own team, one by one, stream in behind her. "Any one of you athletes want to call me old again?" she challenged, ignoring the stitch in her side and the burn in her lungs that came from forgoing her own warm-up.

Her team members answered her with belabored breaths and hands pressed against their knees as they tried to collect themselves. She wasn't sure who made the original comment, but judging by the way one of her athletes stared daggers at her with arms crossed, her pinched brows fighting against the pull of her tight, dark French braids, Haddie had a guess.

"That was pretty savage, Coach Martin," Levi mused, striding up beside her. "And impressive," he added. "I barely made it through roll call on my roster before you clocked an entire mile."

Haddie swallowed, trying to lubricate her throat enough to speak since her water bottle was all the way over on the bench, and she seemed to be stuck in a game of chicken with the girl in French braids, neither daring to break eye contact first.

"I either really impressed them," she finally replied. "Or just made eighteen new enemies."

Levi laughed. "Good thing you still have the better part of three hours to figure it out." He nudged her shoulder with his own. "I'll take the south end of the field," he told her, nodding toward the opposite end of where they stood.

Haddie squinted as she noticed one lone member of Levi's team who had *not* joined the rest to gawk at the *old* lady racing a pack of teens. He dribbled a soccer ball between his feet, occasionally bringing it up to volley from one knee to the other.

"Who's that?" she asked.

"According to my roster, he's a senior named Billy McMannus, but all I got when I called his name was a grunt, so I took it as acknowledgment that he was the guy on my list. According to the not-so-tight-lipped rest of my team, Billy is an ace player who rarely gets off the bench due to frequent academic ineligibility." Levi shrugged. "Not really sure what to make of that."

Haddie finally relinquished the staring contest to turn toward her fellow coach. "Don't let other people tell his story. School year hasn't even started yet. My advice? Try not to label him before you're even sure of his name." Her words came out harsher than she'd intended. She saw a muscle pulse in Levi's jaw, but when she opened her mouth to apologize, he beat her to the punch by grabbing the whistle around his neck, turning back toward his team, and blowing loudly to get their attention.

"Track's all yours, gentlemen!" he bellowed. "If you're waiting for an invitation to hit the pavement, consider yourselves invited!" He blew the whistle again. "Move! Move! Move!" he shouted. "Do *not* show up back to the field until you hit a full mile in equal or *less* time than it took Coach Martin's team!"

As his team snapped to attention and broke into sprints, Levi turned back to Haddie and gave her a curt nod. "Thanks for the advice, Coach," he told her, his voice gruff. Then he strode past her onto the field and headed toward Billy McMannus, who either hadn't heard or, more likely, had ignored his impossible-not-to-hear coach.

Two hours and plenty of dribbling, shooting, and passing drills later, Haddie was ready to split her team for a nine-on-nine scrimmage. Sure, it wouldn't be a full team match, but it would give her athletes a chance to challenge each other and give their coach the opportunity to see who worked best in which position. But when a soccer ball whizzed by her from center field, headed straight to where Sarah Ramirez—the name of Haddie's staring contest opponent—had dropped to a squat to tie one of her cleats, Haddie froze but only for a beat. Her heart thumped against her chest as the ball hurtled toward Sarah's head. In a split second, her instincts kicked in, and without thinking, she sprinted toward

Sarah, pushing her out of the way while simultaneously blocking the ball with her torso.

She collapsed onto her back with a grunt, ball hugged to her chest as a crowd gathered around her.

"No goal," she croaked, then heard a whistle blow in the distance.

"Holy shit!" someone remarked.

Haddie squinted, the sun obscuring her vision.

"Language," she squeaked, still catching her breath and assessing the damage. Her ribs ached, but nothing felt broken.

Finally letting the ball roll out of her grasp, she pushed herself up onto her elbows. A figure extended a hand to help her up, and Haddie gripped it tight, letting whoever it was pull her to her feet.

"Sarah!" Haddie remarked with surprise. Loose grass tangled with the student's disheveled left braid, the side on which she must have fallen when Haddie pushed her out of the way. Other than that, the girl looked no worse for the wear.

Jogging toward them with his team in tow was Levi, though she noticed a limp in his gait as he approached.

"McMannus!" Levi barked. "I think there's something you want to say to Coach Martin."

A tall, lean-muscled kid with a mop of sandy hair hanging over his eyes shrugged and nodded toward Haddie.

"Nice reflexes, Coach Martin," he told her in a low, deep voice.

Haddie picked up the ball and tossed it back to him. "Nice shot," she replied. "Just not quite nice *enough*."

A chorus of *oohs* and *aahs* rang out among both teams. Levi opened his mouth, but Haddie caught his eye and shook her head. She didn't know what Billy McMannus's story was either, or why he shot that ball at an unsuspecting player, but they weren't going to figure that out here and certainly not now. The only thing they could assess at the moment was how well their first day of camp had gone.

"What do you say we work this out on the field, Coach Rourke?" she challenged.

Levi's eyes widened. "You mean a scrimmage?" He leaned a little closer. "Right now?" he added, only loud enough for her to hear.

Haddie laughed. "The *kids*," she clarified.

Levi cleared his throat and straightened. "Right. Of course. I knew that."

Haddie shrugged. "It's better than splitting my team in half and not having enough players on the field. You're not afraid of a little friendly competition, are you?"

More *oohs* and *aahs* erupted from both teams as Levi considered her. Something flashed in his eyes before a smile spread across his face, and Haddie could have sworn that for a split second, he *was* afraid of the challenge. But why?

"You're on, Coach Martin." He lifted his visor from his head, ran a hand through his disheveled hair, and then pulled the bill back down to shield his eyes. "May the best team win."

Haddie winked at him. "Oh…we will."

They shook hands, Haddie's eyes twinkling with mischief. "My girls are ready to give you a run for your money."

"Is that so?" Levi raised an eyebrow, the corners of his mouth turning up in a grin. "Well, I guess we'll just have to see about that."

"Guess so," Haddie agreed, smiling. As she watched Levi walk back to his team, she couldn't help but feel a pang of sympathy for him. He came home to coach football, and he'd been given the school's soccer team instead. Her pang didn't last long, though. Because when it came to the sport she loved—and to proving herself in a new job, at a new school, in a brand-freaking-new town— Haddie Martin wasn't pulling any punches.

"Remember, team," Haddie called out as her first eleven players took their spots on the field, her voice laced with determination. "It's all about teamwork and communication!"

"Let's do this!" Levi echoed, his gaze meeting hers for a brief moment, and there it was again, the flicker of uncertainty before he blew his whistle, signaling the kickoff.

Despite McMannus's powerful kick that sent the ball hurtling toward Haddie's team's goal, Levi's team fumbled on the field, their lack of coordination and communication evident in every missed pass and misstep. Haddie watched intently, her gaze sharp as she studied their movements. The sun cast playful shadows on the grass beneath them, but the actual *playing* sent a whole new pang straight to Haddie's heart—*guilt*.

Billy McMannus might be a power forward, but other than that, Levi's team was a mess. As soon as Haddie's team gained possession of the ball, it was only a matter of seconds until they scored their first goal—before the other team's goalie even knew what happened.

They were going to annihilate Levi's team, which would *not* bode well for anyone's spirit the very first day of the season.

"Time out!" Haddie cried after the teams began to reset following the goal. "Coaches'…um…coaches' conference!" she added, then grabbed Levi's elbow and pulled him onto the track.

"What's going on?" she whisper-shouted.

"What do you mean?" he replied through gritted teeth, which told her he knew *exactly* what she meant.

"*Levi.*" She backhanded him on the shoulder. "That was *not* soccer out there. That was… That was…"

"The *worst*," he admitted. "They're going to get their asses handed to them."

She threw her hands in the air, keenly aware that all eyes were on her wild gesticulations and that all ears were probably straining to hear what they were saying. She knew *Levi* knew nothing about soccer, but she couldn't believe Coach Crawford tossed him a team where almost every player seemed to know even less.

He lifted his visor again and scratched the back of his neck. Sweat glistened on the dark hair at his temples.

Why, of all thoughts that could possibly be roaming around in her head right now, was she thinking about how the combination of a sweaty, frustrated, vulnerable Levi was one of the sexiest things she'd ever seen?

Shut. Up. Brain. This was a man in crisis with a *team* in crisis, and Haddie wanted to help. Instead she found herself wondering where else he was sweating and how a man like him might like to— *ahem*—work out his frustrations.

"Your players need to work on their positioning. They're bunching up too much, making it easy for my team to intercept the ball," she blurted out, forcing her thoughts back toward soccer.

He nodded once. "Are you coaching me, Coach?" he asked, but he wasn't smiling, and Haddie couldn't gauge his tone.

She crossed and uncrossed her arms, then cleared her throat. "Don't you *want* me to coach you?"

"I thought it was going to be one-on-one," Levi replied. "If my team finds out…" His voice trailed off as he lowered his visor back on his head and mirrored her crossed-arm stance. "I'm a good coach," he assured her. "And I know the basic rules. But I know football better than I knew my own name. I can coach it in my sleep. Hell, sometimes I do. I'm not used to…uh…" He sighed. "This is going to make me sound like a real asshole, but I'm not used to *not* being good at something." He winced. "See? *Asshole.*"

Haddie laughed. "It took some very *non*-asshole vulnerability for you to even admit that, so I'm going to have to disagree, Coach Rourke. Tossing the asshole call out." She shrugged. "Sorry to disappoint you." She took a step closer, just to make sure no one trying to eavesdrop could hear what she said next. "Look, if we keep up this scrimmage like we're doing, my team is going to wipe the floor with yours. But if you follow my lead, let me give you some pointers, I think we can give your guys a fighting chance to hold their own."

Levi held out his hand, and Haddie gave it a firm shake.

"Deal," he told her.

Haddie grinned, then grabbed the whistle around his neck, tugged it between her lips, and blew. "Let's play!" she called toward

the teams still waiting on the field. Then, whistle still in her hand—
and still wrapped around Levi's neck—she glanced at her fellow
coach whose eyes were still squeezed shut.

She winced. "That was loud, huh?" she asked.

Levi nodded.

"And I didn't give you any warning, did I?" she added.

He shook his head.

"Should I step away now?" Haddie asked with a nervous smile.

Levi finally opened his eyes. He raised his brows as he stared
down at the instrument of ear torture still pinched between her
thumb and forefinger.

"Right!" Haddie dropped the whistle. "Sorry!"

He shook his head and let out a rueful laugh. "I can't believe
you did that."

Haddie snorted and backhanded him on the shoulder, and Levi
laughed too. Just like that, they'd somehow leveled the playing field,
pushing Haddie's less-than-roommately thoughts into the recesses
of her brain.

Together they pivoted back toward the field and strode toward
their teams.

"Today we'll focus on positioning and studying your opponent," she told him as they strode toward their teams. "No one is
so good yet that they need to be double-teamed or anything like
that. So tell your defense to follow whoever they are guarding rather
than the ball and to study that player's strengths and weaknesses.
Tomorrow we'll work on passing. Wednesday, setting up and running plays. Thursday, we'll record our scrimmage, and Friday we'll

kick it off by watching and analyzing the recording. Sound like a plan?"

Levi stopped mid-stride and stared at her for a long moment.

"What?" she asked, stumbling to a halt herself.

He shook his head. "Nothing," he told her with a grin. "Just—"

"Are we playing or what, Coach Martin?" Sarah called from the girls' team's goal area.

Both coaches jogged toward center field.

"Okay, folks!" Haddie called as they approached. "Bring it in for a second!"

Both teams jogged toward the center, forming a huddle on each side of the center-field line.

She nodded toward Levi. "What's our focus today, Coach?"

Levi's eyes widened, but then he clapped his hands together, and she watched him morph to laser-focused. "Today is all about covering your opponent and your spot on the field. Worry about the ball when it comes your way, but worry about your counterpart every second you're out there. Got it? Study their strengths and weaknesses and *learn* from them. We'll start tomorrow's camp by demonstrating one thing we learned from our opponents." He blew his whistle. "Positions!"

The players scattered back to their positions, and Haddie gave her opposing coach an appraising nod.

"Nice work, Coach!" she called as she backed toward the sideline.

"Thanks, Coach," he replied with a wink that, had it come from anyone else, would have been cheesy as hell. But from Levi, she knew it was an acknowledgment of what she'd done for him and his team.

"Thanks, Coach!" a group of students—some from *each* team—parroted in a singsong tone.

"You guys are *super* cute together!" one of Haddie's girls added.

What Haddie would have given for a whistle of her own at that moment, but it didn't matter. Nothing was going to burst her bubble today, certainly not a few know-it-all teens who actually knew *nothing* about Haddie and Levi at all.

A warmth spread through her, but this was different from getting hot and bothered by a sweaty, frustrated man. It felt almost like it did when she saw Emma the first time after she'd left Chicago to move back to Summertown. It felt like…affection. For a friend.

So she had a hot roommate. She could live with that. Because she could also tell that he was a good guy, and the kind of friend she wouldn't mind having as she navigated the start of a new life.

"May the best coach win," she told him as they took their positions on the sideline.

Levi nodded. "She will."

CHAPTER 6

evi and Haddie hadn't crossed paths since they drove to campus earlier that morning, and he felt inexplicable relief when he filed into the high school gymnasium to find her sitting with a group of who he guessed were other elementary teachers. He didn't recognize a single one of them from all the high school meetings he'd been in that day.

"Looking for someone?" a voice questioned from behind, and he spun to find Tommy Crawford grinning back at him.

"Commissioner!" Levi exclaimed. "When did you get back in town?"

The two men shook hands and gave each other their usual dude pat on the back.

"Got back late last night. Figured if I was going to do the honeymoon thing right, it meant not dragging my ass back to town until I absolutely had to."

"That was cutting it close, don't you think?" Levi asked his friend.

Tommy shrugged and crossed his arms over his chest. "Teacher in-service and back-to-school night." He sighed. "I'd have cut it closer if I could have, but this was as close as I could get."

Levi laughed. "Come on. A day full of impractical meetings and busywork followed by your dad getting behind the podium to welcome everyone back? What's not to love?"

Tommy groaned, his ever-present grin dimming for just a moment. "You say that as if you know what it's like to have endured it for the past ten years. You're just getting started, my friend."

"Mr. Rourke...Mr. Crawford...how nice of you two to hold up traffic while the rest of the faculty are trying to enter."

Both men spun to find Tommy's father, the man in question, with his brows raised and a stern look on his face. He and Tommy looked so much alike yet couldn't be more different.

They both had brown eyes, the same wavy hair, though Tommy's was sandy-colored where his father's had more salt than anything else these days. They even had the same square jaw, the same winning smiles. Yet Coach Crawford prided himself on the number of trophies he continued to add to the football showcase in the school's entryway while Tommy's speech and debate medals got tucked away in a shoebox in Tommy's childhood bedroom.

Levi and Tommy moved out of the way of the other teachers filing in, and Coach Crawford followed them.

"Sorry about that, Da—" Tommy started but then course corrected with, "I mean, Principal Crawford."

Levi clapped a hand on his friend's shoulder. "I just haven't seen Tommy since the wedding, so we were catching up."

Tommy's father appraised them both and gave them a curt nod.

"How about you two finish catching up in the bleachers with the rest of the faculty. Announcements are starting soon."

"Sure thing, Coach," Levi replied.

"Sure thing, *Coach*," Tommy mimicked, though Coach Crawford either didn't notice or didn't care as he strode off toward the podium that faced the home-team side of the bleachers.

"Yikes," Levi said when Tommy's father was a good enough distance away. "After that speech he gave at your wedding, I thought things were better between you two."

Tommy scoffed and scrubbed a hand across his visibly tanned face. "Coach sure knows how to work a crowd," he admitted. "But the second he sees me on school grounds wearing civilian clothes instead of a coach's polo?" He raised a brow at Levi. "He asks himself the ever-present question of, 'Where did I go wrong that my son turned out like *this*?'"

Levi shook his head and laughed. "Like what? The only teacher in the entire district who has received the Illinois Teacher of the Year award…twice? The only teacher…I hear…who comes up as the most requested when students are filling out their schedule requests for the following year? Or the only coach I know to have smoked his debate opponents *every* time at the state debate meets?"

Tommy laughed. "Okay, now you're just being an asshole to embarrass me."

But Levi shook his head. "You're hot shit, Tommy Crawford. You don't need to throw a pigskin across a field to prove that to anyone." But something in his chest squeezed. Levi believed the words he said to Tommy, but it took Tommy years to believe it about himself, that he could still be *hot shit* in a coach's polo rather than pads and a helmet. Now here he was, knocked down a peg again, a true fish out of water where he used to be king of the ocean.

"Thanks, man." Tommy shrugged, thankfully oblivious to Levi starting to spiral. "Somehow, though, I don't think he ever got the memo. Good thing he always had you around to fill the void, right?"

Tommy smiled as he said the words, but Levi could feel the bitterness behind the grin. Is this what he'd missed being gone for so long? His best friend still feeling less than in his father's eyes all these years later.

"Come on." Tommy nodded toward the bleachers. "Let's stop holding up traffic and let the big guy have his spotlight."

Tommy strode ahead, and Levi followed a couple steps behind, an ache in his gut that seemed to be growing by the minute.

As they approached the bleachers, Haddie's eyes met his, and a smile spread across her face that turned the ache into something warm, something like comfort.

"Hey, Commissioner…" Levi caught up to his friend and back-handed him on the arm. "Come here. There's someone I want you to meet."

Tommy sighed and followed Levi to where Haddie sat, climbing into the empty row above her and the other teachers she sat with.

"Who's your friend, Coach?" Haddie asked, spinning to face them. Her hazel eyes crinkled at the corners when she smiled, and he took a certain pride that after doing this roommate and friend thing for almost two weeks now, he could elicit such an expression from her.

"Haddie Martin, this is Tommy Crawford, my best friend since elementary school."

Haddie's eyes widened. "Well, that is about the most adorable thing I've ever heard. No wonder he asked you to be his best man." She held out a hand, and Tommy shook it.

"Don't fall for that bullshit charm of his," Tommy told her. "He got into his share of trouble back in the day."

Haddie leaned toward them and stage-whispered. "I expect you to tell me all about this trouble you speak of when Levi isn't around."

Tommy laughed and elbowed Levi in the ribs. "I like her," he told his friend. "It's been a while since you've introduced me to someone you're seeing."

Levi choked on a laugh, and Haddie snorted.

"Oh god!" she told Tommy. "We're not dating. We're just living together."

This time Tommy let out his own choking sound. "Excuse me?"

Levi cleared his throat. "Remember when I asked about the apartment? Haddie sort of already had dibs on it but couldn't afford the rent."

"And your best man here didn't want to go halfsies at first," Haddie chimed in.

"You didn't even want to tell me your name," Levi reminded her.

She scoffed, then turned her attention back to Tommy. "I didn't like your friend much initially."

"You mean I didn't like *you*," Levi countered.

"Ha!" Haddie cried. "You liked me so much that you—"

"We came to an agreement, put our mutual dislike aside, and now we're roommates!" Levi blurted out, not wanting to find out how her sentence would have ended or what images it might have conjured in his head.

Shit. Images were already conjuring. Haddie in his bathtub. Haddie naked and wet climbing out of his bathtub. Haddie's lips…

Tommy barked out a laugh. "Sure. *Not* dating. What did she say about 'adorable'?" Tommy asked, nodding his chin toward Haddie. "So… Did you two just meet with the whole apartment thing?" He straightened back to his regular sitting position and glanced back and forth between Levi and Haddie, who were both staring at each other.

"Yep," Levi replied, beating her to the punch. "Met the morning I called you on your honeymoon asking about the apartment."

"Yeppers…" Haddie added. "First time we ever saw each other was in the hardware store."

Tommy glanced at his friend to see if he was buying their story.

"Yeah, well, seems like you've known each other as long as me and Five-Oh-One have," Tommy told Haddie. "Because you push his buttons about as well as I do, and not gonna lie… It's damned funny to see."

Haddie grinned and clapped her hands together. "Five-Oh-One? Okay, that is even more adorable than him introducing you as his BFF from elementary school. Seriously. You two must have been lethal in high school with all that sweet, small-town boyish charm. I bet you both broke a lot of hearts." She laughed. "Or maybe you didn't because you're both too damned adorable."

At this, both Levi and Tommy straightened their posture and jutted out their chins, peacocking for the pretty woman who totally had their number.

"I mean, I broke a heart or two," Tommy said, his voice dropping an octave. "I wasn't that sweet."

"Yeah, same," Levi grunted. "We were total assholes."

Levi was one of the good guys when he was a teen. Sure, maybe football always rode shotgun, but any girl he dated knew that and seemed okay with it. That was high school. Levi never saw himself as book smart like Tommy and Matteo. Football was his shot at a big future, and if that meant putting everything else second, then so be it.

But when it all went to hell—when he lost his mom, his career, and in a way, his brother soon after—that sweet, adorable guy was lost too.

What would Haddie think of the man he'd become since then? And even more so, why did he care?

"Good evening, everyone!" Principal Crawford's voice boomed through the gymnasium's speakers, echoing off the high ceilings.

Haddie gave them both a quick wave and then spun back to face the floor.

"Here we go…" Tommy remarked with a sigh, and he leaned back, resting his elbows on the empty bleacher behind him.

"Welcome back to what I'm sure will be another winning year for the Summertown Muskies."

"Muh-SKIES!" almost everyone in the crowd of faculty roared back in the same chant they'd done at every football game for as long as Levi could remember.

Everyone but Levi, Tommy, and he was pretty sure, Haddie. It had been so long since Levi had been a Muskie. Haddie had never been one. And Tommy... Well, he guessed Tommy was the only one to actively abstain despite the pride Levi knew he had for his school and the students he taught.

"After two more days of working in your classrooms, we welcome our students back on Friday morning not only to what I know will be an award-winning academic year, but also to our first home football game to kick off the season."

Another chorus of "Muh-SKIES!" rang out, but this time the high school and middle school mascot's name turned into a continuous chant, with Coach Crawford basking in the glory of the legacy he'd created.

Finally, Coach Crawford cleared his throat into the microphone, and the chant slowly faded until he had the auditorium's full attention once more.

"It warms my heart to hear the spirit of our town so fervently displayed among the educators of our future leaders. If you're new to Summertown, there are two things you should know. One, our town lives up to its name. Its famous gardens and topiaries and, most recently, outdoor art installations bring visitors from far and wide to witness what some may call a spectacle but what we know as simply summer in Summertown."

Soft murmurs of laughter and recognition emanated from the crowd.

"But once summer ends, our little town's sole draw is its unparalleled football team. For years, we were one of the best in the state...a few times, *the* best."

Tommy raised his brows at Levi, indicating the role Levi played in Summertown's football glory days.

"But…" Coach Crawford continued. Yet after his *But*, he paused long enough for Tommy to groan.

"It's such a show," he mumbled under his breath.

"What is?" Levi asked.

"You don't remember?" Tommy asked. "Ah, that's right. You've never seen behind the curtain."

Before Levi could ask for more clarification, Coach Crawford began speaking again.

"We've been climbing the ranks for years," he continued. "But while we have easily risen to the top of our little pocket of Small-Town USA, in competing with the big-city schools in Chicago, with the affluent suburbs whose tax dollars fund things like new turf, uniforms, and elite training camps, Summertown is still a step behind. That means we need to consolidate our efforts…and our funding to truly put Summertown High School back on the map."

"Muh-SKIES!" a few people chanted, and Coach Crawford let loose a deep, throaty laugh.

"Muskies, indeed," he replied. "And I can tell by the spirit in this room that you all agree that we need to get behind our team… that we need to do what it takes to compete with the bigger districts, with the stronger teams that have been trying to push us out of our rightful place on top!"

"Muh-SKIES!" several more folks chimed in. But Levi couldn't help a growing feeling of unease, like this was all leading to something that would pull the rug out from beneath them.

"And so I want to send you off to embark on this new school year knowing that my goal is for all students to thrive, from kindergarten on up to senior year. But I want this town to thrive as well, and that is why I will put everything I can into our team this year. Thank you in advance for your hard work today and the days to come as we kick off the new year. I'll see you all back here tomorrow morning for a few quick announcements before cutting you loose to prepare for student arrival on Friday. All together now! One... Two... Three..."

"Go, Muskies!"

And with that, the crowd dispersed.

It wasn't until they were outside, heading toward their cars, that Levi's shoulders relaxed.

"That was weird, right?" Tommy broke the silence first.

"*Thank* you!" Levi replied. "I thought it was all in my head."

"What do you mean?" Haddie asked.

They stopped beside Levi's truck.

"So my dad has always had an unwavering love for the football team. That's nothing out of the ordinary," Tommy said.

Haddie grinned. "I'm assuming you played too?"

Tommy laughed. "I wore a uniform and rode the bench in ninth grade until I realized one very key piece of information."

Haddie crossed her arms. "What's that?"

"That I can't stand football. Playing it, I mean. I went to every game, supported my buddies on the team, but I had zero desire to be out there with them." Tommy shrugged. "And so goes the story of how Thomas Crawford the Second, the one and only child of a man who lives and breathes the game, turned out to be a bigger disappointment than anyone could have imagined." He spoke the words in the exaggerated voice of a sports announcer, and again Levi felt like he'd been socked in the gut.

Haddie looked Tommy up and down. "Funny," she told him. "You don't look like a disappointment."

Tommy laughed again, and Levi could tell that this time it was real and genuine. Not that he was surprised. Haddie seemed to bring out that type of reaction in people.

"Thanks," Tommy replied. "I'll remember that the next time my father tries to cut the debate team's budget to pay for the football players to take a Coach bus to sectionals instead of a school bus if they make it this year."

Haddie grimaced. "Yikes."

"Tommy kicks some big-time ass as the head debate coach," Levi added. "He did the same when we were students here. So, if you're looking to lose an argument, look no further than this man right here."

Tommy chuckled and shook his head. "Yeah, yeah. Enough with compliments, all right? I know I'm hot shit. Sometimes, though, it'd be nice for my old man to realize it." He shrugged. "Anyway...I gotta get home to the missus," Tommy added with a grin Levi knew was the happiest smile he'd ever seen on his friend's face. "See you kids bright and early tomorrow." He waved to both of them. "Great to meet you, Haddie!" he called as he backed away, then spun on his heel as he headed toward his own car.

Levi tapped the bed of the truck. "Should we head out?" he asked.

Haddie was still staring off in the direction where Tommy had gone. Finally, she turned to face him again.

"You know, you can tell a lot about a guy based on his friends," she told him.

Levi's eyes widened. "Oh yeah? So what does the very little you know about Tommy Crawford tell you about me?"

She pursed her lips and tapped her index finger against them. "He's self-deprecating, which is fine. You could have been the type of guy who leaned into his friend's insecurities and piled on. I've seen guys like that..."

Levi leaned back against the bed of his truck, stretching his arms along the top of it. "I'm not that kind of guy, Haddie."

She shook her head. "No...you're not. You sang his praises like you actually meant it."

His brows pulled together. "I *did* mean it. Does that surprise you?"

She stepped forward and cupped a hand to his cheek, giving it a soft, grandmotherly pat that did not register as such to his insides, his pulse quickening at her touch.

Just friends, just friends, just friends, he reminded himself.

"Lots of things about you surprise me each and every day, Levi Rourke."

She dropped her hand, and he let out a nervous laugh. "In a good way, I hope?"

Haddie grinned. "So far, so good," she told him.

Her stomach growled, and Levi laughed.

"You *heard* that?" she asked, hand flying over her belly.

"Everyone in the parking lot heard that," he told her. "I guess we better get you home and fed."

They tossed their schoolbags in the back of the cab and climbed into the truck. As Levi backed out of the parking space, Haddie's phone chimed.

"Ooh," she said, looking at her screen. "It's an email notification from Principal Crawford. Subject line says, 'Important News.' Seems a little ominous, considering we just left a gymnasium where he could have announced important news to us directly, don't you think?"

Again, Levi got that twisty feeling in his gut, but he pushed it away. What could be worse than being suspended from the job he loved and coming home with his tail between his legs to coach a sport he knew absolutely nothing about?

"I'm sure it's nothing," Levi told her.

Famous last words.

CHAPTER 7

Haddie paced back and forth in front of the television, unable to concentrate on the one thing that usually set her mind at ease… as long as the U.S. Women's National Team was winning its soccer match. But she still couldn't get past the list in Principal Crawford's email.

"I don't think stewing about it is going to change anything," Levi told her from where he sat on the couch, nursing an after-dinner beer as he tried to peek around her every time she crossed his line of sight from the couch to the TV. "And I thought you wanted me to *educate* myself on the game some more." He gestured toward the screen. "Or can I give Coaches Lasso and Beard another go?"

"How are you not more upset about this?" she asked, coming to a halt.

Levi shrugged. "I am upset about it," he replied. "I think it sucks that other programs like Tommy's debate team get the short end of the stick so the school can pour everything into the football program, but Coach Crawford isn't wrong about bringing revenue to the town. We're known for football, and the better the varsity team does, the more game tickets we sell, and the better the whole school district does in the long run."

Haddie just stared at him. She was pretty sure that if she were a cartoon, steam would be pouring from her ears and nostrils.

"Short end of the stick?" she cried. "*Short. End. Of. The. Stick?* Levi, he's getting *rid* of the soccer program after this school year. The *whole* program. He's not going to tell the students or families until after the season is over and he's got the school board's support, and there's nothing we can do about it if we want to keep our jobs, which means there is nothing they can do about it either! Tommy might have a little bit less in his team's activity account, but he gets to keep his debate team. But our teams?" She couldn't form the right words to articulate all of the emotions she was feeling or why she was feeling them. All she knew was that Principal Crawford's "By the way, here are some upcoming budget cuts" email had knocked the wind out of her, and Levi's response had been nothing more than a shrug accompanied by, "That really sucks."

He finished his beer, set it on the end table, and then leaned forward, resting his elbows on his knees with a sigh. "I know," he admitted with at least a hint of feeling in his tone. "But what's done is done. Coach Crawford has been running this district since we were kids, and his word is pretty much law. I mean, when it goes to the school board, anyone against it can attend the meeting and protest, but I've never seen a board not do Coach Crawford's bidding. That's life in Summertown."

Haddie scoffed, hoping the hot sting of tears would take a back seat to her unmitigated anger. "So that's it? You're just going to sit back and let him steamroll a whole program because 'What's done is done'?" She crossed and uncrossed her arms, waiting for him to respond with something that would prove she hadn't misjudged him, that the Levi she'd begun to know was more than just a really good first impression. But when too many seconds had gone by and all he could do was offer her another sigh, she stormed into her room, slammed the door, and quickly changed into her running gear.

When she emerged barely five minutes later in her green fitted athletic tank and matching leggings, his only response was, "Where are you going?"

"I need to clear my head," she told him, positioning her phone in her armband and inserting her earbuds. "Remember what I said in the parking lot about you surprising me each and every day?"

His brown eyes darkened and his jaw tightened. "I remember," he replied coolly.

Haddie shrugged. "This time it's not in a good way."

She hit Play on her music app, and even though she saw Levi's mouth open to respond, she didn't give him a chance. She'd let him in, just the tiniest bit, and already she felt blindsided by how easily this new friendship could turn into hurt.

So she shook her head, swallowed the lump in her throat, and headed out the door.

She'd expected to be alone on the track, all the faculty having gone home for the night and no practices scheduled until tomorrow afternoon. But a lone figure circled the football field, and on the team bench she could see that lone figure's sole spectator.

"Emma!" she called out, hitting Pause on her playlist, and her best friend looked up from her laptop, her face splitting into a grin when she saw Haddie.

"Hads!" Emma tossed her laptop to the bench and sprang to her feet, jogging across the field to meet Haddie where she stood in the end zone.

The two women embraced, and though Haddie was disappointed not to have some quiet time to process the recent events of the evening, she realized maybe this was better because the knot in her stomach was already starting to loosen just from Emma's presence.

"I'm sorry we keep missing each other," Haddie told her friend.

Emma—dressed in a pair of ripped jeans and a gray T-shirt that read, *I'm not short. I'm just more down to earth than other people*—waved her off.

"I know what back-to-school week is like," Emma told her. "Plus, we're swamped at the inn with the end-of-summer rush, which is why I'm out here doing my *real* day job on my laptop while Matteo does his thing." She waved as Matteo came around their end of the field but kept running, his T-shirt—whatever it might have said—slung around his neck like a towel. "Also," she called to him, "you're superhot, and I'm totally objectifying you every time you pass by! I hope that's okay!"

He pointed to his earbuds and mouthed something along the lines of *I can't hear you* and then waved back as he went on his merry way.

Haddie and Emma burst out laughing.

"Wow. How is it possible that I miss you when you live only, like, two minutes away?" Haddie asked.

Emma shrugged. "Because I'm so very missable. Duh."

Haddie snorted. "This whole being-an-adult-and-working-for-a-living thing sucks sometimes."

The corners of Emma's mouth turned down. "Bad day at the office before the office even opens?"

Haddie sighed. "Kind of?"

Emma held out her arms and spun slowly. "Well, you've got this whole track almost to yourself to blow off some steam. Or… we can go hide out in the press box, and I can listen or try to play therapist. Whatever you need."

Haddie nodded toward the bench where Emma's laptop still lay. "Don't you need to get back to your day job?"

"Day job, schmay job!" Emma exclaimed. "My favorite girl is here, and she needs me. Right?" She pressed her palms to Haddie's cheeks and used her thumb and forefingers to move Haddie's lips up and down. "Yes, I totally need my best friend and don't have to solve all of my problems on my own," Emma added in a caricatured version of what Haddie guessed was meant to be Haddie's voice.

Haddie gingerly grabbed her friend's wrists and lowered her hands with only a tiny bit of an eye roll.

"Fine," Emma said. "I will take your acquiescence to join me in the press box as your way of telling me you need me."

Haddie groaned. "You know you're the only person I'll admit I need, right?"

Emma raised her brows. "And yet, you still haven't actually admitted it."

"I think I did," Haddie replied. "Go get your laptop just in case a mosquito or praying mantis tries to run off with it. I'll take one lap and meet you up there."

Emma smiled and bounced on her toes. "Acquiescence is reading between the lines, and those blank spaces say You. Need. Me. Meet you up there in five."

Emma jogged back to the bench while Haddie took to the track for one quick quarter of a mile to clear her head before meeting her best friend—the one who'd be there for her even if she never admitted how much she needed her—at the top of the Muskies bleachers.

"Okay, first of all…why are we even allowed in here?" Haddie asked as she climbed into the press box and sat down next to Emma in front of the window that looked out onto the field. "Wait. Let me guess," she continued. "No one locks doors in this quaint little town because nothing bad ever happens here."

Emma laughed. "Or…Tommy stole Coach Crawford's key back in high school and made a couple of copies, and Matteo swiped Levi's when we were sophomores and never returned it."

Haddie nodded approvingly. "I knew I liked Tommy the second I met him." Then she winced.

Emma's brows drew together. "Then why do you look like you just ate a lemon wedge?"

Haddie groaned and dropped her head to the announcer's desk, banging it lightly against the damp, peeling wooden ledge. "Because it appears that I am and always will be a terrible judge of character."

Emma slapped her palms on the desk, and Haddie jumped.

"Um...hellooo?" Emma said, pointing at herself with both her thumbs. "I am made 100 percent of extremely good character, no additives or preservatives, and you fell for me the second you met me."

Haddie raised her brows and dipped her head toward Emma's T-shirt. "After I got past the kitschy tees. It was touch and go before that."

Emma stood and adopted an exaggerated runway-esque pose. "Except then you realized the tees make me happy, and that I make you happy, and we both lived happily ever after. The end."

Haddie playfully flicked her friend's messy topknot and sighed. "Yeah, I guess it was true love or soulmates or whatever you want to call it."

Emma collapsed back into her chair. "And from what I know of Tommy Crawford, you're pretty spot-on with your initial assessment of him, so where is this character-assessment doubt coming from?" Her expression grew somber. "And if this is when we talk about Chicago, I promise to stop cracking jokes starting now."

Haddie swallowed a knot in her throat. "You mean my grand-monster? You already know all there is to know." She did her best to keep her voice even.

Emma nodded slowly. "Yeah, your grandmonster," she began gently. "I know you're grieving that loss in your own way. But you're also grieving the loss of a perfectly good job at a perfectly good school in a city I know you loved, and I don't quite get how they're all connected."

Haddie felt all the color drain from her face.

"Hads," Emma continued when Haddie still hadn't formed a response. "I don't want you to feel pressured to talk about anything you're not ready to talk about. But I'm here whenever you are, okay?"

Haddie pressed her lips together and nodded. "I just want to move on, Ems. Here, in my new life with you and Matteo, and my very unexpected new roommate."

Emma gasped, clapped, and bounced once in her seat all at the same time. "Are you two in love? Did he propose with a giant Toblerone? Are you going to be my sister-in-law?"

Haddie snort-laughed, at once aghast but also grateful that Emma knew exactly what she needed in this particular moment—ridiculous suspicions that were laughably off the mark.

"Not even the tiniest bit close, my friend. In fact, I'm pretty sure any lingering attraction I had toward him has effectively been squashed like a sidewalk overrun with cicadas." So what if the man brushed his teeth before bed wearing nothing but a pair of sleep pants and a self-assuredness that silently said, *I know you like the view*? She could still appreciate such a view and at the same time unappreciate his lack of empathy for the school's soccer program.

Emma winced. "Thank you for the nightmare-inducing analogy."

"You're welcome." And then she told Emma everything—from meeting Tommy at the back-to-school event to being impressed at how much Levi wore his affection for his friend on his sleeve to the same man *shrugging off* the notion that the soccer program's budget was not being cut. No, no, no. The program was being dismantled altogether because the teams never made it that far in their conferences, and the program was more of a money suck than a money draw for the district.

"So, you know…" Haddie continued. "Bye-bye to the one thing you might love or that you might be good at, kids. This here's a football town!"

Emma narrowed her eyes at her friend. "Principal Crawford's email did *not* say 'This here's a football town.'"

Haddie threw her arms in the air. "It might as well have. Because that's how it sounded in my head, and…ugh! Levi just washed his hands of the whole situation and said, 'What's done is done.'"

Emma nodded, adding, "Mm-hmm. Mm-hmm," for emphasis. "And how did that make you feel?"

Haddie groaned. "You know you're not actually a therapist, right?"

Her friend shrugged. "I'm getting into character. But also, how *did* it make you feel when he said that? I mean, you two have been living together for almost two weeks now. As friends, right?"

Haddie backhanded her friend on the shoulder. "Yes as friends! How many times are you going to ask me that before you believe me?"

Emma pouted. "I don't know. You're hot. *He's* hot. You're my best friend, and he's my fiancé's brother. How amazing would it be if you and Levi really did fall in love? You could buy the house next door to ours. I don't think it's for sale, but Matteo and I could turn our place into a frat house long enough to drive them away.

I'd totally do that for you. And then we can grow old together like we were meant to."

Haddie pressed the heels of her hands to her eyes and then let out a long exhale. "Ems. I love you. Truly, I do. But Levi Rourke and me? Never gonna happen." Even though it almost had and Haddie still thought about that almost-had at least once a day.

"Right… Right…" Emma replied. "Because that thing he said about cutting the soccer program made you feel…?"

"Betrayed, okay?" Haddie blurted out. "It made me feel betrayed. He knows how excited I am about coaching these kids and how much it means to me, but this year for him is just a quick little detour until he gets back to what he actually *wants* to be doing. Ems, this job and these kids are *it* for me if Coach Crawford doesn't let me go before I make tenure. How am I supposed to tell them that whatever happens this year, it doesn't matter because the program is over before the season even begins." Her eyes widened. "Oh wait. I can't because Coach Crawford said we need to keep everything under wraps until the school board approves his decisions, which he's confident they will."

She blew out a breath. "You want to know what's even shittier than being betrayed? Being the betrayer. I'm the betrayer, Ems." Haddie felt that hot prick behind her eyes again as her throat grew tight. This was exactly why she'd left Chicago, to say goodbye to the hard stuff. Yet here she was, walking right back into it less than a month after starting her life over from scratch.

Emma shrugged, undeterred. "Well… What if you said to hell with Principal Crawford's budget cuts and Levi's lack of support and fought for what you think is important?"

Haddie loved being a teacher. And now she also loved being a coach. But she was as fish out of water as someone could be. She had no idea how to stand up to a guy who basically lorded over the entire, tiny little school district like it was his and his alone. "I wouldn't even know where to begin," she admitted.

"You don't have to figure it out this minute," Emma told her, draping her legs over Haddie's and then flicking on the announcer's microphone sitting on the desk. "You'll think of something in that über-creative brain of yours, and whatever it is, count me in to help."

Haddie tilted her forehead against her friend's. "Thank you," she told Emma with a sigh. But her soft words were amplified by the microphone, pushed out onto the field so that Matteo, even with his earbuds still in, glanced up at them as he rounded the track. "But…why the mic?"

Emma leaned back, flashing her a mischievous grin. "Thought we might serenade my husband-to-be and embarrass the hell out of him."

Haddie's expression brightened. She didn't have to solve her problem tonight. It was enough to have Emma on her side, even if she wasn't sure what came next as far as school was concerned. Embarrassing Matteo, on the other hand…

"Is the mic wireless?" Haddie asked.

Emma nodded.

"'Can't Take My Eyes Off You,' Heath Ledger à la *Ten Things I Hate about You*?" she added.

Emma jumped up, pulling the microphone from its stand, not

wasting a second as she started in on the lyrics about Matteo being too good to be true. And together, she and Haddie danced down the bleachers, turning Matteo's water break either into his worst nightmare or—as Haddie liked to think—yet another reminder of how lucky he was that Emma said *yes*.

Maybe happily ever after wasn't something Haddie would ever find for herself, but it comforted her to know it was out there for people who knew how to be brave with their hearts. People she'd never understand but could admire from a distance. People like Emma.

Levi was already tucked away in his room by the time Haddie returned, so she got ready for bed and climbed beneath the covers. Several minutes of tossing and turning were interrupted by a text notification on her phone.

Haddie grabbed the phone, expecting a few more wise words from Emma, and gasped when she saw the text preview on her lock screen.

Mr. Tux: Awake?

Her heart leaped like she was a kid opening a Christmas gift to find something better than what she could have even imagined that she wanted...which was why she fought every urge to reply, even after the phone buzzed a second time in her hand.

Mr. Tux: Is it weird that we still barely know each other, and I already hate fighting with you?

"I hate fighting with you too," Haddie whispered. But she hated even more what that implied. That they cared about each other and about their friendship enough that they could already hurt and disappoint each other.

Mr. Tux: If you're reading and not responding, don't tell me. My ego's still kinda fragile. So I'm just gonna tell myself you fell asleep as soon as your head hit the pillow.

Haddie couldn't help herself. She tapped the empty text box, typing and deleting the word *Hey* but not knowing what the hell to say next until she finally sighed and dropped her phone facedown on her chest.

It buzzed, making her rib cage vibrate. Or maybe it was just her heart stuttering in her chest.

Mr. Tux: Message received, Birthday Girl. Sleep well.

CHAPTER 8

evi thought giving Haddie her space for a day would be enough. Two max. He figured he needed as much time to get over seeing those three dots appear and disappear in response to his late-night texts. What was he thinking? He'd obviously messed up, so why did he think bombarding her with texts would make it better when she probably just wanted to get some sleep? When he ambled out of his room on Friday morning, the official first day of school, he figured they could finally call a truce. But Haddie was already walking out the door.

And because he apparently wanted to see how many times he could be rejected by a woman he wasn't even romantically involved with, he tried to catch her before she left her classroom at the end of the day. But when he got there, Ms. Darlene, the woman who'd been the librarian since Levi and Tommy were in middle school, was holding down the fort as Haddie's class got ready for dismissal. She squinted at him through rainbow-framed glasses, her hair sitting atop her head in the same bun she wore all those years ago, the one that was somehow held together by a No. 2 pencil.

"Ms. Martin is in a meeting that ran long, so I'm covering for her until she gets back. Should I tell her you stopped by?"

"Who are you?" a tiny but powerful voice inquired from somewhere much closer to the floor. Before he could answer Darlene, the owner of the voice began tugging at his pant leg. "Hey, mister! I asked you a question," she continued.

Levi dipped his head until his eyes met those of a first-grade girl who couldn't have even been three feet tall. Even with her high ponytail of wispy blond hair, she still barely reached his knee.

He dropped to a squat in front of her and grinned.

"I'm Coach Rourke," he told her. "I'm a friend of your teacher's. What's your name?"

The girl narrowed her eyes, assessing him. "I'm Piper. And if you're one of Ms. Martin's friends, why didn't she put anything about you in her favorite things on her All About Me poster?" She pointed toward the back wall of the classroom. Below the row of windows that looked out onto the main entrance of the elementary wing of the Summertown district were posters with stick figure self-portraits and drawings of favorite things like flowers or pets. Levi wasn't sure, but it looked like one student either had a pet dinosaur, really loved dinosaurs, or possibly was aiming to draw a hairless cat. In the middle of all the first-grade creations, he found Haddie's poster. Her own self-portrait was also a stick figure, which, of course, Levi found ridiculously adorable. Then surrounding her portrait were what Levi guessed were the favorite things that told all about Haddie.

A soccer ball.

A pair of running shoes.

A Toblerone.

Two other stick figures, who were clearly Emma and Matteo.

And then rows of much smaller stick figures along with slightly taller ones. Her first grade students and her team.

Piper was right. Levi's brother made the poster, but no mention of Levi himself. Ouch.

He cleared his throat. "Um, Piper... Did Ms. Martin say anything to the class about whether or not she was going to the home-opener football game tonight?"

The young girl crossed her arms. "She said she was going but only to give..." Her brows drew together. "What did she say again? Only to give someone a piece...a piece of her head?"

Levi laughed softly. "A piece of her mind?"

Piper's eyes widened. "YES! That's it! A piece of her mind. Does it hurt to do that?"

Levi shook his head. "It won't hurt Ms. Martin, but whoever is on the receiving end is probably in for a world of hurt." That person was either Coach Crawford, himself, or both. "It was nice to meet you, Piper," he added. Levi's knee began to throb, so he pushed himself back to his full height.

The young girl looked up at him with eyes narrowed. "I know," she replied. "I'm delightful."

Levi laughed, but he was interrupted before he could form a response to Piper's very true statement.

"Okay, everyone!" Darlene called to the class. "Time to line up! If you're taking the bus, please stand behind the yellow star. If you're being picked up in a car, please stand behind the blue star. And if you're being picked up to walk, please stand behind the red star."

She pointed to three large star cutouts taped to the floor in front of the classroom door. As little bodies milled about and settled into place, Levi finally got a full bird's-eye view of the room. Alphabet cards with upper- and lowercase versions of each letter lined the perimeter of the room just below the ceiling. A colorful rug with bright flowers and a train carrying all sorts of woodland animals was framed with yet another alphabet. And then surrounding the rug were five pods of three desks each, a decorative, laminated nameplate taped to each one.

All he had to do was look at the work she'd done in her room to know how much Haddie cared about a school where she'd only taught for one day so far. Levi's prep for his high school health classroom had been nothing more than counting the desks and making sure the number he got matched the number of students listed on his roster.

"If you could tell her I stopped by, Ms. Darlene, I'd really appreciate it. Though you might want to tell her after the students are dismissed, just in case she has any colorful words to say about my visit."

He weaved through the not-quite-single-file lines of first graders to the door and pivoted back to give them all a quick smile and a wave. Then he made his way back to the high school wing to close up shop for the day and hopefully figure out his next move.

Levi knocked on the open classroom door even though he could see Tommy sitting at his desk, eyes trained on his laptop.

"Come in," Tommy replied absently, still not looking up, so—being the grown man that he was—Levi grabbed a forgotten piece of notebook paper from an empty desk, crumpled it into a ball, and launched it right at his friend's head.

It bounced off of Tommy's temple and landed on the desk.

Tommy sighed, glanced up, and rolled his eyes.

Levi grinned and pumped both fists in the air. "Muskies!" he cried in his deepest bro voice. "Come on. Aren't you heading out to the field for the pregame pep rally?"

Tommy sighed. "Did you not see my father's email after the faculty meeting Wednesday night?"

Shit. He'd been so wrapped up in Haddie's reaction to the email that he hadn't stopped to think that Tommy might be hurting too. Man, he was out of practice when it came to this whole friendship thing.

Levi rounded the rows of desks and attempted to take a seat in the front row but then realized he was not really high-school-sized anymore and opted for leaning against the window kitty-corner to Tommy's desk.

"I'm sorry," Levi told him. "But are you surprised? Your dad did exactly what you expected him to do."

Tommy leaned back and crossed his arms. "Look... I get that this job doesn't really mean anything to you. You'll be in and out of here faster than I can blink. But this is my career, man. It's everything to me, just like..." He blew out a defeated breath. "Like football and only football is everything to my father...and I guess you."

Levi winced. "Ouch," he said, this time out loud. "Tommy…" he added, but Levi wasn't sure what to say next.

"It's not just a reduced budget for the debate team," Tommy continued. "We used to partner with the middle school teachers to do a fall play and a spring musical. He dropped it down to one production a year. Speaking of music? Did you see there will no longer be a stipend for early-morning choir rehearsals at the elementary school? That means there's either no choir, or the music teacher has to do it on a volunteer basis." He scrubbed a hand across his jaw. "How are you not pissed about the soccer program?"

Levi's expression fell. "Tommy…" he said again. "I don't know this school or these kids, not anymore. How am I supposed to react?"

Tommy shrugged. "Like you're not another one of my father's yes-men. That would be a start."

Except that's exactly who Levi was. He didn't have a choice. Levi's possible reinstatement hung in the balance. Any wrong move could tip the scale against him. But any argument or explanation of his sentencing right now would only make Levi look more selfish than he already felt.

"I'm sorry, Tommy," he told his friend. "I really am. But I'm not sure what else I can do."

Tommy pressed his lips into a thin line and nodded. "Yeah. Me neither. And to your earlier question? No. I'm not heading to the pregame rally."

Levi sighed. "I get where you're coming from. But the kids who will be out on that field tonight? They didn't do anything wrong by choosing to play the game. Same goes for the ones in the stands who are supporting them. Some of them are your students, right?"

Tommy responded with a resigned nod.

Levi strode to where his friend stood and clapped him on the shoulder. "Then maybe support the kids you can right now until we figure out our next move."

Tommy's eyes widened. "Where the hell did that little nugget of wisdom come from?" he asked with a half-hearted laugh.

Levi lifted one shoulder. "Honestly? I'm not sure. But it was pretty impressive, wasn't it?"

This got him a genuine smile. "Yeah, Five-Oh-One. I guess it was."

Levi blew out a relieved breath. "Good, because I wasn't sure I could take two of my favorite people thinking I was a piece of shit." He raised his brows. "So… See you in the bleachers?" He started backing toward the door.

Tommy shook his head ruefully. "Maybe," he replied. "Won't it be weird for you to watch from the stands?"

Levi stopped and smacked his palm against the doorframe. "So freaking weird," he admitted. "But less so if my buddy's there."

Tommy groaned. "Fine. I'll be out there soon." Just as Levi was about to pivot and head back out, his friend added, "Hey…what do you mean about two of your favorite people thinking you're a piece of shit?"

Levi held up his hands as if he had no idea what Tommy was talking about. "Later, Commissioner!" he called out and then spun on his heel and left.

Because what the hell did he mean by that?

CHAPTER 9

"Ms. Martin, we are about to start our pregame practice. Feel free to make an appointment with my assistant during office hours next week."

Principal Crawford turned back to the field where the marching band played what Haddie guessed was the Muskies fight song while cheerleaders were tossed into the air and, thankfully, caught by those standing below.

"I just want to discuss these budget cuts and some possible scenarios that might let Summertown keep its soccer program." Haddie refused to be dismissed, even though she knew they weren't going to solve anything during a pep rally. Would this be a mark on some secret checklist Principal Crawford might use to pink-slip her at the end of the year? Maybe. But as much as she wanted to keep her job, she wanted to earn and keep her team's trust that much more.

The principal sighed but kept his eyes on the field. "Come up with an alternate scenario first, Ms. Martin. And then we'll talk."

"Really?" Haddie bounced on her heels, unable to bite back her grin. She'd pounded a tiny dent into his armor. Even if it was barely progress, it was something.

"Really," he relented.

"Okay!" she replied. "I will. And then I'll make an appointment, and...and we'll talk. About scenarios. And soccer." She was beaming. She couldn't help it. It was a glimmer of hope, and she was going to hang on to it. The school year had just begun. So much could change before summer came around again. And even though no players had taken the field yet, she already considered the night a win.

Principal Crawford glanced in her direction and raised a brow. "Does that mean I can blow my whistle now and start warm-ups?"

Haddie nodded. "Of course. Absolutely. Warm-ups. And I will talk to you next week!" She bounded in the opposite direction, heading back to where she'd left Emma and Matteo in the stands. Only, when she got to their section of the home team bleachers, she found Emma, Matteo, and Levi waiting for her.

"You know what?" she said, backing away from their row as quickly as she'd approached. "I'm in the mood for a hot pretzel. Who wants a pretzel, because pretzels are on me?" Except she didn't wait for anyone to respond. Instead she jogged down the bleacher steps, onto the pavement, and continued back around the stands to where the concession booth was.

Facing the man who decided the future of her career? No biggie. Facing the man whose texts she'd guiltily read and reread the past two nights? Scarier than walking a circus tightrope with no net beneath.

"Haddie!" she heard over her shoulder, and ugh, if the sound of her name on Levi's lips didn't make her want to halt in her tracks.

But she fought against physiology and kept moving, pretending she didn't hear him, which was feasible because there was already a sizable crowd milling around.

Her plan, though, was not foolproof since once she arrived at the concession stand, she had no choice but to stop and get in line. Leaving the group for a sudden desire for a hot pretzel might have been an excuse, but now that hot pretzel was on her brain, her belly really wanted one.

"*Haddie*," Levi said again, this time from right behind her.

She sighed, squared her shoulders, and spun to face him. "Levi!" she exclaimed with entirely too much enthusiasm. "Fancy seeing you here!"

Fancy seeing you here? To what decade had she just retreated?

His brows furrowed. "You're surprised to see me at the home opener football game? Surprised to see me in line to help you carry all those pretzels? Or surprised that you've managed to freeze me out for two whole days, and now you have to talk to me?"

Haddie's squared shoulders took a deep dive into Slumpsville. "The last one, I guess," she admitted with a mumble. "But I'm angry at you, and I don't know how to deal with being angry at someone I live with if that someone isn't my grandmonster who ignored me as much as I ignored her."

Levi's shoulders fell too, and he opened his mouth to say something, but Haddie was quicker on the draw.

"This isn't about me and my grandmonster, so don't look at me like that, okay? This is about you and me and—"

"And *you* get to decide when and where we hash this out?

Haddie...as you've so brilliantly pointed out, we *live* together. And up until a couple of days ago, I thought we were friends."

She sighed. The sincerity in his eyes and the hint of anguish in his tone were melting her frosty exterior.

"We were," she admitted. "I mean...we are. I think. I don't know? What do friends do when they get mad at each other?"

Levi laughed. "You mean when one friend gets mad at the other and then pretends he doesn't exist? Come on, Haddie. You've gotten into fights with friends before." He paused. "Haven't you?"

Haddie swallowed. "So, this is the part where I'm either going to sound cuckoo for Cocoa Puffs or...well...I guess that's the only way I'm going to sound. I've never had a fight with a friend before."

Levi narrowed his eyes. "Not even Emma?"

She scoffed. "Emma and I don't do mad."

He shrugged. "Fine. What about any of your friends back in Chicago? You had to have gotten in a fight or two."

Haddie shook her head slowly. "And before you accuse me of being friendless, I'm not. I mean, I wasn't. I had plenty of people I hung out with in high school and in college, but no one close. No one like Emma." This was the lifestyle she'd cultivated, never planning on someone like Emma who would claw her way over the drawbridge and past her moat. But saying it out loud didn't sound cuckoo for Cocoa Puffs to Haddie's own ears. It sounded... sad. Like she suddenly realized she might have been missing out on more Emmas in her life. Or maybe, possibly, a Levi.

He crossed his arms. "Why do I get the feeling that was by design and not because of how severely unlikable you are?"

Why? How did he see right through her?

"I don't let people get too close, okay?" she told him. "And I think, maybe, I let you claw your way in too soon. You disappointed me, and now I don't know what to do with that."

"Can't get much closer than the bedroom next door," he offered with a tentative grin. "And claw my way in?"

She sighed. "I guess you're like Emma. Scrappy."

He put his hands on his hips and stood like a superhero ready to take flight. "I'm too big and strong to be scrappy."

Haddie laughed, despite the continued feeling of unease that seemed to come hand in hand with being Levi Rourke's roommate and friend.

"Okay," Levi continued, taking a step back and holding up his hands. "I'm not going to push you to talk this out if you still want space, but at least hear me out." He waited a beat, and when she didn't stop him, he went on. "I don't know how much you follow college football news… And I'm guessing by the look of utter disinterest on your face that the answer is not at all. But the reason why I'm here, why I have this job? It's because I did something I shouldn't have, even if I tell myself it was for the right reasons. Everything I do while I'm here bears weight on what I get to do when this year is up."

He ran a hand through his hair, a pained expression on his face. "I don't just get to go back to my job…" He shook his head. "No… my *career*. I have to pay fines. To do court-mandated counseling. I need a letter of recommendation for reinstatement from a trusted reference like Coach Crawford." He let out a mirthless laugh. "My future is basically at his whim. Does that make any sense?"

Haddie's heart squeezed. Of course it made sense. The same man held both of their careers in the palm of his hand. But it didn't change one very simple truth. "What about *their* future?" she asked, motioning toward the bleachers where much of the student body congregated to cheer on the team. "Do you really believe what's done is done?"

"I–I don't have a choice," he admitted. "I have to."

"Then you're right," she told him. "I guess I still need my space."

He nodded, and Haddie hated how much her stomach tied in knots at the wounded resignation in his eyes. "Okay," he finally said. "I understand. I'll let you enjoy the rest of your evening." Then he shoved his hands in his pockets and took a couple of steps backward, until he turned and walked away.

"Can I help you, ma'am?" someone asked, and Haddie spun around to find she was suddenly at the front of the concession line, a PTO parent waiting to take her order.

"Oh!" Haddie replied. "Yes. Um…four soft pretzels, please." Because she wasn't going to be a total jerk and snub a guy she knew probably hadn't eaten dinner like the rest of them.

Ninety seconds later, Haddie awkwardly carried the four paper trays that were wildly too small to hold the gargantuan pretzels back to the bleachers. She should have been surprised when she got back that Levi was gone, but she wasn't.

"Where'd Levi go?" Emma asked.

Matteo held up his phone, brows pinched together. "He just texted. Said something came up and he'll catch us for the next game." His shoulders fell, only a little, but it was enough for Haddie to notice she probably was a total jerk, making him miss a game she was sure he'd been looking forward to all week.

Emma hooked her arm through her fiancé's and rested her head on his shoulder. "I'm sorry, Matty Matt. I know you were hoping to connect better before the wedding."

Haddie passed out the pretzels and collapsed onto the metal bench next to Emma, two giant twists of dough in her own lap. "Everything okay with Matteo and Levi?" she asked softly enough that she hoped only Emma could hear, but Emma waved her off and tore into her pretzel.

"Just…Levi hasn't been home much in the past decade, and all siblings have issues, you know?" she said around a mouthful of dough.

"One of those siblings can hear you," Matteo responded from Emma's other side.

Except Haddie had no idea. Emma was the closest thing she had to a sibling, and they'd only met as fully formed adults. "I'm sorry, Matteo," she called back, further solidifying her total-jerk status.

Emma nudged Haddie's shoulder with her own. "How are *you* doing?"

Haddie laughed. "Are you Joey Tribbiani-ing me?"

"Ha!" Emma replied. "If I am, is it working for you?" She batted her eyes at her friend.

Haddie stared pointedly at Emma's boobs. Or, more specifically, the words written across her boobs on her T-shirt. "Yeah, except I don't think at any point during the show did Joey say, 'Hold on while I overthink this.'"

A second later, Haddie's phone buzzed on the bench beside her with a notification.

She frowned when she picked it up and read Emma's text. "Why are you sending me a calendar request for a meeting at the town hall?"

Emma grimaced. "Okay, so I thought I programmed that email to go out at 7:00 *a.m.* and not *p.m.* My bad?"

Haddie tapped open the calendar invite and read the no longer truncated title. "Saturday-Morning Grief Support Group," she read. Then she glanced back up at Emma, her eyes narrowed to slits. "Do I look like I need grief support?"

Emma's head wobbled back and forth from shoulder to shoulder. Then she held her thumb and forefinger up. "Maybe a little?"

"I'm fine," Haddie assured her. "Especially since I'm already making headway with Principal Crawford. If I can come up with a plan for alternate funding, he agreed to meet with me and hear me out."

"Of course you're fine," Emma agreed. "And I'm super happy about Principal Crawford giving you a chance to save the program. But I thought that if you weren't ready to talk to me, then maybe you'd want to meet up with some other people who might understand what you're going through... Not that you're going through anything." She shrugged. "It's not like you have to RSVP. I just wanted to let you know the meeting existed."

Matteo popped his last shred of pretzel in his mouth and rested his head on Emma's shoulder. "My dad and I have gone a few times

109

since I've been home," he chimed in. "Talking about stuff has never been our strong suit, and... I don't know. Even a decade later, it helped."

Haddie sighed and glanced down at her own untouched pretzel growing cold in her lap.

"Running is my therapy," she assured them both, yet the slight waver in her voice made her wonder if maybe it might not be such a bad idea to talk to other people going through something similar.

Emma picked up Haddie's giant pretzel and held it in front of her mouth.

Haddie laughed, sank her teeth into it, and tore off a piece that was almost too big to fit in her mouth.

"Then go for a run tomorrow," Emma told her. "And if you happen to pass the town hall and want to venture inside, I won't stop you."

———————

Maybe Haddie did need more space to figure out this roommate/ friendship thing with Levi, but she also needed to take responsibility for perpetuating their stalemate.

Haddie: Awake?

Three dots appeared immediately, and Haddie waited for them to disappear, for no response to come. She deserved at least that much. But her phone buzzed in her hand a second later.

Mr. Tux: Awake

Haddie: Sorry I made you miss a night hanging with your brother. That kind of makes me the worst.

Mr. Tux: Thanks, Bday Girl. But there is no world I know of where you could ever be the worst.

Haddie's heart and stomach simultaneously fluttered.

Haddie: What if there was a world where I was a supervillain?

Haddie swore she could sense him smile from the other room.

Mr. Tux: Then you'd be the best supervillain. See what I did there?

She laughed.

Haddie: I see. Impressive loophole.

Mr. Tux: Happy to know I haven't lost the ability to impress you yet.

Haddie sighed. "Stop being so charming," she whispered. Because even if she was still a little mad at him, she couldn't ignore there was so much more to Levi Rourke than the Summertown soccer teams—or soon to be lack thereof.

The safest thing to do was put his charm—and both of them—to bed. Separately! Ugh. Even her brain was conspiring against her.

Haddie: Anyway, just wanted to apologize for making you feel like you couldn't hang with Matteo. That wasn't my intent. Sleep tight, Levi.

The telltale three dots appeared and disappeared again until finally a response came through.

Mr. Tux: Apology accepted. And still maintain you could never be the worst. Sleep tight, Bday Girl. Thanks for the text.

She set her phone on her nightstand and sighed.

Thanks for being scrappy, Mr. Tux, she thought and then drifted off to sleep.

CHAPTER 10

Levi looked at the paper sign taped next to the meeting room's door and then back at his most recent text from Eden Frankel, his lawyer.

> **Eden:** Yes. The judge will accept group counseling as long as you attend at least fifteen sessions, the group is led by an actual counselor, and the counselor signs off on your attendance and progress.

Even via text, Eden sounded like a lawyer, despite her having known Levi and having worked with his university's football program for the better part of a decade.

He sighed, scratched the stubble on his cheek, and pushed open the door.

"Oh good!" called a woman who was in the middle of converting rows of folding chairs into a large circle. "The doorstop keeps losing the war against the door. Do you think you can wedge it in there a little better? An open door is always a much more welcoming door."

"Uh…sure," Levi replied. He found the doorstop, toed it with his sneaker to the open door, and gave it a good kick to wedge it underneath. When he let go of the door and it stayed, he gave himself a mental pat on the back and decided this was a sign of better things to come today after his and Haddie's text exchange last night.

"Can I help?" he asked, striding toward the woman and her mess of chairs. He held his hand out as he approached "I'm—"

"Levi Rourke," she interrupted, giving him a hearty shake.

His eyes widened. "Have…um…have we met?" She looked at him from behind tortoiseshell, cat's-eye frames, her long brown hair in a braid hanging over one shoulder. She looked around his age, which meant they could have gone to school together, which in a town this small, would make him the hugest asshole known to man for not recognizing her.

She laughed. "Hope Ellis," she told him, grabbing his hand and giving it a firm shake. "And no. We haven't met. I just set up my practice about six months ago. The…uh…pro bono group thing is kinda my marketing tactic. But you're not one of my regulars, and I had a chat yesterday with Eden Frankel…" Her voice trailed off.

Levi cleared his throat and dropped her hand. "She had you google the incident. Didn't she?"

Hope replied with a sympathetic smile, which made him groan. "Well…there goes my anonymity."

She laughed, and they continued to set up the chairs.

"This isn't like AA," she told him. "It's not a secret meeting. It's grief counseling. Some members of the group even meet up on their own socially."

Levi carried two chairs across the growing circle and set them in place. "Yeah, sure. That's fine," he said. "Just to be clear, I don't really *need* grief counseling. This is just a formality for my sentencing."

She nodded. "You don't have to share anything you're not comfortable sharing, Levi. But you've got fifteen sessions to decide, right?"

He flashed her a devil-may-care grin and wondered if she bought it.

"Good morning, Hope!" a woman called from the entryway, and Levi let out a sigh of relief. But when he spun to see who his savior was, he stumbled back a step.

"Mrs. Higginson?"

His father's girlfriend beamed and strode toward him with open arms. "Levi!" Before he had time to process the fact that anonymity was truly out of the question, she'd already enveloped him in a hug. "And it's *Tilly*," she reminded him.

Levi let out a nervous laugh, and Tilly finally released her embrace.

He wasn't sure who it was that Tilly was grieving. Hell, she didn't seem all that grief-stricken. But since she'd called Hope by name, Levi guessed she was a regular, which meant he'd likely find out more than he'd ever bargained for when it came to his father's love life.

"Good morning, Hope," more voices called as people filed in. Levi recognized Old Man Wilton, a widower who was now dating Mrs. Pinkney, owner of the town sweet shop aptly named Sweet, and who was a widow herself. Dawson Hayes, the former deputy sheriff who graduated with Levi, strolled in.

"Levi Rourke, as I live and breathe," Dawson said, striding toward him. "Heard you were back in town and coaching soccer?" The statement came out like a question.

"Hayes..." Levi replied. "I heard about your dad. I'm sorry."

The deputy crossed his arms and his jaw pulsed. "You don't have to say that. You and your brother know he wasn't a good man."

Maybe he wasn't, but if Dawson was here, that meant he was grieving.

Levi cleared his throat. "Well, I'm sorry if things have been hard since his passing."

Dawson gave him a curt nod, seemingly satisfied with Levi's amended response, and then strolled to an empty seat in the growing circle of group members.

When all was said and done, nine people plus Hope sat in the circle with five empty seats for the *just in case-ers*, as Hope called them.

"Good morning, everyone. I trust you all had a good night watching the Muskies take their first win of the season?"

There were some soft hoots and hollers in recognition of the football win that Levi had listened to from his truck in the parking lot.

He understood why Haddie wanted her space, yet at the same time *didn't* understand why—if they really were friends—they couldn't hash it out and move on.

"So, let's start how we always do, with introductions, especially since we might have a new member or two today," Hope continued.

At the mention of a new member, every head turned in Levi's direction, which told him he was the *only* new member today.

"Remember to state your name and one thing about yourself that you want to share. It can be anything from the reason why you're here to your favorite color. Whatever makes you comfortable."

"I'll start!" Tilly cried, waving her hand in the air.

Hope nodded for the other woman to continue.

"Hi, everyone!" Tilly said with glee. "I'm Tilly Higginson, and I'm here because I lost my husband."

Levi's brows pulled together. "Wait, your husband died?" he asked, suddenly afraid he was stating the obvious. But Levi had met Tilly's *ex*-husband, and he didn't remember hearing anything about both his father *and* Tilly being widows.

She waved him off with a sweep of her hand. "Of course not," she said. "But if you wish for something hard enough, it can happen, right?"

The small gathering of people laughed.

"You set her up for that one, Levi," Hope commented. "But then again, she baited you." She sighed. "So he doesn't think we are a bunch of theoretical mourners—or *non*-mourners—do you feel comfortable sharing the actual reason you're here?"

Tilly sighed. "I'm lucky. I don't know yet what it's like to lose someone close to me. But the man I love lost *his* wife about a decade ago, and I'm just trying to understand him better by talking with all of you."

Levi's chest squeezed. Wow. He was *not* expecting that, the love part or that she would give up her Saturday mornings to learn more about his father from people who've experienced something close to what his father experienced in losing Levi and Matteo's mother.

"Does my father know you do this?" Levi asked tentatively, and Tilly nodded.

"He and Matteo used to come together, when Hope first got here." Tilly shrugged. "One day Denny asked if I wanted to come along, and I've been coming ever since."

Levi's throat tightened. His father and Matteo did grief counseling. *Together*. And Levi had no idea. Suddenly, despite being back in Summertown for the first time in years, he felt a million miles away.

"They still attend," Hope added, directing her attention to the still-stunned Levi. "But only on occasion, when they feel like they have something to work out."

The air in the otherwise spacious room felt thinner, like he couldn't fill his lungs enough to form words. So he nodded, letting everyone know he'd heard what Hope had said, but that was all he had in him at the moment.

"Why don't we go around the circle from Tilly," Hope suggested. "Clockwise, so we can give our new member a few minutes to get ready to share." She smiled encouragingly at Levi, and he forced what he hoped resembled a smile in return.

Around the circle they went, Old Man Wilton explaining what a wonderful woman his wife was and having been perfectly content to live out the rest of his years with the animals on his farm—until he'd wandered into Mrs. Pinkney's sweet shop with a hankering for one of her almond-coconut clusters just before closing, and she invited him to dinner.

"I was tired of eating alone," Old Man Wilton told them. "Turned out she was too."

Dawson Hayes grunted something about losing his father. The woman next to him—Levi was pretty sure she owned the candle shop—had recently lost an aunt. Another claimed to be from Middleton, the next town over and sometimes Summertown rival. She was mourning her twenty-year-old dachshund named Oscar... as in *Mayer Weiner*.

Everyone there so readily shared a quick snippet about the person—or pet—they missed. Tilly Higginson was the only one there to support a loved one who'd experienced loss. And finally, it was Levi's turn.

All eyes were on him, which shouldn't have mattered. He'd stood up in front of five classes of judgmental teens the day before and barely flinched when he went over the syllabus with his health class and had to mention the word *prophylactic*. Hell, on NCAA football game days, he didn't even notice the ESPN cameras anymore. But this was...a lot.

"Whenever you're ready, Levi," Hope told him when he still hadn't uttered a sound.

He drew in a breath and opened his mouth, but he was upstaged by a metal crash and clatter just outside the door. The whole group rubbernecked in the direction of the disturbance.

Levi caught sight of a familiar running shoe and purple spandex-clad leg as the disturber tried to flee.

"Haddie?" he called.

Hope was already out of her seat and striding toward the door where a folding chair—one Levi remembered passing as he strode through the door—now lay toppled in front of the entryway.

"Hello," Hope said as a pink-cheeked Haddie spun back toward the door, a chagrined smile on her face. She lifted the chair and set it back in its upright position beside the door and let out a nervous laugh.

"I wasn't..." Haddie started. "I didn't mean to eavesdrop." She shrugged. "Figured I could just lurk for a bit before deciding whether or not I wanted to come in."

Hope held out a hand, and Haddie shook it. "You're welcome to lurk *inside*," Hope assured her in a reassuring tone. "We still have a few more chairs to fill."

Haddie's eyes met Levi's, then darted away just as quickly.

What was Haddie even doing here? Had she followed him? He wasn't sure that was even possible, considering her running shoes weren't in their usual resting spot beside the front door when he'd left, which meant she'd already been gone. But then... *why?*

Haddie untied the hoodie around her waist and shrugged it over her shoulders, shoving her hands in the kangaroo pocket as she let Hope lead her inside. She chose a chair that was neither near Levi nor in his direct line of sight, but it didn't matter. Her presence was suddenly true north, and Levi the needle of a compass with no choice but to follow.

"Feel free to introduce yourself and tell what brings you to the group," Hope encouraged after taking her own seat again. "Or you can get your bearings while Levi does his introduction since it's technically *his* turn."

"She can go first," Levi blurted out. "I'm totally okay with that."

Haddie's eyes met his, and she raised her brows. Then she straightened in her seat, rising to the challenge.

"Sure," Haddie replied. "Might as well after *that* entrance."

Soft laughter traveled around the circle. She had them wrapped around her finger already, Levi included. "Hi...everyone," she continued. "So, yeah. I'm Haddie. The lurker." More laughter. "And my friends Emma and Matteo, who I'm sure you all know, recommended the group since I...um...just lost my grandmon..." She cleared her throat and shook her head. "I lost my grand*mother* a couple of weeks ago. I'm new in town, and I just started teaching at Summertown Elementary. I was really looking forward to starting fresh, but things haven't exactly been going according to plan."

"You mean the budget cuts?" Tilly Higginson asked.

Haddie's eyes widened, worrying she'd just endangered her job more than she'd meant.

"Oh, don't worry, honey!" Tilly continued, waving her off. "It's almost impossible to keep a secret in this town, even if you are Coach Crawford."

Haddie let loose a relieved breath and then decided to go for broke since the cat was already out of the bag. Her words picked up both volume and momentum as she went on. "And I know football is everything to Summertown, but there are other important sports... I mean *programs*," she amended, and Levi realized she understood that program cuts weren't exactly public as far as she knew. "And those *programs* are important to the kids who are in them and the faculty who sponsor them." She smiled nervously. "What was I supposed to share again?"

Hope pressed her lips into a grin. "Your name and why you're here. I think you covered that."

"Right," Haddie replied. "Anyone else want to overshare?"

Levi felt the air rush from his lungs as it all hit him at once. Haddie in the hotel bar, the black dress that had seemed so out of place for someone who wasn't a guest at Tommy's wedding. He hadn't simply met Haddie on her birthday. He'd met her on the day she'd buried her grandmother. How had this never come up? It hit him then that despite having already lived with the woman for two weeks, he barely knew any more about her than he did that first night. And now here was Coach Crawford taking away one more thing that she loved, and Levi had basically shrugged it off. He really was an asshole.

"I'm sorry for your loss," Hope told her.

Haddie gave her a painful smile. "Thank you."

"A car wash!" Tilly Higginson chimed in.

"A what?" Haddie asked, confused.

"A *car* wash!" Tilly repeated. "Whatever programs need money, you should organize a car wash. It's fun for the students, and I guarantee you that anyone in town who drives will be downright delighted, considering the nearest place to get a professional wash is a half hour outside of town."

She let out a breath and smiled. "Thank you, Tilly. That is an excellent idea." And while all eyes but hers seemed to pivot back to Levi, he was still staring at Haddie. Finally she turned to face him and shrugged, as if to say, *Surprise!*

"Levi?" Hope said, and Levi had to deliberately peel his gaze away from Haddie, trying his best to collect himself as he did.

"Right," Levi replied, scratching the back of his neck. "I'm Levi, and I'm here because a judge says I have to be," he added coolly. Might as well lead with the truth, right? "I'm sure most of you have seen the YouTube video, or at least clips of it, floating around social media." He scrubbed a hand across his face. "I did something wrong, something I've never done before, and a judge who'd never met me before my sentencing decided that I had anger management issues stemming from unresolved grief." He let out a bitter laugh. "So… There you go."

He waited for nods of understanding and received a few, but a quiet scoff made him flinch.

He cleared his throat and turned his direction back to his roommate, brows knitted together. "I'm sorry, but do you…have a problem with why I'm here?"

Haddie sighed. "No. I mean…okay…yes?"

"Yes?" he parroted.

"It's just… That's…it?" she continued. "Like…for real?" Her tone was gentle, yet he immediately went into defense mode. "This is a grief support group, you know? We grieve." She pumped two fists in the air like *We grieve* was the latest Muskies cheer. "I guess I figured that if there's anywhere you should feel safe to drop the everything-rolls-off-my-shoulders act, don't you think it's here?" She winced at her own words, which meant she knew she'd stepped over the line.

He barked out a bitter laugh. "Says the woman who just rattled off her own grandmother's passing in a very matter-of-fact list of what's been going on in the past two weeks."

"Levi!" Tilly Higginson cried in a tone that brought back such a visceral memory of his mom that he nearly lost it, and Levi didn't lose it—except when asshole refs made bad calls.

"It's fine," Haddie said. "He's right. I shouldn't have pushed."

"See?" he replied, not sure if he was directing the ridiculously childish-sounding response to Tilly or Haddie or anyone else who was listening. What. Was. Happening? These meetings were supposed to be a formality, not the relaunching of whatever sort of battle kept brewing beneath the surface of his and Haddie's relationship.

Wait. Not relationship. Roommateship? That was a thing, right? Whatever it was, after their texts last night, he'd thought… What the hell *did* he think? When he and Haddie were able to hide behind a screen, it almost felt like they were making progress. But whenever they came face-to-face? *POW! BANG!* It was like a comic-book battle between hero and villain, and he couldn't keep track of who was who. When she didn't immediately respond, he continued. "There is nothing in my court order that specifies what I have to share at these meetings. I'm here, aren't I? Doesn't that count for something?"

"Of course it does," Hope interjected. "But maybe this is about something else?" She motioned between Levi and Haddie.

"What?" they both cried in unison. "She's just my roommate," Levi added. "That's it." He gestured like he was a ref calling a slide into home plate safe.

"Right," Haddie agreed with less conviction in her voice. "Just roommates. That's it."

She sounded…hurt? But that was it, right? That was what they agreed to, and they'd both stuck to that agreement.

He threw his hands in the air. "What do you actually want from me, Haddie?" he pleaded. "I said I was sorry. I gave you your space. And then last night…last night…" He groaned. "Why does my grief or lack thereof mean so much to you? You barely know me."

"I don't know, Levi," she replied, more gently this time. "But you could maybe tell us why it meant so much to a judge."

He tilted his head toward the ceiling and pinched the bridge of his nose. Then he straightened and let loose a long sigh. "Because my very public mistake is very publicly available for anyone to see. It's not a story worth telling."

"I haven't seen it," Haddie admitted. "Maybe I want to hear it," she added, her tone softer this time. "From you."

When he finally looked at her again, all accusation had left her eyes. And despite knowing that they were sitting in a room full of other people, at that moment, Levi felt like it was only him and Haddie. No one else—not Matteo, not his father—had *asked* what happened. They took what they saw as the whole story.

"Fine," he relented, his voice as soft as hers. "You win." He drew in a breath, and then he told her—and the group—everything.

CHAPTER II

"There's not much to say," Levi started, and Haddie found herself sliding forward on her metal folding chair, elbows resting on her knees and her chin in her hands. "A ref made a bad call on one of my players right before halftime, and I challenged it because it would have cost us possession of the ball that I knew we'd earned." He shrugged. "The other officials confirmed I was right. Stuff like this happens all the time."

Levi had been on both the winning and losing end of challenging a call. That was just how it went. It wasn't supposed to get personal, and even if it did, he wasn't supposed to react. "The clock ran out," he continued, "and we broke for halftime, which should have been the end of it. But as we were heading off the field, that particular referee said something ugly about the player in question, so I decked him." He cleared his throat. "The referee...just in case there was any confusion."

This earned him a few sympathetic nods, a couple of soft laughs, but no one said a word, so Levi continued.

"Here's the thing..." Levi cleared his throat as his chest

squeezed. "Doesn't matter how many times I tell myself I did it to protect my player. I wasn't doing anyone any favors by laying that guy out. And then social media made a spectacle of the whole thing, my arrest included." Levi let out a bitter laugh. "I'm really just a selfish prick, right? And according to a judge and a court-appointed psychologist, an angry, supposedly grieving selfish prick at that."

He was wearing basketball shorts and a purple Muskies T-shirt, and when he pressed his hands to his knees, Haddie caught a glimpse of the thin pink line that ran from an inch below his kneecap to an inch above it, a forever reminder of the night she knew—thanks to knowing Emma and Matteo's history—Levi and Matteo had lost their mom. Was the judge right? Had Levi never processed that grief like he should have? But also, what the hell was *should have*? How could someone put rules around an impossibly painful emotion?

Levi's jaw clenched as he continued. "That is the only time I've ever raised a hand to someone else. I am not a violent man, and I don't condone violence as a means to any sort of end. It just…happened."

"No," Hope said.

Levi's eyes darted toward her. "No? What do you mean, *no?*"

"I mean no," she replied matter-of-factly. "You made a choice. It might have been a split-second choice, and in your head, you might have made yourself believe that choice came with noble intent, but it didn't just happen." Hope leaned forward, resting her elbows on her knees as she pinned Levi with her gaze. "Why did the judge think you were grieving, Levi?"

"You already know the answer. You've seen the paperwork from my lawyer."

Hope nodded sagely. "Why don't you tell the group?"

He gritted his teeth. "I'm not the only one here, right? Why don't you give someone else a turn?"

"Hope!" Haddie blurted out, literally launching herself out of her seat. "Come on. Give him a break."

Levi didn't look at Haddie, though. This time he kept his eyes trained on the woman who seemed to be holding him emotionally captive.

"Because it was the ten-year anniversary of my mother's death, okay?" he relented. "And instead of being here with my father and brother to honor or celebrate her life, I was on the football field worried about a stupid play. Surprise. I'm just as much of a selfish piece of shit now as I was then. On the field when she died and on the field again ten years after." He huffed out a breath. "This was a mistake." Then he rose, stepped around his seat, and strode toward the door.

"It doesn't count as a session if you don't stay for the full hour!" Hope called after him, but Levi didn't pause, didn't look back, didn't do a thing except keep on walking until he was out of sight.

Haddie chewed on her bottom lip, but she was already standing, so the next move was to go after him, right? She had no clue what she would say when she caught up to him. *If* she caught up to him. She hadn't seen his truck outside, but maybe he'd parked around a corner. Maybe he was already on the road heading who knew where. All Haddie knew was that she'd set the ball in motion for Hope to goad him into sharing before he was ready.

"I should…" She winced, glancing at the rest of the group

who'd barely gotten started thanks to her and Levi. "I'm sorry for eavesdropping and leaving, but I just want to make sure he's okay."

Hope smiled at her, as did Tilly Higginson, and a few others nodded.

As Haddie crossed toward the other side of the circle, Hope gently grabbed her wrist before Haddie made it across the perimeter.

"Yeah?" Haddie asked nervously. "I'm so sorry. Am I supposed to pay you or something?"

Hope laughed. "Last time I checked, free was still free. Just… tell Levi that if he comes back next week and *stays*, I'll put this session back on the log."

"Oh!" Haddie replied. "That is really nice of you. Thank you." Then she hesitated for a second. "But maybe next time, not so much tough love?"

Hope shrugged. "He shared, though, didn't he?"

The woman wasn't wrong. Haddie learned more about Levi in the past ten minutes than she had in the past two weeks.

"Right," Haddie admitted. "Again…thanks."

In that moment, Haddie realized that Hope wasn't only nice but also really pretty. And even though she knew, logically, that Hope could or *should* only have a professional interest in Levi, she was shocked by a wave of jealousy at the possibility of her interest being otherwise.

Which was ridiculous, of course. Because Haddie and Levi were friends. *Only* friends. Although they'd been attracted to each other that night in the hotel, they'd both agreed nothing like should ever happen again between them. Yet it somehow only occurred to

Haddie *now* that eventually—likely sooner rather than later—Levi would be attracted to someone else. The thought dropped like a stone in her gut, and she did not like the feeling.

"You're welcome," Hope replied, jolting Haddie back to the moment. She let go of Haddie's wrist, freeing her to run after Levi and say…what? She'd simply have to figure it out when she got there.

Grateful she was dressed for a run, she jogged up the stairs and out the door, ready to break into a sprint but instead having to pull the brakes the second she reached the bottom of the town hall steps, lest she plow face-first into what she knew was a solid wall of muscle. *Levi* muscle.

She pinwheeled her arms, trying to keep from pitching forward, when he caught her by both wrists.

"Whoa," he said softly, his big hands absorbing her body's momentum and sending a shock of electricity straight to her toes.

She wriggled free as soon as she found her footing, and Levi took a step back, palms up in surrender.

"Sorry," he added. "Was just trying to help."

Haddie threw her arms in the air. "What kind of a person makes a dramatic exit like that only to—I don't know—stop and take in the sights?"

Why was she angry? Or was she exasperated? *Frustrated?* What *was* she?

Instead of answering her with words, he nodded toward something above Haddie's head, so she turned around to see whatever it was he was seeing.

"Oh," she said softly, glancing up at the town hall's painted pillars. Its yellow-and-black candy-cane-*striped* pillars to be exact, the tops punctuated by overlapping hubcaps painted pink, yellow, and orange to look like the wispy foliage of the trees from Dr. Seuss's *The Lorax*, though Haddie always thought they looked more like troll doll hair. "I was here last summer when those popped up. I kind of forget they're new for some people."

Levi crossed his arms and kept his gaze trained on the art installation Mayor Green had once called vandalism. Now he called it what it really was—a lucrative tourist attraction, thanks to the still-unnamed artist everyone knew only as the Gardener.

"I thought I was going to be late this morning, so I just kind of rushed inside without taking the time to let it sink in. Is it true no one knows who it really is? I mean, no one believes it was Old Man Wilton, right?" he asked, referring to the mayor's insistence that the so-called vandal come forward after he and the Gardener struck a deal via social media. The old farmer stepped forward claiming it was him, but all someone had to do was look to the top of the town hall columns to know there was zero chance the man had climbed so far as the building's roof to finish the job.

Haddie squinted, the fiery eye of the sun making the colors dance in her vision.

"It's like walking around in a—"

"Tim Burton movie," Levi interrupted.

Haddie gave him an approving grin. "And here I thought all you knew was Pixar."

This earned her a laugh. "Hey. Don't knock where your name-sake comes from, Dash."

The nickname he'd used as an accusation the morning after their meeting now felt like a cozy, warm hug even though Haddie was so not a hugger.

"I'm sorry about what happened in there," she told him, nodding toward the building. "And I'm sorry about your mom."

"I'm sorry about your grandma," he countered, but she waved him off.

"I'm out here to check on *you*," she told him.

Levi blew out a breath. "It was more than a decade ago. I should be over it by now, right?"

Haddie shook her head, and without thinking about what she was doing—because apparently she just acted these days and threw thinking out the window—she pressed a palm to the left side of his chest.

Levi's eyes grew wide as he glanced down at her hand where she could feel his heart thump faster against her palm.

"What are you doing?" he asked, tilting his incredulous gaze back up to meet hers.

"Wow. Your heart is going a mile a minute," she told him. "I knew I was right."

"Right about what?"

He took a step back, but Haddie just followed, taking a step forward.

"You, sir, have feelings."

He scoffed, and this time he wrapped a gentle hand around

her wrist and lowered it to her side. "I never claimed to be a robot, Haddie."

No, she thought. *That's me.* Because Haddie did rattle off her grandmother's death like it was just this thing that happened a couple of weeks ago. But this moment was about Levi, wasn't it? If she could get him to open up, then wasn't it a win for feeling your feelings no matter who was feeling them? That was totally sound logic.

"And I never claimed you were a robot," she told him. "You know, I didn't like Hope pushing you like that…" She paused for a moment. "Even if I kind of gave her the opening to do so…" Another pause as she grimaced and waited for Levi to let her have it because hadn't she so easily seized an opportunity to deflect attention from her onto someone else? But he didn't let her have it. Instead, he crossed his arms over his chest and the beating heart she'd just felt with her own hand and calmly waited for her to finish. "She was only trying to get you to admit what it looks like a judge already knew."

"Which is what?" he asked, the sudden hoarseness in his voice making Haddie's chest feel like it was squeezed so tightly that her own heart might pop right through her rib cage and onto the sun-drenched sidewalk, which—by the way—would totally kill the moment.

"That there is no expiration date on grief." She grabbed his forearms, and good god they were as solid as his chest. Did his muscles have muscles?

Levi could have fought her. In fact, Haddie was pretty sure she could have kicked both feet up off the ground and hung from those very solid, muscles-with-muscles forearms, but he must have sensed her silent threat to do so because he dropped his arms a second after she gave them a soft tug toward the ground. And then she grabbed his hand and pulled him down the sidewalk that was not, thankfully, strewn with her exploding heart.

"Where are we going?" he asked, confusion knitting his brow.

Haddie swore that palm to palm, skin to skin, she felt her pulse mingle with his. Except hers was racing, as if it was trying to outrun his, and she found herself so invested in whether or not he—or his pulse—would catch up, that she hadn't realized her non-answer until Levi asked the question again.

"*Where* are we going? Or are you kidnapping me?" The corner of his mouth twitched into an almost grin. "Because I'm not sure if you know, but I'm kind of a big deal in this town. If I go missing, the people of Summertown will leave no stone unturned until they find my captor and exact revenge."

She paused briefly and gave him a practical, definitive single nod of her chin. "We need ice cream."

CHAPTER 12

Haddie marched with purpose through the town square, paying no attention to the three giant sunflowers there...made from hubcaps! Levi knew the town had changed in the decade plus since he'd lived here, but part of him felt more like a stranger to the place where he was born and raised than Haddie, a woman who'd only moved to Summertown a couple of weeks ago.

He could have easily kept up with her clipped pace, overtaken her if he wanted. But there was something about her leading him where she wanted to go. There was something about her wanting to provide something he needed, even if he didn't exactly feel like he *needed* ice cream.

She finally stopped in front of Sweet, the shop that, yes, carried every kind of sweet you could imagine, including ice cream.

Mrs. Pinkney, Sweet's owner and proprietor since Levi's birth and likely before, was just flipping the CLOSED sign to OPEN when they approached.

She opened the door, a bell jingling overhead as happened in most—if not all—other stores in town, and greeted them with a warm, ear-to-ear grin.

"Levi Rourke, as I live and breathe!" the older woman said, pulling him unexpectedly into a warm embrace.

For a moment he simply stood there, not knowing how to react. It wasn't like the folks of Summertown weren't huggers. On the contrary. Everyone here was like one big family. It was just that Levi hadn't been hugged in…in… Levi couldn't remember the last time he'd been hugged.

After a stunned moment while he breathed in Mrs. Pinkney's telltale scent of sugar, butter, and a hint of cinnamon, he returned the embrace, albeit a bit stiffly and a lot awkwardly.

She pushed him back to arm's length and took a good look at him. "Still as handsome as ever, aren't you?"

Levi felt his cheeks grow warm, and he could feel Haddie smiling at him—likely in a laughing way—in his peripheral vision.

"I bet that college-coaches calendar sells out each year just because of your picture!" Mrs. Pinkney continued, motioning for them to enter the shop.

"Coaches calendar?" Haddie cried, and now he could see that she certainly was sporting a laughing smile. "I'm sorry… What?"

Levi rolled his eyes as Mrs. Pinkney led them to a table and then pulled a smartphone out of her pristine white apron. "It's right here on Amazon," she told Haddie, and the pride in her voice made Levi blush even more, which only made him roll his eyes harder—at himself. He was a grown-ass adult man, for crying out loud, which meant he was way too old to blush like some lovesick teenager.

Not that he was lovesick. Christ. No. He was just…embarrassed. That was all.

"Oh. My. God," Haddie said with a mixture of surprise and reverence. "Levi Rourke, did they…oil up your torso for this?"

Levi pinched the bridge of his nose and collapsed into a chair, swearing under his breath.

"Wait!" Haddie continued. "Did you wax your chest for this before they oiled you up?"

He didn't have to look at the image Haddie was staring at to know what she was referring to. He might not have been invited to participate in the most recent year's calendar due to the whole legal circus surrounding his suspension, but he remembered what the photographer and stylist had dressed him in the year before when the theme was Hometown Beginnings.

The stylist had somehow procured a pair of purple Muskie football pants and matching helmet with his high school number, 23, painted on it. It was only because of the bottle of whiskey at the studio that Levi was able to relax enough to hold that helmet and—yes—let the stylist oil him up.

"Any proceeds went to a combined scholarship fund for incoming athletes from all participating universities," he grumbled. "They still do."

He glanced up to see Haddie thumbing the screen on her own phone now, a goofy grin on her face. "There!" she declared, then set her phone onto the table. "I'm now a proud supporter of the NCAA Hometown Beginnings Scholarship Fund."

Mrs. Pinkney clapped. "Wonderful! Always happy to turn

another donor on to such a worthy cause." Then she winked at Haddie, who responded with a curtsy.

"Mrs. Pinkney," Haddie responded with triumph in her voice. "We will each take a double scoop of salted-caramel pretzel crunch, please!"

The other woman responded with a curt nod and then disappeared behind the candy/pastry/ice cream counter.

Haddie lowered herself to her seat and leaned across the tiny table so her eyes—and every other part of her face, for that matter—were an inch from Levi's.

"I'm going to pin this calendar to the wall right above my headboard and keep it on the lovely month of June for all twelve months of the year," she teased, referring to the month he appeared in the calendar, which was also the month of his own birthday.

Calamondin orange blossoms.

"Cala *what?*" Haddie asked.

"What?" Levi parroted, and she was still right there, right in front of him, her nose crinkled and her soft pink lips pursed in a pout. "Did I say something?" Because he thought he'd only *thought* the thought.

"Something about orange blossoms," she replied, dropping back into her seat.

Levi swallowed. "Your shampoo or perfume or whatever," he replied, affecting as much nonchalance as he could muster while momentarily drunk on her scent. "It smells like this orange tree my mom used to grow."

Haddie looked at him like he'd just sprouted a second head.

"Look, I know just about everyone in this town has a greener thumb than I'll ever have—I mean, I've killed succulents—but I'm pretty sure orange trees are pretty hard to grow in Illinois, what with that thing we have called *winter*."

Levi shook his head, coming out of his trance and straightening in his seat. "So, there is this citrus fruit, the calamondin, which is something between, like, an orange and a kumquat?" His brows drew together before he nodded to himself. "Yeah. A kumquat. And it grows on this smaller, indoor-outdoor tree that you can bring inside during the winter months. It was my mom's favorite plant. And when she brought it inside..." He closed his eyes and took in a deep breath through his nose. "It smelled like summer whenever you walked by the tree, even if it was twenty below and grayer than gray outside. It smelled like...you."

"Oh," Haddie said softly, the teasing grin from her recent calendar discovery melting into a soft sort of reverence. "It's a set," she told him, her voice a bit hoarse so that she had to clear her throat. "Shampoo, conditioner, body spray. I get it at this little boutique around the corner from my apart—" But she cut herself off. "I used to get it there. Guess I'll be in the market for a new scent soon." She gave him a one-shoulder shrug.

"No!" Levi blurted out. "I mean, Chicago's still a great place to visit, right? We could... er... You could always swing by the shop the next time you're in town. If you wanted to. Because it suits you. The scent."

Stop talking. Stop talking. Stop talking, he warned himself.

"Here we go!" Mrs. Pinkney cried from behind the counter,

saving him from himself. But before he glanced up at the shop proprietor and the monstrous bowls of ice cream she'd just slid across the counter, he caught Haddie smiling shyly down at nothing in particular in her lap.

"I'll grab those," he mumbled, then ambled the two steps to the counter to retrieve the largest servings of ice cream he'd ever encountered. When he returned, setting down the mountains of ice cream on the table, Haddie seemed to have recovered from whatever was keeping her from meeting his gaze before.

"Yes!" she cried, clapping her hands together.

"Yes?" Levi asked. "No person should consume this much ice cream in one sitting, and I'm talking about just one of these bowls, split between us."

Haddie scoffed and waved him off. "The words coming out of your mouth right now are words of a man who has never had salted-caramel pretzel-crunch ice cream, and you grew up here, Coach! There's no way in hell you escaped the best thing to ever touch your tongue!" She squeezed her eyes shut and shook her head. "You know what I mean!"

He laughed while simultaneously trying to banish the thought of Haddie mentioning his tongue.

"I was...um...very strict about keeping my body healthy," Levi admitted. "I hope you know I was joking before about calling myself a big deal around here, but the truth was—or I guess still is—that the Summertown football team is one of the most important things to this town. And when I was on that team—"

"The *star* of that team..." Haddie blurted out.

140

Levi sighed. "I didn't take my responsibility lightly, which meant treating my body like a temple and only feeding it what it needed to stay strong and healthy."

"But you drink beer," Haddie said through an incredulous laugh.

"Yeah...*now*. But not in high school."

She filled her spoon with a heaping mound of vanilla-chocolate swirl ice cream that dripped with golden caramel and—he assumed—with a hidden hunk of pretzel as well. "Levi, you've been out of high school for almost fifteen years, and you're telling me that in all that time, you've never eaten a bowl of Mrs. Pinkney's salted-caramel pretzel-crunch ice cream?"

"Not once that I can recall!" Mrs. Pinkney chimed in from behind the pastry case where she was organizing her fresh creations.

Levi shrugged. "Some old habits die harder than the rest, and I never really got into sweets, and I'm not about to start with a basin of ice cream that will no doubt turn me lactose intolerant if I'm not already."

Haddie snorted and then, without warning, shoved her already dripping spoon against his lips so that he had no choice but to open wide or else possibly chip a tooth.

He coughed as her spoon came dangerously close to his uvula and then clamped his lips shut around the utensil, his tongue and teeth and roof of his mouth wiping it clean before releasing their grip and effectively giving the spoon back to its rightful owner.

It took a couple of seconds for the brain freeze to subside and the mix of flavors—vanilla bean; rich, fudgy chocolate; buttery caramel; and the savory pretzel crunch—to register. But when it did...

"Holy fuck," Levi's frozen and still full mouth attempted to say, but instead it came out as more of a *Hoe-wee fuh*.

"Language, Levi..." Mrs. Pinkney warned. "This is a family establishment that will be overrun with children before you finish that bowl."

Levi nodded and gave her a thumbs-up as he swallowed. "Yes, ma'am!"

Haddie dropped her spoon in her bowl, dusted off her hands, and crossed her arms. "Best thing to ever touch your tongue, right?" she asked with a self-satisfied *I told you so. When I'm right I'm right* kind of smile.

"Yes," he admitted. "Hell fucking yes." Then he covered his mouth as Mrs. Pinkney shot him a reprimanding glare. "Sorry!"

And even though he slightly regretted his life choices later that day, Levi Rourke polished off the entire bowl of ice cream and maybe a little of Haddie's too.

Asleep? he texted late that night when a nagging thought would not let him fall asleep.

Birthday Girl: Almost

He should have let it go, should have dealt with the fact that he wasn't going to sleep that night rather than unburden his burden onto Haddie's shoulders and make the knowledge her burden too. But there was some reckless part of him—after all, he consumed basins of ice cream now—that wanted her to know.

Levi: I lied before. Earlier today, I mean.

The three dots appeared and disappeared, then appeared again.

Birthday Girl: About...what?

He should definitely abort this mission. He'd already made her nervous. But now, if he didn't follow through, she'd grill him until he did. So, in the name of honesty and a bit of selfish assholery, he told her.

Levi: Salted-caramel pretzel crunch is the second-best thing to ever touch my tongue.

Three dots…there and gone. There and gone. There and gone. If she didn't respond, he'd leave it be. That was the silent promise he made to her. But after an interminable several seconds more, her text came through.

Birthday Girl: What is the first?
Levi: You

CHAPTER 13

evi watched the clock run out after the final goal was scored. He clapped four times, his jaw tight before he called out, "Good game, Muskies! Good game!" to no one in particular. The two teams did their high five/handshake thing as they walked off the field, and then Levi led his team to an empty section of the already mostly empty bleachers as their few spectators filed out. "You too, McMannus!" Levi called over his shoulder to his one benchwarmer who hadn't left the bench with the others.

One full week of school, and as predicted, the guy was already on academic probation. Levi wasn't even sure how that was possible, but he was forced to bench his best player for their first game, and it hadn't gone well. For any of them.

He kept his eyes on Billy McMannus until the kid slowly rose from the bench and moved even more slowly toward the section of the bleachers Levi had deemed their postgame meeting spot.

"Thanks for joining us, McMannus," Levi told him.

Billy mumbled something under his breath and joined the rest of the team on the bleachers.

Levi sighed and adjusted his visor, which was no longer nec-essary considering the sky full of stars blanketing them from over-head. But *not* wearing his lucky visor? Yeah, that was never going to happen, even if the luck was still catching up to him from the college circuit.

"Listen up, team!" Levi began. "This was our first game and—"

"We *ate* shit," Teddy Kostas interrupted.

"Watch it, Kostas," Levi warned.

"Sorry, Coach," Teddy replied with a sigh.

"All right," Levi continued, addressing the entirety of his team. "We *did* eat shit tonight, but does anyone know why?"

Billy McMannus's name rose in a shallow murmur among the team members.

Levi nodded appraisingly. "Yes," he agreed. "We were missing our best player tonight. But…what if there *were* no Billy McMannus on this team to begin with?"

"Uh… Thanks, Coach?" Billy replied drily, and the rest of the team chuckled softly.

Levi narrowed his eyes at his star player who was so far living up to his not-so-stellar academic reputation, and Billy held up his hands in defense but said nothing else.

"You *all* have your talents," Levi continued, addressing the entire team. And he meant it. Even the players who weren't starters *could* be with the right discipline, the right coach. But was *he* that guy? Levi didn't know. And he still had a hard time wrapping his head around trying to become that guy when he knew after this year it wouldn't even matter.

But they *don't know that*, a voice in his head whispered, one that sounded a lot like a roommate he knew who was finally warming back up to the two of them being friends.

Levi sighed. "It was a rough start, and you all need your rest, so I'm going to let you all head home. But I'm giving you an assignment to work on before Monday afternoon's practice." This earned him a chorus of grumbles. He lifted his whistle to his lips in warning, and the grumbling died down. "If *I* have to work this weekend to figure out where we need help, then so do you. So, come Monday afternoon, I want one page, *handwritten*, with what you think *you* could have done differently in tonight's game. The focus is on *you*, meaning I don't want one page telling me how you think one of your teammates could have made *your* life easier. The only person you can control out there is yourself. So that's who I want to hear about, okay?"

Murmurs of "Yes, Coach" bubbled up from the stands from all except one player. For the first time that night, Billy McMannus was smiling as he leaned back on his elbows like he was kicking back in on a chaise at an all-inclusive resort.

"What's with the face, McMannus?" Levi asked, and Billy let loose a soft laugh.

"What's the matter, Coach? Can't the one guy who has 'no homework' this weekend take a second to gloat?" He put air quotes around *no homework*.

Levi shrugged. "He could, if such a guy existed. But last I checked, you're still a part of this team, and if you had done something differently, you would have been out on that field tonight. So there is no way you're off the hook for this, my friend. One page. What could *you* have done?"

Billy's smile fell, and though Levi knew the others were probably dying to taunt him about the shutdown, he was happy to see that the tone of his voice was enough to warn them not to.

"Grab your kits and get out of here," Levi told them after several moments of silence. "I'll see you on the track for warm-ups after school on Monday."

"Yes, Coach!" they responded in unison but with far less enthusiasm than he'd have liked. For tonight he'd let it go. They'd all been through enough.

They jogged to the sideline, packing up their kits and then heading off the field. Before he left, Billy McMannus glanced back at Levi with his jaw set and his eyes dark and narrowed.

Levi responded with a single nod.

Don't let other people tell his story, Haddie's voice reminded him as the advice crept back to the front of his thoughts, and Levi tried to shake the sound of it away. One stupid text almost a week ago, to which she of course did not respond, and now his inner monologue belonged to her.

That didn't mean he'd been thinking about her all week and what her nonresponse meant. Or that he'd been thinking about the fact that exactly zero late-night texts had appeared since. All it meant, Levi reasoned, was that Haddie gave some good advice when it came to soccer and getting to know his students. His admitting to her—like a complete idiot—that she was basically the best thing he'd ever tasted had nothing to do with it.

Who was he kidding? Of course what he'd said had everything to do with it. And now, as his team trailed off the field, he found himself wondering not just how her game went or if she was having a similar talk with her team but instead if he'd royally fucked their friendship beyond repair.

She'd acted perfectly roommatey the whole week. She'd simply never broached the subject of the ill-fated text, and he had certainly followed suit.

Levi startled the second he walked through his apartment door when he found Haddie literally standing just on the other side of their doormat, hands behind her back.

"Holy shit!" he exclaimed. "How long have you been waiting there like a freaking horror-movie creeper."

Haddie beamed. "Actually, I was sitting. Then I was pacing. Then I heard your key in the door, and—as you know—I'm a runner and pretty fast, so…"

Levi kicked off his shoes, but he was basically trapped against the door because Haddie still hadn't moved.

"We won!" she finally blurted. "And I don't just mean *won*. We *owned* Middleton. Three to zero. It was amazing, Levi. I can't even explain it. I mean, I've played the sport. I've watched it all my life. But coaching it? Do you know what it's like to coach a sport that you love with your whole heart and watch your players succeed?"

After a beat of silence, Haddie's words seemed to catch up with her brain, and her smile faltered.

"Sorry," she added with a wince. "Of course you know, and I'm an asshole. I just... It's the biggest adrenaline rush I've ever had, and I couldn't wait to share it with..." She hesitated and bit her bottom lip. "I couldn't wait to tell you." She rocked back and forth on her heels, then produced two opened bottles of beer from behind her back, offering one up to him. "How did your game go?"

"Holy shit," he said again, taking the offered beer. "You really are fast."

Levi's chest tightened as he took a swig, the cool, hoppy beverage somehow warming him from the inside out. He wasn't sure if it was because of how he felt about the night *he'd* had or because Haddie had come straight home after what he knew was her best night in a long time because she wanted to share her win with him.

Had he really not messed it all up?

Levi forced a smile and huffed out a laugh. "We got owned," he admitted. "But I'm really happy your team won." He meant it too. There was something about seeing Haddie smile like that, with her whole body, that made the bitter taste in his mouth sweeten.

Haddie finally backed up into the main living area, allowing him to move.

Levi strode to the couch and collapsed into the far corner, leaving room for Haddie on the other side.

She followed his lead and dropped down opposite him, lips pressed together like they were a dam, the words behind them begging to be set free.

He bit back a grin and gave her a single nod. "It's okay," he told her, and he meant it. "Tell me everything."

And she did. The dam burst, and Haddie told him everything from the kickoff to the final goal, to Sarah Ramirez not letting one ball past her goal line. To Middleton's defense being run ragged as Haddie's offense kept them running from one fakeout to another, kept them diving toward their own goal in an attempt to stop the unstoppable.

He'd never seen her like this before, and her complete and utter glee was infectious. Levi found his disappointment fading behind the smile taking over his features. Maybe this program wouldn't mean anything to him a year from now, but it would mean something to Haddie. It meant something to her now.

"We should do that car-wash thing," he said. The words rushed out of his mouth before he realized they were coming.

Haddie halted mid-sip, her eyes wide. "Are you serious?" she asked. "You... You want to do a fundraiser for the soccer program?"

Levi nodded and drained the rest of his beer. "I don't know if there's anything we can do to change Coach Crawford's mind," he admitted. "But I guess it doesn't hurt to try, right?" Plus, he told himself, it would look great on his résumé of look-at-all-the-great-things-I've-done-to-make-me-worthy-of-reinstatement, which wouldn't be such a terrible by-product of helping out the program, right?

Haddie set her beer on the end table and launched herself at him, wrapping her arms around his neck as he tried not to drop the empty bottle still in his hand.

"Thank you! Thank you! Thank you!" she exclaimed, her breath warm on his neck.

He coughed out a response, and she flew back, her cheeks

flushed and a nervous smile on her face. "Sorry!" she cried. "I should have given you some warning before crushing your lungs like that."

"It's okay," he told her, his voice strained as he pushed himself further into the corner and willed himself to *stop* reacting to her warm, soft curves having just been pressed against him.

Aunt Lorna's hairy mole. Aunt Lorna's hairy mole, he chanted silently in his head, remembering the great aunt whose upper-lip mole always bristled against his and Matteo's childhood cheeks when she greeted them with a hug.

Slowly his below-the-belt reaction receded, and Levi let out a relieved breath.

"I swear I'm not a hugger," she continued. "Though I know recent evidence does not support this assessment."

He laughed nervously, praying her eyes stayed trained on his and didn't dip any lower until... Okay. He sighed. Crisis fully averted. "Guess I...uh...just bring it out in you."

She shrugged, blissfully unaware that Levi had unexpectedly and immediately hardened at her touch. "It's weird, you know?" she continued. "The only person I've ever shown physical affection to in, like, the past decade...is Emma. Guess that means you're entering the inner circle," she teased.

"Inner...circle?" he asked, lowering his empty bottle so it casually rested against his zipper just in case anything she said reawakened his...stirrings.

Haddie nodded. "Of friends I trust."

A stone landed with a thud in the center of his gut. "Emma is the only person you trust?" he asked, wanting to ask if that was still the case when her grandmother was alive. But Haddie hadn't mentioned anything that had gone down in the grief group since their reconciliation last week, and Levi hadn't wanted to pry.

Haddie smiled at him but shook her head. "Not anymore, Levi Rourke. Welcome to the inner circle."

Haddie Martin's inner circle hadn't even existed for him three weeks ago, and now he found himself making a silent promise to never do anything that would get him kicked out of such a place.

He grinned. "Thank you," he told her. "It's an honor to be here." And he meant it. "Does...um...this mean that you forgive me?" he dared to ask, and Haddie's brows knit together.

"For what? I thought we were past all the before-the-ice-cream stuff," she said, but then her eyes widened as the elephant in the room revealed itself to her. "Ooh," she added. "Right. The ice cream."

Levi couldn't read her expression. "Because I would like to officially—on the record—apologize for the stupid, inconsiderate, selfish thing I texted you that night that has basically put an end to our little nighttime texting thing that I sort of enjoyed and maybe—if I'm being honest—sort of miss."

Haddie nodded sagely and then tapped a finger against her pursed lips. "I guess," she began, "that I've just been wondering how to respond and whether or not, in this circumstance, honesty was, in fact, better than pretending you never sent that text at all."

"Yes!" Levi blurted out. "Please. Honesty. Tell me I'm an asshole and then let me off the hook so I can get out of my head and we can get back to the way things were."

But instead of responding to him verbally, Haddie grabbed her phone from the end table, and a couple seconds later, Levi's phone buzzed in his pocket.

Birthday Girl: Salted-caramel pretzel crunch is the second-best thing to ever touch my tongue too. But we can't do anything about that. So you're off the hook, can get out of your head, and we can go back to the way things were.

Levi finished reading the text and then glanced up so his eyes met hers. Haddie pressed her lips into a resigned smile and shrugged as if to say, *Sorry, Champ. It's just not in the cards for us.*

She was right. Of course she was right. They'd both be jeopardizing their careers for something that already had an expiration date. So he did the only thing left to do and fired off a text of his own.

Levi: Great. Glad we're on the same page. Sorry for the momentary loss of sanity. Glad for things to get back to normal.

Except, despite them parting ways soon after and disappearing into the safety of their rooms, he couldn't help but wonder what it might be like if one day, something—or someone—mattered just a bit more than his career.

And that was how Levi Rourke set himself up for another sleepless night, getting tangled in his own meandering brain. But this time he played by the rules and kept his thoughts squarely to himself.

CHAPTER 14

Haddie watched from across the room as Levi raised a fist, ready to knock on the opened door when Piper, her blond, springy corkscrew pigtails bouncing as she walked, paused in front of the seemingly giant man in the opened classroom doorway and placed her hands on her hips.

"Miss Martin!" Piper called as Haddie continued to stare in Levi's direction. "The big man who is not on your favorite-things poster is at the door again!" She pointed accusingly at Levi, and Haddie pushed herself up from where she'd been crouching beside another student from Piper's pod, helping him color his paper towel.

She swiped a hand across her forehead, then realized that hand was freshly stained with wet purple marker and wondered what she'd just inadvertently painted across her face, not that there was any time to deal with accidental face painting when she had a whole gaggle of six-year-olds who were probably doing the same.

"Levi... I mean... Mr. Rourke!" she called above the din of her miniature humans coloring, chatting, and a small chorus of them singing Taylor Swift's "Me!" "Keep working on your rainbows, everyone, while I talk to Mr. Rourke for a second," she added.

She strode toward where he stood grinning at the scene before him, despite Piper having loudly reminded him of his very visible absence from Haddie's favorite things. Okay, so maybe she'd initially left him off the poster in the hopes that he'd see it and know she was mad at him about the whole *What's done is done* situation with the soccer teams. But now that they'd lived together for almost a month and had once again pumped the brakes on the attraction that hadn't exactly simmered like she'd hoped it would, his absence from her poster felt like a safety net, reminding her that no matter how good something tastes, that doesn't necessarily mean it's good *for* you.

"Sorry," she told him as she approached. "We're in the middle of a science experiment." Her brows drew together. "Wait… What are you doing here?"

Levi laughed, and while logic told her, *Hey! It's just a laugh. Everyone has one, and they do it every day,* that didn't stop her stomach from reacting with a slight flip and flutter at the sound of his chuckle.

"The flyer?" he said. "For the car wash?"

Shit! The flyer! Haddie was still getting used to the fact that Levi was all in on the fundraising effort that she'd forgotten all about offering to throw together a quick flyer that Levi would then post throughout the high school where they guessed they'd get most of their potential customers. There was also the matter of a room full of six-year-olds and tables filled with cups of water, markers, and not always entirely good intentions.

Haddie smacked her marker-stained hand against what she was sure was her marker-stained forehead.

"Right!" she said. "I totally meant to do that when the kids were at recess, but then I remembered I hadn't cut the paper towels yet for growing our rainbows, and I totally forgot. I promise I'll email it by the end of the day. Do you have a color printer on your side of the campus?" Haddie glanced up at the clock and then back to Levi. "Wait. Don't you have class right now?"

His smile broadened. "Turns out the guidance counselor is meeting with the seniors today during P.E. to talk about the college admissions process. Means I have a bonus free period before lunch."

"Miss Martin! Christopher is coloring his lips with our blue marker again!" someone called from behind.

"Shit," Haddie hissed under her breath. "That's the second marker he's used as lipstick today. I wouldn't care so much if it didn't dry the damned thing out so quickly," she added in a stage whisper, then turned over her shoulder. "Christopher! Your pod's rainbow needs to be on the paper towel, not on your mouth, for the experiment to work!"

Levi's eyes widened in horror as Haddie pivoted back to face him. "Isn't that, like, toxic or something?" he asked.

Haddie snorted. "They're not Sharpies or paint pens," she assured him. "Washable Crayolas are nontoxic, but I'm still going to have to do some explaining to Christopher's parents. Again."

A small hand tugged on Haddie's pinkie finger. "Miss Martin, I think the big man should help us grow a rainbow so you don't have to work so hard."

Piper stared up at Haddie with a smug expression that told her teacher she knew Haddie was reaching the end of her rope with their growing-a-rainbow activity, something that had looked like pure fun on one of her favorite teacher Pinterest boards and that was, instead, pure chaos.

Haddie sighed, her shoulders relaxing as if Piper had just presented her with the answer to all of her problems. True, Levi probably knew less about first grade science than he did about coaching soccer, but this was an all-hands-on-deck sort of situation, and Levi was standing right there, sporting two perfectly capable hands. For science. Capable hands for *sci-ence*.

"You do have an extra free period," Haddie reminded him with her brows raised. "Want to join us?"

She didn't have to warn him that first graders were way different than high schoolers, did she? Just as she was about to open her mouth to explain as much, Levi crossed his arms and declared, "Sure! Why not?"

Piper changed her grip from Haddie's pinkie to Levi's and gave him a soft tug. "Come *on*, Mister. My table is almost ready to go. We'll show you what to do."

Haddie huffed out a laugh and shrugged as Levi let Piper lead him to her seat where, despite the empty, miniature-sized chair where Haddie had just been perched, Levi opted for kneeling, which she appreciated since there was no way the chair would survive an attempt to support Levi's full body weight.

"Here's what we're doing," Piper began, and Haddie grinned, letting out a breath of relief just as she bent down to whisper in his ear.

Were those...goose bumps on his neck? Maybe the air-conditioning was set cooler than normal. It wasn't as if she could tell. She'd been perspiring since the activity began.

"You're in good hands," she assured him, and then strode past him to Christopher's pod, dropping down next to her student who she could only describe as looking like a vampire who'd just feasted on Smurf blood. That was, of course, assuming Smurfs bled blue.

"Come here, buddy," she said to Christopher and then pulled a wet wipe from the dispenser in the center of their pod and used her time scrubbing Christopher's lips once again as an opportunity to eavesdrop on the pod behind her, Piper's pod.

"Are you listening, Mister?" Piper asked, and Haddie's shoulder's shook with silent laughter.

"Are you laughing at my bwoo wips?" Christopher asked, and Haddie shook her head.

"Of course not," she assured him. "Want to know a secret?"

At this, Christopher beamed and nodded his head.

Haddie stage-whispered, "I don't think Mr. Rourke knows what he's doing, so it's funny to watch him try to figure it out...or watch Piper tell him what to do."

"Piper tells evweeone what to do," Christopher replied. "She's bossy. Like you."

Haddie heard a snort from behind her—a very masculine snort.

"Well," Haddie replied, holding her head high. "Then I guess if she wants, Piper can be a great teacher someday."

Christopher nodded like, *Ah yes. I see what you did there, Miss Martin.*

"Misterrrr!" Piper called again. "Are you even listening to me?"

This time Haddie had to repress a snort. She glanced over her shoulder to find an exasperated Piper, hands on her hips, staring through narrowed eyes at Levi.

"What?" he asked. " I mean, no. Sorry, Piper. I was distracted," he admitted with a sigh. "Sorry. I was distracted by Christopher's artistic expression," he told her, but Levi's eyes caught Haddie's instead of Christopher and his painted lips.

"He's just doing it to get my attention, but *I'm* not gonna look." Piper groaned. "Are you sure you're not looking at my teacher? Because it looks like you're looking at my teacher and not Christopher." Then Piper giggled. "Are you going to paint *your* lips so Miss Martin will pay more attention to you?"

Levi coughed and then replied with an emphatic "No."

Haddie turned back toward Christopher and his rainbow while silently willing Piper to continue her line of questioning.

"No you're not looking at Miss Martin, or no you're not going to paint your lips to get her attention? Do you think Miss Martin is pretty?"

Haddie felt her pulse quicken and her cheeks warm as she waited for Levi's response.

"I don't think students are supposed to ask teachers those kinds of questions," Levi told her.

"Sure they can," Piper assured him. "My mom and I read the classroom policy and procedure book together because we like to know all the rules, and there was nothing in the book about asking one teacher if they think another teacher is pretty. Right, Miss Martin?"

Haddie hoped the color in her cheeks had receded when she turned to face Piper and Levi again. "What's that, Piper? I was over here keeping an eye on Christopher's markers. Did you say something?"

Levi scoffed. "You heard, you little eavesdropper," he teased.

Haddie looked at her watch and gasped. "Oh wow! Look at the time! Piper, make sure Mr. Rourke and your table are finishing their rainbows, okay? I'm not sure our visitor knows how to do the project." She raised her brows, redirecting Piper into miniature teacher mode, a mode the young girl loved almost as much as being line leader.

"Okay," Levi said to Piper and the three other kids in her little pod. "How are we growing a rainbow?"

Haddie stood and pretended to check on the rest of the pods. But she made a point to glide past Levi's pod more than was necessary, especially with Piper at the helm. She watched from a distance as Levi's group of children gave him his own precut and folded section of paper towel and showed him how they were laying it horizontally and then coloring each edge with six one-inch bars of color: red, orange, yellow, green, blue, and purple.

"You have to color all the way to the end," Piper told him. "And it's okay if it gets on the desk because it washes off, but that doesn't mean it's okay to color on the desk on purpose." She gave him a stern look.

Levi nodded once. "Got it, Boss. Color to the edge, but don't color on the desk on purpose."

The girl next to Piper giggled. "She's not your *boss*!" she told Levi.

Levi's mouth fell open in mock surprise. "She's not?" he replied.
"Well, then who is?"

"Miss *Martin!*" the whole pod answered in unison.

They all glanced toward Haddie, who was of course already staring at them, which meant she was caught red-handed. So she simply shrugged and then busied herself straightening piles of papers on her desk.

Levi got back to work among his giggling cohort. Piper nodded toward the small plastic cups of water in front of him. "Do this," she began, demonstrating with her own rainbow-edged paper towel. She laid the folded towel over the side-by-side lips of the cups, gently dipping the rainbow edges into each respective cup but leaving the white middle flat and facing up.

"How did you know what to do?" Levi asked, sounding genuinely awed at the small girl who was effectively teaching the activity.

Piper shrugged. "I'm table leader this week. And for all table activities, Miss Martin lets the table leaders help out when she does her demonstration so we can show our tables what to do. But next week? I get to be *line* leader, which is even better because I get to lead the class through the halls and to our specials classes. Specials means music, art, library, and physical education, in case you didn't know."

Levi nodded sagely and followed his table leader's directions, as did the rest of the group. Once she'd assessed that the other pods were doing just fine, Haddie meandered among her clumps of students until she stopped at Levi's clump.

For several seconds, they all simply stared at the *nothing* that was happening on the paper towels. Haddie knew what was coming, but they didn't. And she loved seeing students' reactions to a new lesson, especially when it went according to plan and wasn't a teacher Pinterest fail.

A moment later, a collective gasp rose from the members of the pod, Levi included.

"The colors are *moving*," he stage-whispered. "So freaking cool!"

"I don't think you're supposed to say 'freaking,'" the boy to Levi's right accused.

Levi waved him off. "It's okay," he assured the kid. "Last time I checked the policy and procedures handbook, 'freaking' was not a swear." He glanced up at Haddie and gave her a conspiratorial wink.

The boy relaxed into his chair and stared at his own rainbow as it started to grow from the outside in. "So freaking cool," he parroted, and Levi's mouth fell open.

Haddie returned his wink with a glare that she hoped conveyed, *I'm going to have fun fielding that parent phone call this afternoon.*

"But maybe only say it here?" Levi amended, and Haddie really hoped the kid would take him up on the suggestion.

For the next several minutes, the whole class seemed to watch in rapt silence as tiny rainbows bloomed from equally tiny glasses of water.

A phone timer sounded, and Haddie practically leaped toward the front of the room. "Okay, my little scientists," she called. "Clap once if you can hear me."

The whole class—Levi included—clapped once.

"Clap *twice* if you can hear me," Haddie said this time.

Everyone—Levi included—clapped twice.

"Good job, scientists," she told them. "But it is time to head to music! You can leave your rainbows where they are and let them continue to grow. After music, we'll talk about weather and storms and how—even though storms can sometimes *sound* scary—when they're done, we get to see the amazing effects of refraction, reflection, and dispersion. Or...what I like to call a rainbow!"

The class cheered and clapped as they stood, pushed in their chairs, stormed toward the door, and filed into one very impressive line.

Levi climbed to his feet, and Haddie caught him wincing as he put weight on his left. Did he hurt his knee? Was he not supposed to kneel?

"Do you have a second?" she asked, bruising past him as she followed the kids to the door. "I just need to walk them to the music room, and then I'll be right back!" she called over her shoulder. Then she stepped past her students and out into the hallway, holding a finger to her lips as a silent reminder to...well...stay silent in the halls.

In unison, each student mimed zipping their lips and tossing away the key. And while some of them giggled *not* silently as they filed through the door, Haddie couldn't help but feel proud of how her students behaved with their unexpected visitor. She was also a little proud of herself, having already fallen into a groove with new students in a new school in an equally new town. Things were... good, and Haddie couldn't help smiling as she led her students the rest of the way down the hall and to the music room.

Levi was facing the windows, inspecting the All About Me posters when Haddie quietly strode up behind him.

"It takes a lot to earn a spot on a poster like that," she said softly over his shoulder.

Levi nodded, his eyes landing on what they both knew was the poster in question.

"Does anyone ever add to their posters at a later date?" he inquired.

Haddie hummed her contemplation. "I haven't seen it happen yet, but it only takes one to set a precedent."

They were both quiet for several seconds before Haddie spoke again.

"I was mad at you when I made that poster," she admitted.

The corner of Levi's mouth twitched. "I know."

"And I barely knew you back then." She let out a nervous laugh. "We barely know each other now," she added.

Levi nodded. And then finally, he turned around.

"Aren't you wondering?" he asked.

Haddie's brows furrowed. "Wondering what?" she asked.

"How long it will take to earn the coveted spot of being one of *my* favorite people." He flashed her a sly grin and then brushed past her as he pivoted and backed toward the door.

"I'm already one of your favorite people, aren't I?" she asked, crossing her arms and feigning a confidence she hoped he believed.

"Definitely too soon to tell," he deadpanned. "Oh, we do have a color printer across campus, and I've got an Uncrustable with my name on it waiting for me at my desk, so I better head out."

Haddie shook her head and laughed. "That is a child's lunch."

Levi shrugged. "Doesn't make it any less delicious." He paused in the doorway. "Thanks for letting me watch you in action. That rainbow activity is definitely a favorite."

Haddie rolled her eyes. "And I am…?" she drawled.

"A great roommate." He tapped the doorframe twice and then shoved his hands in his pockets. "I look forward to your email and attachment, Roomie."

"Guess I walked right into that one." Haddie laughed. "Goodbye, *Roomie!*"

He spun on his heel and headed back toward the library and the hallway Haddie knew led to the secondary campus.

I'm already one of your favorite people, aren't I?

She was already wading into dangerous waters by asking the question, even in jest. But that wasn't the worst of it. The worst of it was that she so very much wanted it to be true, which meant she might have already plunged into the deep, and the question was, would she sink or swim?

CHAPTER 15

Haddie stumbled through the apartment door with her school backpack over one shoulder, her soccer gear over the other, and forearms lined with grocery bags from her "quick" stop at the market on the way home.

Levi sprung up from where he sat at the table.

"Hey there…" He quickly emptied one of her arms of bags and set them on the kitchen counter. "Why didn't you text from downstairs? I could have helped you bring everything up."

She maneuvered past Levi and into the kitchen herself, depositing the rest of the groceries on the other side of the stove and letting her schoolbags fall to the floor.

"I thought I had it," she told him. "I didn't have it."

"What is all this?" Levi asked.

Haddie glanced through the galley kitchen's window and out to the table strewn with loose sheets of paper where Levi had been sitting. "What's all *that?*" she countered.

He groaned. "After losing our first game Friday night, I gave the team a weekend assignment: write one page about something you could have done differently that might have changed the trajectory of the game. Past Levi thought he was a genius for coming up with the idea. Present Levi, who has to read the submissions and make sense of it all, isn't sure he agrees." He held his hands out to indicate the mess of bags in the kitchen. "And now back to our regularly scheduled program. What's going on? I thought grocery day was Thursday, not Monday."

Haddie felt her cheeks grow warm and cleared her throat. "I... uh...wanted to make you dinner. I mean, make us dinner. As a thank-you for helping out during the grow-a-rainbow activity. I think the kids really liked you."

Levi barked out a laugh. "Piper doesn't like me. She tolerates me, though, and is happy to keep reminding me that I was not included on your favorite things poster."

Haddie rolled her eyes. "I stand by my assessment that three weeks isn't enough time to know if a person is one of your favorite people." She shrugged. "I guess you'll have to keep trying. Also, I hope you're a pasta fan because that's all I really know how to make." She shooed him out of the small kitchen. "Go read your essays and figure out how to coach your team better. I've got plenty here to keep me busy."

"Really?" Levi asked. "Because I could help."

Haddie narrowed her eyes. "You know what would be a *huge* help?"

"What?" he asked, smiling at her like a golden retriever. If any other gorgeous man was looking at her like that, it might do things to her insides that would have her thinking about much more than just making him dinner. But Levi Rourke was no real golden retriever. He was simply playing the part and would soon be on his way to bigger and better things than a placeholder job in a placeholder town. And so, as she'd learned to do in the almost month of knowing him, Haddie ignored the tiny stirrings and the whisper in her head that asked *What if?* every time he surprised her in a way she wished he wouldn't. But…she could make him dinner.

"Staying out of my way!" she told him. Haddie laughed and grabbed him by the shoulders—by his huge shoulders—and pushed him out of the narrow galley and back into their front entryway. "Read. Your. Essays."

"Okay, okay." He relented, holding his hands up in defeat. "But you're going to have a hard time beating that Uncrustable I had for lunch."

Haddie glared at him and pointed to the table, and with a chuckle, he got back to work.

She was by no means a chef under any definition of the word. But she'd been on her own long enough to perfect a couple of go-to meals. Tonight? Tuscan chicken pasta.

She quickly unpacked the groceries, leaving out only the ingredients she needed for the meal. She put a large pot of salted water on one burner. While waiting for it to boil, she chopped up spinach and sun-dried tomatoes, minced a few cloves of garlic, and diced four chicken breasts. Soon, the pasta was boiling and the chicken sautéing with the garlic and spices.

"Holy shit," Levi mumbled from where he sat.

"Someone knock your socks off with the written word?" Haddie called over her shoulder.

"Not yet," he replied. "But I don't think I've ever smelled anything so good in my life. Like, *ever*."

Again Haddie's cheeks warmed, or maybe it was just the steam from the boiling water. "You said 'ever' twice."

"Yep," Levi admitted. "What*ever* you're making over there deserved a second 'ever.'"

Haddie lowered the heat on her pan and slowly added the light cream sauce she'd whisked together. She willed the heat creeping up her neck to lower as well. She needed a distraction.

"I know it's a Monday, and we have a *whole* week ahead of us," she began, her back still to him. "But I feel like anything I cook tastes better with wine. I think there's a bottle of red on the counter but…my hands are kind of full."

"On it!" Levi called .

Haddie smiled to herself as she heard a rustling of papers and then caught Levi's approach out of the corner of her eye. Back to back, and— she guessed—both of them trying not to let body parts brush that shouldn't brush, Haddie cooked while Levi retrieved two wineglasses from the cabinet above the sink.

It was a strange relief to come home from a new job to an apartment in a new town to find she wasn't alone once the day ended. As hard as it was to admit to herself, she *liked* having Levi around like she liked having Emma. She took it for granted that her homebody friend would always be there when Haddie needed, and Emma was always there…to an extent. But now she was getting married. She had a life, a career, her family's inn…and Matteo. Haddie was so, so happy for her friend. But it also made her realize that somewhere along the way, Haddie's resolve to keep everyone at a safe distance had a long-term side effect. She was lonely.

Coming home to Levi every day felt like a warm, familiar blanket you wanted to snuggle up with on the couch, even if it was too warm to need it.

Not that Haddie needed Levi. Or anyone, for that matter. But maybe a warm, snuggly feeling wasn't so bad, even if it was only temporary. As long as Haddie knew this friendship was only temporary, she could banish all other expectations from her mind and just enjoy the moment.

She heard the unmistakable sound of a cork popping behind her, liquid sloshing into one glass and then another. And then she felt his chest against her back, felt and heard his slow, shaky inhale.

"That smells incredible," he whispered, an arm reaching around to offer her the stemless glass.

Even among the garlic and other spices, Haddie could smell the fresh, woodsy scent of Levi's soap, which meant he'd showered after practice.

It's just soap, she reminded herself. But something about how it mixed with his own *Levi*-ness made her wish there was a window she could open so she could gulp a breath of non-Levi air.

Haddie grabbed the wine with her free hand and fought the urge to drain it in one long sip. She killed the heat on the pasta and slid to her right so she could turn around without them having to be chest to chest.

"I need to…" She nodded toward the sink where a colander waited for her pasta.

"Right," he said, staring at her for a beat, but then he didn't move. "Sorry," he added as if reading her thoughts. "You just have some flour…" He brushed his thumb over the tip of her nose. "There!" he added, triumphant. "All clean." Then he grinned and sidestepped out of the kitchen as if he hadn't just been so casually sexy to a woman who was already overheating for too many reasons to count.

"You suggested the wine, genius," she mumbled under her breath.

"Did you say something?" Levi asked, already back in the other room.

"Nope!" Haddie lied. "But clear the table. I'm about to plate everything up!"

Two minutes later, she met him at the table with two full plates, shocked to find that Levi had stealthily set the table with napkins and silverware he'd somehow snuck out of the kitchen when her back was turned. And for the love of Toblerones, the man was standing behind what had quickly become Haddie's regular chair, holding it out for her to sit.

She swallowed, set down the two plates, and stepped in front of her chair.

"Um… Thank you?" she told him with a nervous smile.

Levi stepped out of her way so she could slide her chair closer to the table. He reached through the kitchen window and grabbed her almost empty wineglass from the counter, refilled it from the bottle on the table, and then returned to his usual seat. He shrugged. "Figured if you were going to cook for me that I could at least do the heavy lifting of grabbing a couple of forks and making it infinitely easier for you to sit down."

Haddie laughed. "I was really worried about how I was going to coordinate all of those difficult tasks. I don't know what I would do without you," she teased, then clasped her hands under her chin and batted her lashes at him. "My hero."

Levi held up his own refilled glass of wine and nodded for Haddie to do the same. "To Mondays?" he asked.

Haddie wrinkled her nose. "I'm not sure I want to say cheers to the most dreaded day of the week."

Levi raised a brow. "I don't know. So far, it's my favorite day of this week."

Haddie laughed. "Because you're the first P.E. teacher and coach to realize he loves reading essays?"

"No," he replied, a surety in his tone that made Haddie's stomach tighten. "Because no one has ever cooked for me before just for coloring on a paper towel, and I'm guessing you don't cook for people unless you really like them…unless they're one of your favorite people."

Haddie groaned. "You're impossible."

"In a one-of-my-favorite-people kind of way?"

She groaned. "If I say, 'To Mondays,' will you cease being impossible?"

"If you say, 'To Mondays,' does that mean I'm right? About the favorite thing?" he countered.

Haddie straightened in her chair and jutted out her chin. "How about, 'To roommates who better finish their toast and eat their dinner before it gets cold'?"

Levi laughed. "'To Mondays' it is!" He clinked his glass against hers and they both took a sip. Then he set down his glass, picked up his fork, and shoveled a mouthful of pasta into his mouth.

He tilted his head back and moaned in a way that Haddie was sure wasn't a sound Levi usually reserved for culinary delights.

"It's just pasta," she told him, the words coming out more defensive than she'd intended.

Levi's brown eyes fluttered open as he swallowed and took a swig of his wine before responding.

"Confession," he began. "I was lying when I said people don't usually cook for me just for coloring rainbows. Haddie, people don't...cook for me."

Haddie's brows furrowed, and she lowered the fork that had only made it halfway to her mouth. "No one has ever cooked for you?" she inquired with a laugh. "I find that hard to believe."

"I mean, not in my grown-ass-man-living-on-his-own years, which have been a lot of years." He scratched the back of his neck and chewed on his top lip. Was he...nervous?

Her expression softened. "You can say whatever it is," she assured him. "No judgment here. Just a meal between roommates."

He laughed. "Right. Which is why I feel like a total asshole for what I'm about to admit." He blew out a breath. "I have always lived alone." He motioned between them. "And this type of thing usually happens in a...you know...relationship. But I–I mean, I traveled a lot for my job, and when I was on campus for any length of time—even in the offseason—I was knee-deep in preseason or postseason training, in strategizing, in..." He hesitated, but Haddie nodded eagerly, not wanting him to lose his momentum, especially if she was about to get a glimpse of vulnerable Levi again. "In focusing on the one thing I was good at, which was football." He clasped his hands behind his head and stared at the ceiling before meeting her gaze again. "I never let relationships get to the point where someone might want to make me dinner."

Haddie nodded while absently swirling the wine in her glass.

"See?" Levi added after a long beat of silence. "You think I'm a dick."

But she shook her head, finally focusing her eyes on his again. "If you're a dick, then I guess that makes me one too because aside from a recent lapse in judgment that will never happen again, I, sir, wrote the book on casual."

How was it that three weeks ago she'd had every intention of making this man a nameless one night stand, and now she was telling him things about herself she'd never actually voiced out loud?

"Do you want to talk about that recent lapse in—"

"No!" she blurted out, and Levi nodded once.

"Fair enough," he told her, a muscle ticking in his jaw.

"Are you...mad?" she asked, brows furrowed.

"Nope."

Except his *nope* sounded a lot like a misspelled *yep*.

"It's just that it's in the past, and it's not something I want to dwell on or really even think about ever again, so maybe just forget I said anything. Okay?"

His dark-brown eyes softened, and he nodded. "Yeah, okay. Just, if you ever change your mind…"

"I won't," Haddie told him and then painted her smile back on and raised her glass. "What should we drink to?" she asked, hoping they could find their way back to normal. Again. Because they really were having the hardest time staying on the path they'd both agreed to travel.

"Um…" Levi began, scratching his chin. "To being afraid of commitment?" He shrugged and raised his brows.

"Now that is something worthy of a raised glass, don't you think?" she asked with enough forced enthusiasm that she almost believed she was excited that Levi was just as much of a mess as she was.

The bottle of wine was empty, and their wineglasses were well on their way. Haddie was so not going to be productive tonight with lesson planning, but she didn't care. The food was good (if she didn't say so herself). The wine was good. And the company? Well, once they got past the bump in the road, it was the best she'd had in a long time, possibly bordering on favorite.

Maybe she and Levi didn't see eye to eye on the way Principal Crawford was dealing with the school budget, or on whether or not they were the type of roommates that talked about anything other than today, tomorrow, and—when they got there—the next day. But they seemed to get each other in a way Haddie hadn't felt gotten before.

175

"To being a dick!" Haddie declared, raising her glass.

Levi barked out a laugh and lifted his glass as well. "To being a dick, I guess," he agreed, tapping his glass against hers before they both finished what was left of the wine.

CHAPTER 16

Levi tossed in his bed, unable to find the right position. The combination of the wine at dinner and the soothing sound of the light drizzle outside his cracked window should have lulled him to sleep, but tonight he couldn't put his jumble of thoughts to rest.

He and Haddie had eaten dinner together on more than one occasion, but it usually consisted of him tossing a pizza in the oven while Haddie concocted one of her many "girl dinners," which was what she called it when she tossed a hodgepodge of whatever was in the fridge onto a plate. Sometimes it was half of a sliced cucumber, a couple of torn-up pitas and a tub of hummus. Sometimes it was a handful of chips, a couple of hard-boiled eggs, and whatever fruit she could find.

"That's just Lunchables for grown-ups," he often teased her, to which she'd counter that adding extra cheese to his store-bought pizza and baking it on a stone did not, in fact, make it artisan.

But tonight she'd *cooked* for him, which took preparation and care, and Levi wasn't used to someone taking care of him, at least not since he was a teen before his mom got sick.

Levi wasn't oblivious to the carefully constructed walls he'd put in place since then. Here was the paradox of Levi Rourke. The game was everything to him as a kid, a teen, and a young adult. It came before everything and everyone, and because of that, he wasn't at his mother's side when she took her last breath. He chose to believe her when she called him at school from the hospital bed that had taken up residence in their living room. "Go win this one for me. I'll see you when you come home next weekend," she'd told him. But those were the last words she ever said to him.

Now the game was Levi's protection. It was his penance. He might have enjoyed tonight's dinner, but he'd never in a million years find himself deserving of such treatment. Haddie had thought him worthy, though. Why?

He grabbed his phone from the nightstand and looked at the time. 11:37 p.m. When it vibrated with a text and Haddie's nickname popped up, he legit launched the device halfway across the room.

"Shit!" he hissed, scrambling out of bed to retrieve it. Some higher power must have been smiling down on him because it landed on a small pile of laundry that hadn't quite made its way to his basket yet.

Birthday Girl: Awake?

Dammit…why did he love that a single, usually meaningless word had become their own secret greeting?

Levi: Nope. Fast asleep. This is just a dream.

Birthday Girl: How do you know it's not a nightmare?

Levi: Because you, Haddie Martin, could only ever be a good dream.

Why he was pushing the boundaries again, Levi didn't know. But at the same time, he imagined her biting back a grin, her cheeks flushed, and it gave him an indescribable rush to be the architect of an insuppressible smile.

Levi adjusted his pillows against the wall and pushed himself to sitting. After tossing and turning and *wanting* to fall asleep, now he found himself doing whatever he needed to stay awake.

Three dots appeared and disappeared. Appeared and disappeared. Never in his many years of experience with the English language and punctuation had an ellipsis made his heart race and his palms sweat. The anticipation was both agonizing and euphoric because he knew—at least he hoped he knew—that whatever Haddie said next would leave him with the insuppressible grin.

Birthday Girl: Tell me one thing you learned from your students' essays.

Levi's brows furrowed. Okay…so not even close to what he was expecting. Or maybe it was. Because Haddie seemed to be the one constantly keeping them in line, reminding Levi that no matter what they felt…that regardless of what chemistry might still be bubbling beneath the surface...roommates was the furthest their connection could go.

He sighed, got his head out of the fucking clouds, and brought himself back down to earth.

Levi: McMannus is already ineligible because of Tommy's class.

Of all his players' responses about playing better defense or practicing running a specific play more to make it second nature, it had been Billy McMannus's response that kept turning over in his mind: *I thought Mr. Crawford's introductory assignment was bullshit, so I didn't do it. Now I'm benched. But that doesn't surprise you, Coach. Does it? You believed what you heard about me, and I delivered on your expectations.*

Despite Billy's tone, his few paragraphs were articulate and well written. And his underlying accusation of Levi's expectations were—he hated to admit—on the nose.

Birthday Girl: Maybe it's time to dig a little deeper into Billy's story.

She was right. Levi pictured Haddie in her own bed with a different kind of smile on her face, smugly thinking *Told you so.* And then he shook his head with a soft laugh, telling himself that no scenario where he was picturing Haddie in her bed ended with him getting a good night's sleep.

Levi: Maybe. Hey...tell me about the rainbow thing your class did today. Do you teach weather? Just realizing you have to know all the things to teach the miniature humans. All I need to know is how to unlock the equipment closet.

Birthday Girl: LOL. I think you know more things than that. My weather unit isn't 'til spring, but I tossed in the rainbow activity for a student who started circle time by telling me he was afraid of the storm his mom said was coming tonight. Figured if I taught the class one of the upsides of a little rain, they might be a little less scared.

Levi listened to the calm tapping of rain against his window and laughed. *Some storm.* But then he thought of Haddie forgetting about the car wash flyer so she could prep an activity that wasn't even on her agenda, just because she cared.

Levi: You're kind of amazing at your job, aren't you?

Birthday Girl: I guess I just love those little rug rats, even when they're using my Crayolas as lip stains.

His chest squeezed, and Levi swore he felt a twinge of something like...jealousy.

Levi: They earn their favoritism pretty quickly, huh?

Birthday Girl: Yes.

Her reply came quicker than Levi could blink.

Birthday Girl: Every one of my students is my favorite the second they walk through my door on day one. They're the only ones who get to break my wait-and-see approach.

Levi: You're a little marshmallow, aren't u?

Birthday Girl: Take that back.

Levi: Never

Birthday Girl: Levi...

Levi: Yes...ooey, gooey marshmallow of a bday girl?

He heard her groan through the wall, and he laughed. How was it that on a random rainy Monday in September, sitting in his bed doing nothing than texting, Levi felt...happy?

His phone buzzed in his hand.

Birthday Girl: Also, if you were anyone other than you, it would be hot that you used the correct "you're"

Levi: Wait... What? YOU think that I'm hot? ME, your roommate. Hot. (plz take note of yet a second correct "your")

Birthday Girl: I think no such thing. I said that IT was hot. The correct usage. Proper grammar is hot regardless of user.

Light flickered in Levi's otherwise dark room. A few seconds later, a distant crash of thunder announced what he guessed was a storm after all.

Levi: Guess your student's mom was right

182

Three dots appeared, then disappeared, then appeared again.

Birthday Girl: But there's a chance it could miss us, right?

Another flicker of light with the thunder closer behind said otherwise. He checked the weather app on his phone and saw the storm was moving pretty fast in Summertown's direction. It would likely hit them within minutes but last less than an hour before it headed to its next destination.

Levi: Don't think so

This time the thunder came less than a second after lightning lit up Levi's room, followed by a scream.

Before he knew what he was doing, Levi was out of bed and bolting for Haddie's door. With his hand on the doorknob, he stopped short of barging inside.

"Haddie? Are you okay?"

"My window!" Haddie called. "Something hit it, and I think it cracked!"

A lightning-thunder combo crashed so loudly that the floor shook beneath Levi's bare feet, and Haddie yelped again.

"I'm coming in!" he warned, and when she didn't protest, he threw open her door as lightning illuminated the shape of a human curled into a ball beneath Haddie's bedding.

He flipped on her light to confirm a long, jagged crack in the window's upper pane of glass.

"I'll be right back," he assured her and then quickly padded into the kitchen to retrieve a roll of duct tape from the junk drawer. When he returned, Haddie still hadn't moved. "Hey. Haddie," he said softly. "I'm just going to climb on the bed to tape up your window, okay?"

He saw movement beneath the blanket resembling a nod. So he tore off a long piece of tape, held it between his teeth, and crawled across the mattress to the window where he pressed the tape along the seam of the break.

"Shit!" he hissed when an unexpected raised portion of the seam sliced through the tape and the pad of his finger on the other side.

"What happened?" Haddie asked, poking her eyes and nose out from the top of the blanket.

Levi expected paper-cut-level trauma, so when he saw the blood trickling from the gash, he swore again.

"Oh my god!" Haddie cried, scrambling out from her tangle of blanket and sheet and grabbing him by the wrist of his injured hand. "Come on," she told him, and gave him a forceful tug. Levi complied, scooting to the edge of the bed and hopping off as Haddie led him to the bathroom.

"*Sit*," she ordered, pointing at the toilet.

Levi lowered the lid and did as he was told.

Haddie turned on the faucet and let it run. "Give me your hand," she told him.

Levi complied, sighing as the cool water soothed the sting of the open wound.

She left him like that as she rummaged in the cabinet, finally producing a small first aid kit. Haddie nudged his hand away from the stream of water and proceeded to wash her own hands. Then she turned off the water, dried her hands, and removed a square paper package from the kit, tearing it open to produce a large piece of gauze. She folded the gauze until it was only slightly bigger than the pad of his finger.

"Hold this against the cut with some decent pressure, and let's give it a few minutes to dry. If the bleeding slows after that, we'll bandage you up, and you'll be as good as new."

"And if it doesn't slow?" he asked, trying to contain his complete and utter wonder at how she could go from terrified to grace under pressure in the span of a lightning strike. For the record, there had been two since they'd fled her room, and Haddie hadn't so much as flinched.

She shrugged. "ER for a few stitches?"

Levi scoffed. "For a tiny cut on the tip of my finger? I don't think so." But when he glanced down to see the bright red blooming through the layers of gauze, he swallowed back his bravado.

Haddie slid down the wall opposite the toilet and pulled her knees to her chest. "It's still wet from the water. Give it a few. I'm sure it's fine, and if it's not?" She shrugged. "You've got a plus-one for the emergency room."

Levi rested his elbows on his knees, making sure to keep pressure on what he hoped was nothing more than a superficial wound. Stitches didn't scare him, but a hospital? That was another story.

"Why didn't you tell me *you* were afraid of storms?" he asked softly.

Haddie smiled nervously, hugging her knees tighter. "I was getting there. I mean, I did text to see if you were up when the rain started. I guess the storm beat me to it." Her eyes widened as if she was just registering him sitting in front of her.

"What?" he asked.

"You're in your underwear!" she told him.

Levi glanced down at his nearly naked body and then back up at her with the same delayed reaction as he took in her fitted tank top and bikini briefs.

"So are you!" he informed her, then squeezed his eyes shut, focusing on the feeling of his heartbeat in the tip of his finger instead of on Haddie's long, bare legs or the braless breasts he knew were barely hidden behind her knees beneath the thin cotton of her tank.

Lean in to the pain, he told himself. The tiny cut hurt enough to notice, so he focused on that, on the throbbing *ba-BUMP, ba-BUMP, ba-BUMP* of the blood pumping through his extremities and praying to every deity in existence that his blood did not rush anywhere *else.*

For a nonreligious man, Levi had certainly taken to praying in recent weeks like he never had before.

"It's *fine,*" Haddie assured him. "I was just caught off guard. We're both mature adults, right? And all of our delicate spots are covered, so you can open your eyes."

Levi hesitated, then opened only one eye to start. When Haddie backhanded him on the knee, he finally opened the other.

"What's the matter?" she teased. "Are you worried you'll be turned on by a disheveled, thirty-one-year-old woman who is afraid of storms? Because let me tell you how *not* hot that is."

She rose onto her knees, and Levi looked past her rather than at her. "Look...Haddie..." he finally said. "Setting aside the argument that you are unequivocally hot no matter what you are wearing or what you are afraid of, I don't want to mess up this friendship. But sometimes my...um...physiology takes a second to catch up to my brain. And I would feel like the biggest asshole to ever asshole if a physiological reaction to your unequivocal hotness made you feel uncomfortable or unsafe. So...yeah. I am afraid I'll be turned on by all of those other things you said."

"Oh," Haddie replied. She swallowed. "Let's...um...take a look at that cut."

She wrapped her hand around his and urged him to lift the gauze from the wound.

"Good news," she said, and he could hear her smile without seeing it.

"Yeah?" he asked, still glancing over her shoulder.

"Yeah," she assured him. "We don't have to amputate. So I'm just gonna..." She grabbed a couple more items from the first aid kit, and Levi finally allowed himself to at least watch whatever was going on on the counter.

A Band-Aid was opened and ready to go, but first she squeezed a dab of antibacterial ointment on her index finger. Then she gently spread it across the length of the cut before wrapping the bandage tightly around the wound and taping it closed.

"Good as new!" she said, then climbed to her feet.

There was nowhere to avert his eyes when she was just there. In front of him. Taking up his whole field of view.

He wanted to tell her that *hot* was too basic a word to describe someone who, without even realizing it, put someone else's needs before her own basic need for safety. Or would it be too bold of him to imagine that she was able to do so because she felt safe with him? Either way, Haddie Martin was stunning inside and out—whether she was preparing a meal, hiding under a blanket, or growing rainbows.

Levi felt suddenly overwhelmed with the urge to run as far as he could from this apartment, this town, this planet that felt too small to contain whatever wanted to break free inside him. But bolting through the streets of Summertown in his underwear wasn't an option, especially since the last thing he needed was another scandal.

Finally, he met her expectant gaze and simply said, "Thank you."

Haddie pressed her lips into a smile. "You're welcome. Thank you for taping my window."

He nodded. They were close. So damned close he could smell her citrus shampoo in her still-damp hair. So close he could count the freckles on her nose and the few sprinkling onto her cheeks. Seventeen. So close that if he didn't care about her as much as he did, he'd ask if she'd thought about their kiss in his hotel room since that night. He'd admit that he couldn't forget it no matter how damned hard he tried.

But he did care about Haddie, which was why he never would.

"We can pop by the hardware store tomorrow after work," he told her instead. "Tommy's uncle Pete can probably fix it by the end of the week. Until then, you probably shouldn't sleep in there, just in case the tape doesn't hold."

Haddie nodded. "Right," she said. "Of course. I can crash on the couch until then. Just in case the tape doesn't hold up."

Levi smiled. His first instinct was to offer his bed and for him to take the couch, but he'd never fit if he stretched to his full height, and he knew Haddie wouldn't hear of it. He could offer to share his bed. It was a king, after all, and there was plenty of room, but how did he even suggest such an idea without it winding its way back to his newfound fear of erections. So he simply said, "Okay," and helped her gather her bedding and repurpose it on the couch.

"Good night, Levi," she said sleepily as she burrowed beneath her blankets, the storm already miles away from Summertown once again.

"Good night, Haddie," he replied as he backed into his room and pushed his door shut.

His chest squeezed as he collapsed back into his bed, and he wondered how hard he'd have to beg the powers that be to stop what he feared had already started.

Levi was falling for his roommate.

CHAPTER 17

Levi and Haddie stood in front of their teams, their eyes shining with excitement. It was Friday afternoon, and the sun was just beginning to set over the horizon. Haddie couldn't believe they'd pulled the fundraiser together in only a week and that they had a roster of customers prepaid and ready to arrive.

Haddie stepped forward, in her purple Muskies soccer T-shirt and shorts, grateful for the lingering warm weather even midway through September.

"Okay, everyone!" she called, her voice clear and strong. "This is how it's going to work. Levi and I are in charge of the hose. You need your bucket filled? You come to us. You need your bucket *re*filled? Again, you come to us. Do you get where I'm going here?"

"Yes, Coach…" they sang in disappointed unison. Haddie had no doubt there would be at least one, if not several, water fights at some point during the day, but it wouldn't be because a student got their hands on the hose.

"Your assigned group will be given a bucket, a sponge, and a stack of car-drying towels. Levi and I will be around supervising, but it's up to you guys to get the job done. Got it?"

This earned her a slightly more enthusiastic, "Yes, Coach!" Haddie squinted through her sunglasses at the line of cars already entering the parking lot. Adrenaline coursed through her like electricity. If her first fundraiser was as successful as it was easy, she might have a real shot at saving the soccer program.

"You heard the boss, everyone!" Levi called out. "Let's get moving. The car wash is officially open!"

The teams quickly got to work, some of them already flinging wet, soapy towels at each other to the surprise of absolutely no one, least of all, Haddie.

Haddie and Levi moved between them, offering tips here and there on how to be quick and efficient but also thorough.

As they worked, Haddie couldn't help but steal glances at her roommate, admiring the way he joked with his students like they were bros but also commanded their respect when he needed to get them back in line.

She caught Levi looking too and flashed him a knowing grin, a spark of something passing between them. They weren't flirting because that would be ridiculous. And dangerous. They'd established and reestablished that too many times to count. It had been almost two weeks since the night of the storm, and Haddie still couldn't stop thinking about how close they'd come to kissing in their bathroom…how if Levi hadn't stepped on the brakes, Haddie wasn't sure she could have. Just look at the man, for Pete's sake! She'd have to be a troll hiding under a bridge not to notice Levi's own

Muskies tee ride up when he used the hose to spray down one of the taller SUVs. Was Haddie supposed to not look at the patch of exposed skin above the elastic band of his shorts?

His looks weren't the real problem though, were they? He'd protected her from the storm. He'd flat out told her that he wanted her to feel safe, and with a friend like him on the other side of her bedroom wall—a *friend*, dammit—how could she not feel safer than she had in years?

That was the problem. Levi Rourke was beautiful inside and out, and that is one lethal combination.

It was Sarah Ramirez, Haddie's star goalie, who waved her hand in front of her coach's face to interrupt her gaze.

"Um…Coach?" Sarah asked, and it sounded like maybe not the first time she'd tried to get Haddie's attention.

"Huh?" Haddie asked, blinking several times before her vision focused on the student in front of her instead of the man a few cars away.

"Oh. My. God." Sarah said softly. "You were totally checking Coach Rourke out!"

Haddie felt her face flush as she scoffed. "I was not!" She let out a nervous laugh, sounding like the guiltiest guilty to ever guilty.

"Coach *Martin!*" Sarah replied. "You are sweet on Coach Rourke! I knew it!"

Haddie rolled her eyes. "We're colleagues," Haddie insisted. "And roommates who are just friends. Also, I don't know why I'm explaining this to you. A student shouldn't be making inappropriate assumptions about two faculty members."

"There is nothing in the Summertown High School Policy and Procedure Handbook that says students cannot speculate about two consenting adults possibly being sweet on each other."

Haddie's mouth fell open. "You *read* that?"

Sarah groaned. "You made us all sign off saying that we did!"

Haddie laughed. "I guess I didn't think you all actually did it."

Sarah's eyes widened. "Wait, wait, wait, wait, WAIT. Did you say that you and Coach Rourke *live* together?"

Warning alarms sounded in Haddie's head. Sarah already knew she was full of shit, and now Haddie was adding more fuel to the fire by letting it slip that she and Levi were roommates.

"Platonically!" Haddie whisper-shouted so no other students would hear.

But deep down, Haddie knew their relationship was teetering on a line between platonic and something more. Living with Levi started out awkward, then turned to something comfortable, but lately was starting to feel like torture, all thanks to a stupid broken window.

Tommy's uncle Pete came up to the apartment the next day and measured the glass, and less than twenty-four hours later, she had a brand-new window, and the tree culprit was trimmed. That meant Haddie only had to suffer two nights on the couch, tormented by the muffled sounds of a naked Levi tossing and turning in his bed while she tried to sleep. Okay, nearly naked, but what was left to the imagination had been haunting her dreams ever since. And now those dreams were a waking nightmare.

"And what do you mean you knew it?" Haddie asked Sarah.

Her student shrugged. "There's just some of us on the team who've been speculating, but we had no idea you guys lived together!"

"Who lives together?" Teddy Kostas asked as he strolled over with a noticeably empty bucket.

"Coach and Coach," Sarah informed him, and Haddie groaned.

"No shit!" Teddy exclaimed. "Go, Coach Rourke!"

Haddie shuddered. "Teddy, I am going to pretend you did not just say that and forbid you from ever saying it again. Sarah? If I had begged you not to tell Teddy a second before he showed up, would you have complied?"

Sarah pursed her lips and shook her head. "This is too good not to share."

Haddie filled Teddy's bucket while she pondered the situation.

"What's it going to take to have you two keep your mouths shut about this?" she asked. "Not that I need to defend my purely platonic friendship with Coach Rourke to either of you, but if the rest of your teammates find out, the focus of our practices will no longer be the games, and I'm pretty sure *you* want to continue winning games…" She glared at Sarah. "And *you* probably want to start winning games, correct?" This time she directed her attention at Teddy.

"Harsh, Coach," Teddy replied with a sigh. "The truth hurts, but she's got a point," he told Sarah. "Guys my age have zero maturity when it comes to shit like this. I should know. I'm a guy my age, and my brain is already on overdrive with totes inappropriate speculations." Haddie gasped, and Teddy held up his hands in defense. "What? I didn't say, 'Go, Coach Rourke,' again!"

Haddie groaned. She'd brought this on herself, and now she needed to fix it. "Please, you two. I really need you to keep our living situation in the vault." If a handful of students were speculating about the two of them after barely a month of school, how long would it be before they were the talk of the district? Or even the town? Haddie needed to shut this down before it went any further. "If you do this for me, I'll…" She sighed. "I'll buy you both coffee for a week."

Sarah raised her brows. "Well, this just got interesting."

"I know, right?" Teddy agreed with a dude bro laugh. "I was ready to comply just based on the whole respect-your-elders thing my mom is always telling me, but I'll take free caffeine."

Respect your elders? Haddie didn't even know where to begin with that one. But this wasn't about her ego. It was about protecting her privacy and Levi's too.

"Fine," Sarah replied, but Haddie could see the wheels turning in her head. "But we get to choose the beverage type, size, and when it is delivered."

Haddie's mouth fell open. But then she reminded herself that she was the grown-up here…or the *elder* with authority that they both needed to respect.

"This is how it's going to go down," she told them. "The elementary school starts earlier than the high school, so I will have your drinks made to order and waiting for you on a chair outside my classroom door. If you want the drinks fresh from the coffee shop, you'll be at my door at eight sharp. If you order iced and don't mind it a little watered down or hot and don't mind a little cool off, pop by before first period. You'll email me your five orders by Sunday evening, and after that, no changes, take backs, or swaps. Got it?"

Teddy stood at attention and gave her a salute. "Got it, Coach!"

Sarah held her gaze for a couple of beats more before letting out a breath and saying, "Got it, Coach." But the lilt in her voice and the glint in Sarah's eye set off a tiny alarm in the back of Haddie's mind. Something told her this wasn't her goalie's first rodeo when it came to blackmail, and that was both impressive and terrifying, especially since Haddie thought blackmail was only something that happened in fiction.

"Okay, then," Haddie said. "Your bucket is full, so get back to work."

Teddy saluted her again and grabbed the bucket by the handle. "Got it, Coach!" he said and took off back to his and Sarah's station. That was when Haddie realized that Sarah had approached her before Teddy showed up with the bucket.

"Did you need something else, Sarah?" Haddie asked.

Sarah gave her a mischievous smile. "Nope," she said, then spun on her heel and sauntered away.

"Shit," Haddie mumbled, and then she shrieked as a blast of icy water sprinkled the back of her tank. She spun to find Levi absently staring at the sky as he refilled another group's bucket, a grin tugging at the corners of his mouth.

Don't be flirty, she silently warned him, hoping he might get the hint. But when she glanced to where Teddy and Sarah were working with their latest car-wash customer, she found Sarah staring right back over the frames of her sunglasses. From here on out, Haddie and Levi would have to watch their every move because as long as they were on school grounds or at a school event, someone would be watching them.

CHAPTER 18

On Sunday afternoon, Levi was still nursing his wounds from his team's second loss when he and Haddie showed up at the formal-wear shop, effectively named Posh. Since the weather was still warm, he and Haddie had decided to walk.

"We can talk strategy tonight if you want," she told him. "I mean, I know I'm still new to the whole coaching gig, but we *have* won twice."

"Ouch," Levi replied. "But yeah…maybe we can practice together this week so my guys can see what your team is doing right?"

Haddie nodded absently, but she was looking past him and across the square.

"So that's where the coffee shop is," she mumbled. "Note…to…self."

Levi paused outside the shop door. "I thought you liked to save money by brewing at home."

"Huh?" she asked. "Right! I do. I was just thinking that it's almost pumpkin-spice-latte season, so it's always a good plan to know where to get one."

Levi nodded. "I didn't know you were a latte person."

"I'm not!" Haddie blurted out, then laughed nervously. "But... you know. Sometimes I like to switch it up. Which reminds me... I think for this week, I'm going to drive myself to school. I've got some early-morning meetings, so you might as well sleep in."

"Haddie, I don't mind—"

"No, it's cool!" she interrupted. "We don't always need to ride together, right?"

Levi pulled open the glass door, brows furrowed. "Everything okay with you?"

"You're here!" Emma exclaimed, popping out from behind a rack of ginormous white dresses that looked like they weighed as much as Levi did.

In a white T-shirt that read *I'm the freaking bride!* in plain black letters, Emma bounded toward Haddie and wrapped her in a giant hug.

Levi watched quizzically as, for a second, Haddie stood still as a statue, but then her shoulders relaxed and she reciprocated the display of affection for her friend.

He spun slowly, taking in his surroundings and realizing that—other than a corner of brightly colored garments he guessed were for bridesmaids—he was surrounded, wall to wall and rack to rack with varying shades of white and cream in varying levels of poofiness.

"Um...Emma?" Levi began. "I don't see my brother or anything remotely resembling a tuxedo. Should I be worried about what I've committed to wearing as far as best-man attire?" Levi certainly didn't fault anyone who felt comfortable wearing a dress.

He just wasn't one of those people, especially when he was pretty sure the best man was not supposed to upstage the bride.

As if being summoned, Matteo appeared from behind a red velvet curtain on the opposite side of the shop, clearing his throat. They all turned to find him decked out in everything from a top hat to shiny leather wing tips.

Haddie made a choking sound.

Levi snorted. "I swear to god if there is a rabbit in that hat, I might piss myself laughing."

Matteo's jaw clenched. "Ems..." the younger Rourke said through gritted teeth. "I don't think this is the one."

Emma winced. "Next one, Layla!" she called to the person Levi guessed was responsible for his brother's current look. "A little less magician this time!" Then she directed her attention back to her fiancé. "Remember how much you love me, okay?" she pleaded, but Levi could tell she was also trying not to laugh.

"Trust me," Matteo replied. "That is the only reason you don't see a Matteo-shaped cutout in the door."

Emma blew him a kiss, and Matteo disappeared back behind the curtain.

"So...yeah." She turned to face Haddie and Levi. "That was the funniest thing I've ever seen."

"I think that makes three of us," Haddie agreed.

"There's a small rack in back with the tuxedo options," Emma continued. "Layla doesn't really keep those on display since they don't take up much space and the dresses need a lot more room to breathe. Layla and I have already pulled the maid of honor and groomsman options and put them in fitting rooms for you. So all you have to do is try them on, let me know what you think, and we'll all make the final decision together." Her cheeks flushed. "I found my dress months ago, so no worries about Matteo seeing anything he shouldn't before the big day."

Haddie pouted. "Do *I* get to see it before the big day?"

Emma beamed. "Of course! My mom is going to meet us here in about ten minutes so I can show you both. I just wanted to get the boys started first." She backed up toward the curtain and pulled it part of the way open. "Right this way, bridal party of two. Your wardrobe awaits!"

Levi and Matteo, relegated to the shop side of the curtain while still in their tuxedos, stared at each other for several seconds.

"I might have snapped a stealth photo of you doing birthday-party magician cosplay," Levi admitted.

"You're an asshole," Matteo replied.

Levi laughed. "I know."

"Emma, honey," they heard Layla say. "When you're ready, I'm going to have you hop on the platform in front of the three-way mirror."

"Out in a second!" Emma called.

Levi gave his brother a single nod. "You gonna peek?"

Matteo shook his head. "Are you kidding? Emma will kill me. Plus...I kind of want to be surprised on the big day."

Levi backhanded his brother on the shoulder. "Look at you being all traditional and shit."

Matteo shrugged. "If I'm lucky enough to get a second chance with her, I'm gonna do it right."

Levi could hear in his brother's voice that Matteo still didn't believe he deserved that second chance. The thought filled his chest with a hollow ache for all that his brother went through to get to this day.

"You don't look like a magician in this one," he said, gently grabbing Matteo's lapels.

Matteo huffed out a laugh. "Is that big brother speak for *I clean up good?*"

Levi took a step back and crossed his arms. "Something like that."

"Oh my god," they heard Emma's mom say, followed by a choking sound.

"It's perfect, right?" Layla replied. "Like it was made for her."

"You look stunning, sweetheart," Mrs. Woods continued, and Levi could tell the woman was crying.

"Thank you." The sound of his fiancée's voice made Matteo stand at attention. "I am a freaking smoke show in this thing, right?"

Haddie laughed, her voice thick, and Levi wondered if she was crying too, something he'd never witnessed her do, even the night of the storm when she'd been so scared he could see her body trembling beneath her blanket.

He watched a glassy sheen grow over Matteo's eyes.

"What the hell is it like?" Levi asked, and Matteo turned to face him again.

"What is what like?"

"Being that happy," Levi admitted.

Matteo shrugged. "When was the last time you were in love?"

"I wasn't," Levi blurted out. "I mean, I don't think I've ever been." So why was a name ping-ponging through his brain, making it hard to think straight?

"Then you can't know," his brother replied plainly. "Until you know."

Levi was trying to let the notion sink in when the curtain flew open, and even though they hadn't peeked, he felt like they were somehow busted.

"What are you doing?" Haddie asked, accusation in her tone.

Matteo held his hands up in defense. "We saw nothing," he assured her. "But nobody said anything about us *not* eavesdropping."

Levi wanted to back his brother up, but he was too busy staring at the strapless green dress Haddie was wearing, and the soft skin of her breasts threatening to spill out over the top of the fabric. Attempting to look away, his eyes traveled the length of her slender torso. The rest of the dress fit her like a glove all the way down to her knees where it finally flared out over her shins and feet.

"I know," Haddie said, rolling her eyes. "It's too tight. But Emma loves the cut and the color, so Layla's going to take it a bit up here, which means having to move the zipper, but then I'll at least be able to breathe."

At least somebody was thinking about breathing, Levi thought. Because he was pretty sure he was holding his breath.

Emma popped out from behind a fitting room door, back in her T-shirt and shorts.

"That's a wrap, everyone! Get your clothes back on. Layla's closing up shop for the day, and we're all going to have high tea at the inn to celebrate getting everyone outfitted for the wedding! We've got the dining room to ourselves until four when it opens to the public again."

"I'm going to head out first!" Mrs. Woods said, pushing past Haddie and through the curtain. "Want to make sure your father doesn't need help with the finger sandwiches." She blew everyone kisses and basically floated through the door like the beaming mother of the bride she was apparently meant to be.

Layla gestured for the two men to join Haddie and Emma back behind the curtain. "Just leave everything on the hangers in your fitting rooms," she told them. "I have to run home and take the puppy out for a quick walk before meeting you back at the inn, so I'm going to head out, lock the shop door, and you all can leave through the back if that works okay. The back door locks automatically."

Emma pulled Layla into a hug and thanked her as the rest of them retreated to their respective fitting rooms.

Levi took his time untying his tie and unbuttoning his vest as his body—having…uh…physiologically reacted to Haddie in that dress—caught up to his brain.

Not long after they'd disappeared behind their doors, Levi heard one click open. Then he heard hushed whispers and what he was pretty sure sounded like kissing coming from beyond his door.

"Get a room, you two!" he called to his brother and Emma.

Emma laughed. "Busted!" she admitted. "You guys almost done?"

"Uh-huh!" Haddie replied. "Just need to shimmy out of this thing!"

"Same here," Levi added. "I mean...minus the shimmying. Feel free to go on ahead of us if you want to get started on those finger sandwiches. We're right behind you!" Levi had no idea what finger sandwiches were, but he hoped they were something that excited Emma and Matteo enough to stop waiting so he could buy himself a few more minutes to...*relax*.

"Okay!" Emma called. "We'll see you at the inn!"

A few seconds later, he heard a heavy door snick shut. A few seconds after *that*, he heard Haddie swear.

"Everything okay over there?" he asked, elbowing the wall he shared with Haddie.

"You have to help me," Haddie replied, her voice straining with exasperation.

Something about the need in her tone brought Levi's relaxing to a halt. He swallowed hard. "Um...what do you need?" he managed to say, his voice tight.

"My zipper is stuck. I got it only part of the way down, and then it just stopped, and I'm afraid I might actually pass out if I don't get to take a full breath in the next thirty seconds."

Levi had just let his shirt fall to the floor, and he was standing there in nothing but his unbuttoned tuxedo pants. "I'll be right there," he told her. "I just need to—"

"Levi!" she called with a whimper. "Please? It's so tight, and I'm starting to panic, and..." She gasped. "I can't...breathe!"

He threw open his fitting room and rounded the corner toward

Haddie's, bursting through the propped-open door and accidentally sandwiching her between himself and the mirror when her door hit him on the ass and clicked shut.

"Sorry!" he exclaimed and then backed up against the door.

Haddie's shoulders heaved as she tried desperately to suck in a breath.

Without another thought, he pressed a palm to her hip for purchase and yanked on the zipper, but the damned thing wouldn't budge.

"Try pulling it back up!" she pleaded, and the strain in her voice sent his pulse into overdrive.

He tugged the zipper up, and it moved, but the second he tried to pull it back down, it stopped right in the same spot.

She pressed her arms against the three-way mirror and let her forehead fall against her arm.

"Levi…" she pleaded.

He growled. "I'm going to have to rip it."

"Then rip the freaking thing! Layla has to take it off and put it back on anyway." Her knees buckled, and Levi caught her around the waist.

"I got you, Birthday Girl," he assured her, and with his free hand, he grabbed one side of the partially opened dress and tore.

Haddie gulped in a mouth of air, and then another, and one more after that. Finally, her breathing steadied, and she straightened. But Levi still hadn't let go.

She pressed a palm over his hand, which lay splayed across her abdomen.

"Can you open the door?" she asked with a shaky breath, tilting her head up to look at him through the mirror. "It's getting a little claustrophobic in here."

That was when he finally noticed the dress was now hanging forward, her bare breasts exposed. Yet her hand hadn't left his, and her green eyes seemed to flicker with an unexpected heat.

Levi reached behind him and twisted the handle to the fitting room door, but it didn't move.

"Um...Haddie?"

She suddenly spun to face him. "The pen!" she cried.

"What pen?"

"The one holding open the broken door," she added.

Levi pinched the bridge of his nose and squeezed his eyes shut. "Tell me we are not stuck in here like this." Since the walls did not go all the way to the ceiling, Levi gripped the tops of the ones on either side of him and hung his head, eyes still closed.

"You're not wearing a shirt," Haddie said softly.

He let out an incredulous laugh. "Neither are you."

Levi heard the unmistakable sound of Haddie licking her lips.

A warm palm pressed against his chest, and Levi swore. "Haddie," he growled. "What are you doing?" He let out a shaky breath.

"I don't know," she whispered. "You're...trembling."

He squeezed the tops of the walls harder, feeling his knuckles go white. "Because I've been trying to hold it together since the second you opened that curtain and told me and Matteo we could come back inside."

"*Levi…*" Her hand traveled up to his cheek, and she pressed it against his fiery skin. "You saved me from fainting."

"I know," he ground out. His heart thrashed against his rib cage, trying to keep the feelings he'd been struggling to ignore at bay.

"And you called me 'Birthday Girl,'" she added.

"I am also aware of this," he told her, doing everything in his power not to lean into her touch.

She brushed a thumb across the stubble on his jaw, and Levi was sure if he let go of the walls at his sides, he'd dissolve into a puddle, right there on the spot.

"Do you want to know the two reasons I didn't want to tell you my name that night?"

"No," he said, but he could feel his head nodding.

Haddie laughed, but it was a strangled sound. "You charmed me more than any man had a right to charm me in so little time. I was afraid that if I heard you say my name, I might never leave that hotel room."

"*Jesus*, Haddie…" he hissed, but he made no move to stop her. He wanted to know everything about her and, at the same time, nothing at all. Because the more he knew, the more he wanted. But what if… Did she want too? He couldn't stop the words even if he tried. "What's the other reason?"

She sighed, and her warm, sweet breath brushed against his neck, sending a shock of electricity down his spine, the surge so strong that he shuddered.

"Because I'd never let any man close enough to come up with

a nickname for me, and you gave me one right on the spot. I felt—special."

He opened his eyes, knowing that once he did, he would be a goner. But Levi didn't care.

"You *are* special," he told her. "You know that, don't you?"

She pressed her lips together and shrugged, giving him a sad smile.

Levi let go of the walls he swore were holding him up and dared to cup her cheeks in his palms.

"Tell me not to kiss you, Haddie. I'm fucking begging you. Please tell me not to."

"Don't kiss me," she whispered, tilting her head up toward his.

"Tell me and mean it," he whispered back.

But Haddie shook her head. "I can't."

Fuuuck. "You said you don't date men you work with."

She nodded. "I love my job, but I'm not going to complicate it with some selfish jerk who will eventually outgrow me, promising me a boozy brunch and surprising me with his parents instead."

Levi's brows furrowed. "I feel like I'm missing a huge chunk of the story here. I'll own the selfish jerk part. That's why I'm here. Not in this fitting room, but Summertown. You know what I mean. But the boozy-brunch thing and the ridiculous idea of outgrowing you? Nope. Not ringing a bell."

She waved him off. "Not you, silly. Just someone from before I knew you."

Levi didn't even know the guy's name, and he already hated him.

"And you're not selfish or a jerk, Levi," she continued. "You're still grieving. It's different. *You're* different." She cupped his cheek with her hand, and it took everything—every fucking ounce of his will—not to just lean into her touch, to kiss her palm, and to let their pent-up need take over from there.

Levi didn't realize until now how much he'd continued to want her from that very first night. Now he knew that his need had been growing beneath the surface, like a virus without any known cure. He'd simply been pretending, lying to himself, and for a few short weeks he'd tricked himself into believing he'd found a remedy.

Still, he hesitated. "Haddie, I don't think I can go back if we do this," he admitted.

"Neither can I."

Whether she only wanted him right now or for every other day to come, Levi didn't care.

"And Coach Crawford?" he asked. "Our jobs. What if he…?" But Levi's job—the one he was trying to get back—felt a million miles away while Haddie Martin was right here in his fucking arms.

"Our entanglement," she whispered. "Our business."

Then you can't know…until you know.

Matteo's words echoed in the back of his head as Levi brought his lips to hers.

She hummed sweetly against him, and for a few seconds, that was all the kiss was—sweet. She tasted like coffee and cinnamon, like rainy nights and broken windows and wounds mended with care. But then her arms snaked around his neck, and her dress fell to the floor so that they were skin to skin, heat against heat, two wild hearts bursting from captivity.

He pulled back, gasping. Where before he was afraid to look, now he drank her in. "My god, you're beautiful," he told her, his voice rough as gravel.

"Awww… I bet you say that to all the half-naked girls," she teased.

He shook his head, and she narrowed her eyes at him.

"Okay…" he answered with a laugh. "Maybe I've said it once or twice, but I've never meant it like this. I've never…*known* someone like I know you. When I say it to you, it means something entirely different."

Her gaze softened, and Levi let out a relieved breath.

"Do you think we should be calling someone for help?" he asked, remembering that people were actually expecting them to show up at the inn in the not-too-distant future.

Haddie answered him by taking a step back and having the nerve to slide her bikini briefs down her thighs and over her knees until she kicked them out from under her.

"Oh…my…goddess…" he ground out.

She glanced down to where his erection protruded from his unbuttoned pants. "I have been waiting to see what's on the other side of those boxer briefs for *weeks*. Something tells me the little guy is *not* going to disappoint."

Levi winced. "I'm a fairly confident man," he told her. "But my *guy* might be sensitive to—uh—inaccurate nicknames."

Haddie hooked her finger behind his elastic waistband and

lowered the briefs to take in the view. Her eyes grew wide. "My apologies, *Big Guy*." She gripped him in her palm, and something feral tore from his chest as his back slammed against the locked door.

"No...condom..." he managed as she stroked him from root to tip. His blood felt like fire, and Haddie's touch only stoked the flame.

She bent down and grabbed her dress with her free hand and tossed it over his shoulder so it hung over the top of the door. Then she let go of him and took a step back.

"Do the same with your pants," she ordered.

Levi's mouth fell open. "Did you catch what I just said?" he asked.

She nodded and gave him a wicked smile, and Levi physically ached not to be touching her. Holy hell, what had he gotten himself into?

"Yep," Haddie replied. "*You* don't have a condom. But *I* do."

CHAPTER 19

Levi blinked at her. "Who *are* you?"

Haddie raised her brows. "Do you or do you not want to have sex with me right now?"

Levi swallowed. "I do. Jesus, Haddie." He glanced down at his half-lowered pants and the rock-hard length that she could not believe she'd referred to as little. "But this is a fancy-ass store."

"And?" She crossed her arms over her bare breasts, aware that she was standing naked in a bridal shop dressing room in front of the man she'd been platonically living with for weeks. How? How had she done it and not completely lost her marbles? Haddie was out of her mind with need for this man, but hell, if one of them wasn't going to play it cool here, and it certainly wasn't Mr. Big over there.

Levi let his head fall against the door and groaned. "This isn't how I imagined our first time," he told her.

Haddie wrapped a hand around his wrist and brought his palm to her breast.

Levi hissed in a breath. "Evil, evil woman," he growled.

"But you have imagined our first time?" she asked.

He snatched his hand away and ran it through his hair, tugging at it like it was the only thing keeping him standing.

"Of course I have." He swore, then finally met her gaze again, his eyes dark as storm clouds. "We almost did that night," he reminded her. "And then we didn't. And then we were only supposed to be friends, and we seem to have failed at that too. Now…?" He scrubbed a hand across his face. "I can't believe I'm asking this since I have never asked this of any other woman in the history of my existence, but what is this, Haddie? If we take this step, what the hell does it mean? What happens when I go back to Indiana and eventually back on the road? Are you going to give up what you've started here and come with me? Do we do long distance? Because I'm not sure if you've noticed, but I'm crazy about—"

"Friends with benefits!" Haddie blurted out before letting him finish. Because she couldn't let him say it…couldn't let herself hear it. Levi was right. No matter how he thought he felt right now in this impossible moment they'd somehow found themselves in, he was leaving. That was the way it always went when Haddie cared about someone. So what if they did this without the caring?

His expression fell, and Haddie hated herself for the gut punch she knew she'd just landed. But she would hate even more if she let him fall for her, if she let herself fall for him. Because he was right. Where would they be six months from now?

"Friends with benefits?" he asked, but she could hear the resignation in his tone.

She nodded. "It's the best of both worlds, right? All of the amazing, delicious sex without any of the complications. And no one needs to know, which means no entanglements messing up my first year on the job or you getting Coach Crawford's recommendation for reinstatement." She let out a nervous laugh. "C'est la vie, right?"

Wow, was she good at putting him right back where she wanted him, at arm's length. But wasn't she on to something here? Levi wanted Haddie. Haddie wanted Levi. And neither of them wanted to jeopardize their careers. They could have exactly what they wanted and be no worse for wear when it was time to say goodbye. "This is our redo, Levi. The night that didn't happen can finally happen…here!" Even she could hear the delulu level of eagerness in her voice as she tried to convince him to take her in a bridal shop dressing room. But that was what weeks of burying how she really felt had done to her. Haddie was a shaken two-liter bottle of soda into which someone had dropped an entire roll of Mentos. She would not, could not be contained.

A gust of wind rushed into the fitting area, and their fitting-room door rattled in its frame. In the distance Haddie heard another door slam.

"Hads?" Emma called. "Levi? Are you guys still here?"

"Shit!" Haddie whispered. "Pull up your pants!"

Haddie scrambled back into her underwear and snatched her dress from the door. She wriggled back through the open top, only now seeing the jagged tear where the zipper was once attached and then wasn't. She lost her footing and stumbled back against the mirror, all while Levi did his best to stuff himself back into his pants.

Apparently, she stood corrected on that whole *would not, could not* containment thing.

"Over here, Ems!" Haddie called. "My zipper was stuck, and Levi helped, and then we got locked in! Is Layla with you?"

"No," Emma replied, and Haddie could tell she was right outside the door. "Turns out her puppy ate the corner of her couch, so she had to run to the vet to make sure he didn't swallow anything he couldn't pass. She told me the key code to get back in when I told her you guys hadn't shown up yet." Emma tapped on the door and then added, "And I thought maybe... I mean, I was catching some weird vibes between you two today and wondered if..." Her voice trailed off. "Are you guys really stuck, or did I just interrupt something you didn't want interrupted?"

"Stuck," Levi replied before Haddie even had a chance to open her mouth.

Emma sighed. "Guess it was all in my head. I've definitely got wedding brain going on and will continue to use the wedding as an excuse for my spaciness for months after the fact."

Haddie nodded and gave him what she hoped was an apologetic smile, though she wasn't sure what she was apologizing for.

Emma jiggled the handle. "It's definitely locked," she confirmed.

"You don't happen to have a screwdriver, do you?" Levi asked, turning around to survey the door.

Emma gasped. "I do! I have one of those all-in-one tool things that Matteo makes me carry even though I told him I would never have a use for it!"

"The hinges are on the inside," Levi told her. "Can you pass it to me over the top of the door? Then you might want to call Layla and let her know she'll be coming in to a bit of a mess tomorrow but that I'll set her up with Tommy's uncle Pete to change out the hardware on the door."

Emma held the tool just above the top of the door, and Haddie realized her friend must be on her tiptoes.

Levi grabbed it and immediately got to work. Less than five minutes later, the door dropped a half inch to the floor, and Levi carefully pried it away from the frame enough for him and Haddie to slip through without breaking anything.

"Wow," Emma said when they emerged from their veritable cocoon. "You're shirtless," she said to Levi. "And *fast*...at taking doors off of hinges, I mean."

Levi flashed her a quick grin. "Appreciate you specifying the part about the door." Then he slipped back into his own dressing room while Haddie stood face-to-face with her best friend as she barely held the torn bridesmaid's dress to her torso.

"What the hell?" Emma asked. She grabbed Haddie's forearm and dragged her across the fitting room area, through the red velvet curtain, and out into the main shop area. "Your *dress*, Haddie! What did you do?"

Haddie tried to survey the damage, but every time she craned her neck to try to see what was behind her, she just ended up looking like a dog trying to chase its tail. It didn't matter. She knew it was bad, and it would have been even worse if she not only trashed the dress but then also had sex in Emma's friend's beautiful shop. What was wrong with her? Levi was making her lose all sense of logic.

"I'm sorry, Ems," she finally said, feeling even more guilty that Emma didn't know the half of what Haddie was apologizing for.

"I really am," she continued. "But the dress was so freaking tight. I couldn't breathe. Like, the zipper was stuck, and I was literally about to pass out, so I asked Levi to come and help me." She grimaced. "The zipper was stuck, and I was desperate. So I told him to rip it off of me if he needed to since I knew Kayla was going to have to let the dress out in the bust area anyway." Emma stared at her as if Haddie had just set the whole shop on fire. "I'm sorry. I'll pay for whatever damage we did to the dress, but the door? That's on Layla...and Levi since he's the one who kicked out the pen that was holding it open."

With one hand still holding the dress up, Haddie held out her other and spread her palm into the jazziest of jazz hands. "Ta-da!" she said, but Emma still didn't look amused.

Her friend sighed. "And there's really nothing going on between you and Levi?" she whispered.

Haddie scoffed. "Me and Levi? Please. I know better than to get involved with someone—even casually—who is a colleague in the district where I don't have tenure and where the principal already warned us against any complicated entanglements. Nor do I have any interest in getting involved with a man who's skipping town in less than a year."

"Or..." Emma countered, "who will be the best man at my wedding in a matter of weeks, and I really don't want to have to change your table at the last minute because you broke Levi's heart."

Haddie took a staggering step back, her mouth falling open. "That's what you think of me, Ems? That I'd be so careless as to make your wedding awkward by complicating things with my roommate?"

"Who is Matteo's brother," Emma reminded her.

"Yeah!" Haddie replied. "We've met. He's about yea tall…" She held a hand up high to indicate Levi's massive height. "Athletic build. Really handy with hinges and is apparently a high priority on the bride's list of all things that need protecting, yet somehow I didn't make the cut."

Haddie's throat burned. She knew what she was doing, and she hated every second of it. But she couldn't let out her frustrations on Levi, so Emma would have to do. Granted, it hurt to see her best friend defend her *almost* brother-in-law ahead of Haddie. But the truth was, once Emma and Matteo were married, Levi and Emma *would* be family, and Haddie would still be…well…Haddie.

"*Hads…*" Emma spoke more gently this time, and the sound of her voice made Haddie's heart ache.

"I'm sorry," Haddie replied coolly. "This is all about your big day, and I made it about me. It's just been…" She glanced down at the remains of her dress. "A wardrobe malfunction kind of day, you know?"

Emma laughed, but Haddie could still sense the hint of worry in the sound of it.

"I'm not gonna break his heart, Ems. Okay? Because there's nothing going on between us. Your perfect big day will be your perfect big day. I promise. I'll even keep my dress on for it."

Haddie's best friend sighed, and despite Haddie still barely clothed and clinging to the emerald-green garment, Emma wrapped her arms around her and squeezed.

"I love you, you know," Emma whispered.

"Yeah, yeah…" Haddie replied, finally relenting and leaning into the hug, even if she couldn't hug Emma back without exposing her nearly naked self beneath the dress.

Except Haddie realized that even if she wore nothing at all, Emma wouldn't see all of her. It was true; the Haddie Emma knew *might* break Levi's heart. But if Emma could see everything, she'd know that Levi was in just as much danger of breaking *her* heart.

But that was only if Emma could see, which—of course—she couldn't. Because even when it came to the person she loved most, Haddie still kept her friend just out of reach. It was how Haddie was made. For too long now, it had been what she was hardwired to do. It didn't matter whether she wanted it this way anymore because she had no idea how to change nearly thirty years of programming.

Emma finally let her go.

"You're going to say it one day," Emma told her with a knowing grin.

Haddie scoffed. "I tell you I love you all the time." Though, she did file a mental note that she hadn't said it at this particular moment.

Emma shook her head. "You're going to say it first one day, and then you'll know."

Haddie's brows furrowed. "Know what, ya goof?"

Emma shrugged. "That I'll stay."

CHAPTER 20

W hat is a *finger* sandwich?" Levi mumbled to his brother as they watched Haddie, Emma, and Emma's mom load a cart with some three-tiered-plate contraption on it along with a silver teapot, teacups, and saucers.

Matteo elbowed him in the ribs. "Sandwiches you eat with your *fingers!*" he whispered loudly.

"But what if I want to use my whole hand to eat a sandwich? Or both of my hands?" Levi argued.

He knew his irritation stemmed from somewhere deeper than sandwich etiquette or the fact that he'd never had afternoon tea before and didn't want to look like an asshole in front of Haddie.

After the fitting room fiasco and their subsequent rescue, he'd let Haddie and Emma walk several paces ahead of him on their way to the inn. He used the term *let* loosely, considering the second they made it outside of Layla's shop, Haddie hooked her arm in Emma's and practically sprinted the first block, leaving him and his thoughts in the dust.

Do you or do you not want to have sex with me right now?

Never in his wildest imagination since he and Haddie became roommates had he thought Haddie Martin would say those words to him. And never in his even wilder than wildest imagination did Levi think he would hesitate in order to have the *Where is this going?* chat.

Levi had never been a *Where is this going* kind of guy. In high school, if you knew Levi Rourke, you knew the game came before everything. In college, he was too lost after losing his mom and career to be even remotely present in any relationship. And now that he was a grown-ass adult who should have figured this all out, he realized he was just repeating the same pattern. He'd replaced playing the game with coaching it. And he'd traded his guilt and apparently unprocessed grief for trophies to prove his worth.

But he wasn't worthy, was he? Otherwise Haddie wouldn't have freaked out when he tried to tell her he was crazy about her. Shit. How did he let that happen?

"The sandwiches are too small for your whole hand, dingus," Matteo said, dragging Levi out of his spiral.

Levi glared at his younger brother. "What did you just call me?"

Matteo rolled his eyes. "I have called you several names in the past eleven to fifteen seconds, and that's the one you hear? You are in *deep*, big bro."

"What are you talking about?" Levi let out something between a cough and a laugh. "In what deep? Where? I mean, what?" He grabbed the pitcher of ice water that sat on the table and filled the glass in front of him. Then he drained it in one gigantic gulp. When he finished, his brother stared at him with a one smug-ass smile.

"Shit," Matteo lamented. "Emma was right, and she is never going to let me live this down."

Levi glanced to where the three women seemed to be leaning over the tea cart conspiratorially, and dammit if looking at Haddie didn't turn his blood into something molten.

"Live what down?" Levi asked, but the defensive tone of his voice gave him away. He wasn't an idiot. After what happened in that fitting room today, Levi didn't have the resolve left to hide whatever it was that Haddie Martin was doing to him.

Matteo's only response was to sit back in his seat, cross his arms, and gloat.

"You're going to make me say it, aren't you?" Levi asked with a groan.

His brother shrugged. "Say what…dingus?"

Levi ran a hand up the back of his neck and over the top of his head. "It's complicated," he finally admitted.

"It's actually not," Matteo countered without missing a beat. "'Complicated' is pretending like you don't feel what's all over your damned face."

His brother was right. The pretending drained his focus and his energy. It was probably the reason why he couldn't wrap his head around how to help his team. His brain short-circuited whenever Haddie was around, whether he wanted to admit it to his brother or not.

"Fine," Levi relented. "I have cannonballed off the high dive into the deep end, and I might actually be drowning. Which makes zero sense because we barely know each other."

"Except you feel like you've known her for twenty years," his brother countered.

"Yes! What is that?"

Matteo shrugged, unfazed. "When you live with someone, time moves exponentially faster. When I was...um...locked up..."

Levi winced at his brother's mention of his short time in prison, the worst of the fallout following their mother's death.

Matteo cleared his throat. "Anyway," he continued. "By the end of my first week, I knew the names of all my cellmate's pet rabbits, and I mean *all* of them. Living or dead. Do you want to hear about how Snuffles insisted on sitting on his shoulder like a parrot, even when she was full grown? Or about how Skipper could hop up onto the kitchen counter and wreak havoc with the battery-powered salt and pepper shakers?"

"Rabbits?" Levi asked.

Matteo nodded. "Rabbits. So. Many. Rabbits."

Levi groaned. "Fine. Maybe Haddie and I know each other better than we would if we weren't roommates, but what would even be the point of pursuing this...this..."

"What are we pursuing?" Emma asked, and Levi startled so hard that he almost tipped over his chair but caught himself at the last second.

He sneered at this brother, who was grinning back at him in a way that said, *You were so wrapped up in your feelings about your roommate that you didn't even notice her heading to the table...but I did.*

Levi coughed. "Um...a...strategy for my team to maybe actually *score* at our next game, which is Tuesday right after school."

Haddie made eye contact with him for the first time since the fitting room, and Levi had the sensation of falling all over again, except this time his chair had all four legs on the floor.

"Tuesday?" she said, eyes wide. "Why didn't I realize your game was on Tuesday? We should be home drawing up plays. Or…or on the field so we can demo the plays. Emma and Matteo, you could come too! If I have someone to represent the opposing team, maybe I can finally help get it through Coach Rourke's head what the hell 'offside' means!"

"I thought it was 'off*sides*,'" Levi replied.

Haddie shook her head. "The proper way to say it is 'off*side*,' but of course, America colloquialized it to 'offsides.' But if I'm going to teach you, I'm going to teach you correctly." She crossed her arms and raised her brows.

This was all it took to get her out of her head about what had almost happened between them but didn't…again? Soccer? How was she able to redirect while Levi—who'd been living and breathing football since he was barely able to tie his own shoes—was pretty sure he'd forgotten how many points a field goal was worth.

"Can't," Emma replied, just as Matteo said, "I'm sure we could…"

But Emma cut her fiancé off with a look, solidifying the response to Levi's unanswered question.

He and Haddie weren't hiding shit. Emma and Matteo were betting on the whole *Will they or won't they?* And Levi and Haddie had been too caught up in their own worlds to notice that everyone else was noticing.

"Sorry, Bro," Matteo amended. "I guess you two are on your own for Sunday afternoon P.E. class. Emma and I have—"

"A thing!" Emma interrupted. "For the wedding."

"What wedding thing?" Haddie asked, turning her attention to her friend. "Didn't we just have a wedding thing at the dress shop? And shouldn't the maid of honor be helping with all wedding things?"

"It's...a surprise!" Emma blurted out. "My surprise gift to Matteo."

"What surprise, sweetheart?" Lynette Woods asked as she set the three-tiered stack of finger sandwiches and what Levi could see were also tiny pastries in the center of the table.

"You know, Mom..." Emma replied through gritted teeth. When the other woman opened her mouth to once again express her confusion, her daughter quickly filled it with a tiny sandwich. "I'll remind you about it after I surprise my husband-to-be."

Matteo reached for what looked like a tiny cream puff and popped it into his mouth before leaning back with a conspiratorial grin. "I am very much looking forward to this surprise."

Emma looked at her watch and gasped dramatically.

"What is it?" Haddie asked, stopping midway as she attempted to sit down to likely enjoy her own plate of different tiny foods.

Why was everything so small? Also, why was it called tea if it was more than tea? These were the hard-hitting questions taking up space in Levi's brain because they made about as little sense as soccer or almost having sex with Haddie in a bridal shop fitting room. He had so many questions, and no one would give him a straight answer.

"I just got a calendar reminder for the thing…the surprise. You know what, Hads? We're burning daylight here. How about I make you and Levi an afternoon tea to-go package, and you can head on out to the soccer field for a little one-on-one before nightfall."

Matteo coughed.

Haddie stood all the way up again.

And Levi pressed the heels of his hands to his eyes and wondered how the hell Haddie didn't see what they were doing.

Wait… Haddie didn't see what Emma and Matteo were doing. They were gifting him time alone with her to either finish what they started or put an end to it all together. And if he could also wrap his head around *offside* or *offsides* or whatever it was that kept resulting in the opposing team earning free kicks against the Muskies, then even better. This thing either started or ended *now*.

"You know what?" Levi stood abruptly. "I just realized that I don't even like tea. But I'd be happy to take some tiny treats to go."

"Wait right there!" Emma cried, and she disappeared back the way she'd come, pushing through saloon doors Levi knew led to the Woods Family Inn kitchen. Thirty seconds later, she was back with what looked like a gallon-sized zip-top plastic bag into which she dumped one of the three tiered plates. She sealed it and offered it to Haddie. "Here you go! Tiny treats for you two to enjoy whenever the mood strikes. Maybe you can have a little picnic on the soccer field!" When Haddie didn't immediately accept her offering, Emma shook the bag until she did.

"Okay…you are *weird* when you're trying to surprise someone,"

Haddie told her friend. Then she turned her gaze to Matteo. "I'm kind of a little scared for you."

Matteo laughed, then wrapped his arms around Emma's waist and pulled her into his lap. She yelped and burst into a fit of giggles herself. "I think it's safe to assume we should *all* be a little scared of Emma when she's trying to keep a secret. Sometimes she is *way* too obvious."

"I just wish I remembered what the surprise was…" Emma's mom mused, staring with concentration at the ceiling and mouthing something inaudible to herself as if she was trying to do calculus in her head.

"You two should go." Emma shooed Levi and Haddie with her hands, then laughed when Matteo reached for another cream puff and tried to feed it to her nose.

Haddie's brows furrowed and Levi shrugged. "Guess it can't hurt to work some stuff out in full scale, right? Not like anyone else is scheduled to practice on a Sunday afternoon."

"Right," she agreed, then dangled the bag of small treats between them. "And I guess afternoon tea in the goalie box or something." She pivoted back toward Emma's mom. "Thanks to you and Mr. Woods for making all the goodies. I guess we're going."

Levi nodded toward his brother and fiancée. "Teo…Emma."

"Um…thank you, Lynette," Haddie said to Emma's mother, and less than a minute later, Levi and Haddie found themselves on the sidewalk in front of the Woods Family Inn.

CHAPTER 21

W ell," Haddie said to the bag of small sandwiches and pastries that were now close to a pile of unidentifiable anything. "That was…subtle."

Levi coughed. "Wait…you knew she was full of shit?"

Haddie scoffed. "Emma Woods? Uh…yeah. That woman doesn't have a subtle bone in her body, and the lying gene totally skipped out on her DNA."

Levi crossed his arms and stared at her. "Then why didn't you call her on it if you knew she was throwing us back together to deal with whatever happened at the bridal shop?"

Haddie raised her brows and then started walking in the direction of the Summertown school campus. "Because we're not," she told him with a shrug. "You have a game on Tuesday that you're going to win, but the only way that's going to happen is if we focus. On the *game*."

She walked fast, so much so that he was pretty sure she'd break into a sprint if he wasn't careful. Was she serious? How the hell was he going to be able to focus on a game when he still couldn't figure out why she preferred friends with benefits to him actually admitting he might feel something more. Haddie was more spooked by all of this than even he was. Why?

"Haddie..." He put a hand on her forearm, grateful for his height and long strides so that just in case she *did* decide to run, he could probably keep up for a bit before his knee began to protest.

"We're almost there," she told him, her voice too bright, too cheery. "We really don't need to do this, Levi. We have a game to prepare for. You need to focus." She brandished her fist like she was trying to pep up one of her own players. "You got this!"

Levi spun so he was walking backward, faster than he'd have liked when not watching where he was going, but he guessed he'd just have to trust that Haddie wouldn't let him hurt himself.

"*Haddie...*" he said again, forcing her to look at him.

"*Levi...*" she replied, mimicking his tone but not giving him an inch.

He stepped in front of her and caught her by the shoulders right before she plowed into him. He had to plant his feet, though, to keep from letting her momentum knock them both to the concrete.

"Is that a..." he asked, narrowing his eyes at the topiary at the foot of the driveway next to them.

"Dragon's ass?" she said, filling in his blank. "Yes. Part of the rebuild from last summer's tornado."

Levi barked out a laugh, but when he met Haddie's gaze again, she was glaring at him.

"Come on, Birthday Girl. Shrubbery cut into the tail end of a dragon, and the tail end *only* is funny as hell."

The corner of her mouth twitched, but she fought the smile.

So Levi tentatively let her go so he could back toward the trimmed green haunches and the bulbous behind that extended into a tail that snaked up the perimeter of the driveway. Then, as any grown man would, he hugged the dragon's ass and asked Haddie to take a picture.

With a full-on snort, she broke.

"What is the matter with you?" she asked, grabbing him by the wrist, but Levi shook his head.

"You need to snap a photo first. And then, whenever you think you want to freeze me out, you look at that photo and remember that I embraced a dragon's ass for you with no regard for my own well-being."

She groaned, but she must have known he wasn't going to budge until she complied, so she pulled her phone from her back pocket and, with a groan, snapped a photo.

"There," she told him, flashing her phone's screen at him to show that she had completed the requested task.

Levi straightened and smiled triumphantly. "And now that I have your attention, we're going to talk about the damned fitting room," he told her.

Haddie sighed, and he finally felt like he was making progress. "Fine," she told him. "But not without balls."

He choked. "I'm sorry...what?"

———

After setting the bag of food from Emma on the bench, Haddie dragged the mesh bag of soccer balls from the equipment shed behind the bleachers while Levi carried a stack of orange cones.

Balls.

"You have to shoot a goal without being offside. I don't even care if the ball makes it in the net. Once you get it, we'll talk," she told him as she dropped the mesh bag.

"Why do I feel like you're betting on me to fail?"

She waved him off. "Give me those," she told him, pointing to the cones, so Levi handed them over.

He watched as she put one just inside the goalie box and one several feet in front of the white square painted on the turf in front of the goal.

"These are the opposing team's players," she explained. "The goalie and the defender."

Levi laughed. "Um, I think I can get a goal past a couple of coneheads."

Haddie narrowed her eyes and then jogged back to balls, removed one from the bag, and dribbled it over to the center field line.

"You have to score off of my assist!" she called to him.

Levi still didn't understand why she was making a whole thing out of this. Soccer might not be his sport, but he could trap a ball under his foot and aim it for the goal. It wasn't that much beyond his grasp.

So he held up his hands, palms facing him, and made a motion that told her to *Bring it!*

Haddie kicked the ball. *Hard.* But he could read the trajectory, could tell where it would land, so he raced the ball, lining himself up perfectly to trap it just behind the outermost orange cone.

As soon as he stopped it with his shoe, a whistle blew. His head shot up to see Haddie holding her phone over her head, apparently using a whistle app.

"Offside!" she called.

Shit. Wait… What?

"You passed me the ball!" he called back. "I'm in bounds but offside?" Why didn't he freaking get it?

"Try again!" she replied.

She wasn't going to tell him? What the hell?

She jogged toward him and not only stole the ball out from under his sneaker but also grabbed the outermost cone and took it back with her toward center field. This time she put the cone just behind the line, still on the opposing team's side.

"Come here!" Haddie motioned for him to meet her at center field.

He jogged toward her, albeit slightly annoyed.

"I didn't even get a chance to kick," he grumbled.

Haddie shrugged. "It wouldn't have been your ball to kick anyway. You were offside, so it would have turned over to a free kick for the other team." She backed up and gestured for him to follow her past the center line and onto what would be *their* side of the field, the human-as-opposed-to-orange-cone side.

"Try again," she told him.

Levi glanced from where he stood to the goal. He was a decent shot, but…

"What are we doing?" he asked. "You want me to shoot from here?"

Haddie shrugged. "Shoot from wherever you want once you gain possession of the ball. Just stay onside."

She backed up farther, and Levi rocked on his heels, anticipating another power shot, which was why he was surprised when she started to dribble toward him.

Despite his confusion and frustration, he couldn't help but notice how light she was on her feet, how she faked out nonexistent other players feinting left and then right, trapping the ball with her toe and rolling it to the other side of her body.

Then he saw it, the windup. She was going for it, but if he stood still, the ball would still be airborne by the time it came to him, and he would fumble the shot.

So he backed up two steps, then another few. The second he backed up past the orange cone, Haddie's phone was in the air again, a shrill whistle screaming in the otherwise soundless air.

"Offside!" she exclaimed.

Shocker, Levi told himself. Then he halted where he stood. He looked from Haddie to the "goalie" and then to the defense player she'd moved right up next to the center line. Levi stood between the two cones, and Haddie still had the ball.

An alarm bell went off in his head.

"Haddie…? Where is the rest of the opposing team?"

A smile played at her lips, but she kept it at bay. "They are all teaming up on McMannus, who better be playing on Tuesday," she told him. "They left their poor goalie and his one defender all alone on *their* side of the field."

Levi's eyes widened. "So I'm standing in between the second to last and last players on the defender's side."

Haddie nodded, and he could tell that she was hanging on by

a thread now, that beautiful beaming smile about to break through her last shred of resistance.

"And if I'm where I am without the ball?"

"*Ding! Ding! Ding! Ding! Ding!*" She tapped her nose with one index finger and pointed at Levi triumphantly with the other.

"Fuuuuuck!" he cried, laughing as he jogged toward her.

His team members always apologized after they were at the receiving end of an offside call, and Levi would always tell them to shake it off and not let it happen next time, but the problem was, he didn't *know* what he was looking for to try to head off the penalty before it happened, and his damned ego wouldn't let him ask his students what it was and lose the already fragile trust he'd earned coming to them from the world of football and instead being tossed into soccer.

Without realizing what he was doing until he was already doing it, he scooped Haddie into his arms and spun her.

She yelped and then burst out laughing, and they were both caught up in a moment that Levi realized happened not because Haddie cared more about the game than what happened between them earlier that day, but because she *cared*. About him and his team, and the thought emboldened him enough to lower her back to the ground but keep his arms wrapped around her torso.

"You did it," she told him softly, but she wasn't pulling away.

"*You* did it," he replied, staring down at eyes the color of the grass beneath their feet. "If I would have had more teachers like you when I was in school, maybe I wouldn't have thought football was my only option."

Haddie furrowed her brows at him. "It's not your only option. You're teaching health and P.E. And coaching a whole new sport."

"Terribly," he remarked.

She shook her head and took a step back, so Levi let his hands fall. "When you first shrugged off Principal Crawford cutting the program, I had you pegged. You were here because you had to be, and once you went back to the life you actually cared about, you wouldn't think twice about this program or these kids."

Levi held a fist to his chest like she'd just stabbed him. "Ouch."

Haddie winced. "It was way safer to think that the guy I met in that hotel bar was some fantasy I'd built up in my head." She toed the soccer ball toward her, then rolled it up her shin, and bounced it off her knee. Then she held it against her torso like a shield before blowing out a breath. "But you did the car wash. And you're out here now learning for your students, and…"

And what, Haddie? He wouldn't interrupt her, but Jesus, the ache in his chest was going to swallow him from the inside out.

So he held her gaze even when she looked away, and when her eyes met his again, he gave her a soft, encouraging nod.

She let out a nervous laugh. "You're kind of great."

The corner of his mouth tugged into a lopsided grin. "Last I checked, being kind of great was a good thing. Have the rules changed?"

She tossed the ball at him, which he caught.

"Great doesn't last, Levi. I have a lifetime of experience to back that up. If you're just some guy I live with—along with a few extra benefits—and you leave at the end of the school year, then I'm no worse for wear. But if I care about you and then you go?" Without the ball in her hands, she wrapped her arms around her torso.

Levi could barely keep it together. It should be *his* arms holding her tight. It should be *him* comforting her and telling her that location and distance didn't have to mean loss. But the king of would-haves and should-haves wasn't going to make a promise he knew he couldn't keep. He'd already disappointed the people who mattered most to him, and it would kill him to add Haddie to that list.

He wanted to tell her so many things, but the universe had other plans.

With an unexpected crash and dark-gray clouds obliterating the late-afternoon sun, the sky opened up and drowned out his words.

Together they scrambled to grab the cones and shove the soccer ball back into the mesh bag. They ran through fast-growing puddles to toss the equipment back into the shed. After Levi snapped the padlock closed, he pulled Haddie into the narrow space between the shed and concession stand, where the shallow awnings of both roofs provided temporary shelter from the storm.

They were soaked. Rivulets of water streamed down Haddie's face and over her lips as she stared at him with what looked like a thousand questions pinballing through her brain, the same questions—he guessed—that made his own logic short-circuit every time she was near.

Couldn't and *shouldn't* felt a million miles away when she looked at him like that.

Levi wanted more than friends with benefits, but above all else,

Levi wanted *her*. So he would take what she was willing to give and figure out later...*later*.

"We can run!" he called over the deluge, knowing that, however treacherous, trying to make it home was the logical thing to do.

Haddie shook her head. "I don't want to run anymore!" she replied. "I'm so *tired* of running."

Before he had time to piece together whether or not she meant the physical act of running or something else, her fists clenched his wet shirt, and she tugged him down to her as they crashed together in their own storm of hunger and need.

Their kiss in the fitting room had been wild and unbridled, but this felt like something feral. Like if they didn't devour each other, they'd both disappear.

She pushed his back against the shed so she now stood under the steady waterfall of rain that made its way in between the two roofs. She licked her lips as the water streamed down her face, and Levi groaned. Then she braced her palms against the shed on either side of his shoulders, her body slamming against his.

She rocked her pelvis against his unmistakable erection, and a growl tore from his lips.

Levi slid her soaked shirt up above her bra and cupped her breast, his thumb and finger pinching the taut peak of her nipple. Even amid the storm he could hear her moan, and the sound of her pleasure—of him being the *cause* of that pleasure—set his blood on fire.

"Haddie," he ground out, his own voice unrecognizable to his ears. "Is this... Is it friends with benefits...or more?"

"I don't know," she answered, her lips still against his. "I just can't not do this anymore."

He swore. "Me neither."

They kissed and nipped and tasted, moans and whimpers escaping their lips as Haddie's fingers teased the waistband of his shorts, and he remembered his words in the fitting room.

This isn't how I imagined our first time.

And neither was this.

"We need to get back to the apartment," he said, not believing the words that were coming out of his mouth when he knew instant gratification was only a matter of her hand sliding just a tiny bit lower.

Haddie opened her mouth to protest, but his hand was already around her waist. "Come on!" he called, and then they dove headlong into the storm.

CHAPTER 22

Haddie was breathless, soaked, and shivering by the time they burst through the front door of the apartment. Levi must have been just as cold because goose bumps peppered his arms and legs.

They toed off their muddy shoes and peeled away their wet socks before padding into the living room, small puddles from their dripping clothes forming in their wake.

"We need to dry off," he told her, his voice hoarse. "I'll get us some towels."

He spun toward the bathroom, giving her a moment to think, to wrap her head around all the events of the day that led them to right here. What came next? What happened after they peeled off their soaked clothes?

Haddie knew the ball was in her court. If she chose to call this *friends with benefits*, he'd probably let her. Levi would let her live in her blissful world of make-believe, claiming that whatever they felt wasn't real or wouldn't last. Friends with benefits. Cut their losses before they even happened. Safety. Her line in the sand.

"I'm crazy about you too!" she blurted out instead, and despite the cold, wet clothes clinging to his shivering torso, Levi Rourke stepped out of the bathroom, towel in hand, and smiled the kind of smile that could make the clouds part to reveal the biggest, brightest rainbow she'd ever seen. "Oh la vache," she added, burying her face in her hands.

He laughed. "What *is* that?" he asked.

She met his eyes again. "What is what?"

"The...the thing you just said. Was that French? You did the same thing that night in the hotel and today in the dressing room."

Haddie's cheeks burned. How had he noticed her tell so quickly? Maybe the more astute observation was that Levi had noticed her. He'd seen her, even when he barely knew her.

"When I get flustered...which is not often, by the way...my brain sort of short-circuits and I start spouting aphorisms or idioms in other languages. I got it from...um...from my grandmother." She cleared her throat. "We weren't super close, but when we'd watch soccer together, she used to swear in other languages at bad plays." Haddie shrugged. "Now it's my thing too." He stepped closer, his smile fading, and dabbed the folded-up towel under her eye. "Oh god," she said, a slight tremble in her voice. "Are my eyes leaking? Did I just turn things from romantic and cute to ugh-this-girl-has-issues weird?"

He wrapped the towel around her neck and tugged her close. "I like weird, Haddie. And I like you. But you have to tell me what happens next," he said, his voice layered with hesitation and hope.

Since Haddie was six—*six*—and lost her mom, she'd kept everyone at arm's length, preparing for the moment when they'd eventually disappear. And it still hurt when Emma moved back home. It still leveled her when her grandmonster died, because despite their complicated relationship, they were all the other one had. And what had it gotten her, other than a lonely existence even when the people she was meant to love were right in front of her?

Levi was right in front of her. Would depriving herself of the chance to feel something for him make it any easier to lose him once he was gone?

Haddie's shoulder rose in a small shrug. "Why can't we see where this goes and deal with that when we get there?" She cupped his cheeks in her palms and kissed him softly, drinking in the rainwater on his lips as he sighed against her. Then she stepped back with just enough room to peel off everything she was wearing, letting it fall to a wet heap on the floor.

Levi sucked in a breath as she wordlessly helped him out of his clothes and backed him—naked, hard, beautiful, and hers—into his room.

He lay down on his back, and Haddie crawled over him, staring down at the man she didn't want to run from anymore.

She fell back onto her heels, and he gripped her thighs, drinking her in.

"How did you imagine it?" she asked. "Our first time."

He slid his hand up toward her hips, his thumb pausing to touch her where her pelvis met his.

Haddie gasped at his touch.

"Slower," he told her, tracing a soft circle around her swollen center until she whimpered. "And...preferably not in a locked room the size of a small closet or under the very precarious shelter of an equipment shed's roof where I might get struck by lightning."

She laughed, and her back arched as he slid his thumb against her again.

"What you are doing right now"—she sucked in a sharp breath—"is making it very hard for me to want to go slow."

"And I am enjoying watching you try to restrain yourself." He grinned. "But even more, Haddie, I fucking love that after all these weeks, I finally get to touch you like this."

He slid his upturned palm between them, sank a finger inside her, and Haddie whimpered. Well, two could play this game.

She wrapped her hand around his shaft and slowly stroked upward until she felt him slick against her own thumb. She slowly twisted her grip over his tip before sliding back down.

Levi swore…loudly, and his eyes fell shut. What power to be able to make him feel like this…and for him to trust her with whatever happened next, both in this bed, tomorrow, and the days and months after that.

"Say it again," he whispered, as they both touched and teased and explored.

"I'm *crazy* about you," she admitted once more, and she wished she had the courage to tell him that she'd never said anything even close to that to any other man before.

"Top drawer of my nightstand," he told her, his voice rough, and Haddie grinned as she reached for the drawer, produced a condom, and rolled it down his length.

Levi opened his eyes, slid his hands to her waist, and urged her down to him, his lips brushing against hers.

"Make me promise not to fall in love with you," he whispered.

Haddie's breath caught in her throat. "Don't fall in love with me," she complied, her voice a tremble of words. *Because I won't be able to take it when you fall out.*

He nipped at her bottom lip and smiled against her. "Okay," he replied. "But I should warn you that I'm shitty at keeping promises."

Then he moved his hand between them, positioning himself where she was open, wet, and waiting for him. He lifted her by the hips—good god, the man's upper body strength—and lowered her over his entire length, burying himself inside her.

She cried out, her vision turning to bursts of color as lighting and thunder crashed, illuminating the otherwise dark room.

Haddie Martin didn't know what love was supposed to feel like or if she was even capable of letting herself *be* loved. But if she had to put one word to her jumble of thoughts, to the questions bouncing around in her brain, it would be *Levi*.

Levi.

Levi.

Levi.

"Yeah?" he asked as they moved together, their bodies woven into one, and Haddie realized she'd been saying his name out loud.

"Don't make that promise," she told him, and then gasped as he slipped a hand between them.

"I won't," he replied, and Haddie cried out.

She was so close. So freaking close.

"Because I can't," he admitted.

Haddie felt like she was pitching over a cliff, heart and body tangled together as he moved faster inside her until they were falling together in a sweaty, breathless, euphoric heap.

That night, despite the storm raging outside, Haddie never so much as flinched as she slept in Levi's arms, dreaming about promises she hoped neither of them could keep.

The next morning, Haddie did her best to slide out from Levi's embrace and sneak into the bathroom. All she had to do was make it in and out of the shower without waking him so she could make it to the square in time to pick up the blackmail coffee that was even more important after what happened the night before.

She started the water before realizing she hadn't shut Levi's bedroom door. After popping back out to quietly snick it shut, she made it halfway back to the bathroom when she heard a deep, groggy, sexy voice behind her.

"Shower," he murmured. "Me too."

Haddie huffed out a laugh and turned to face a still-naked Levi, hair askew as he rubbed his eyes, his morning wood on proud display. *She*, at least, was wearing a T-shirt she'd stolen from his drawer before sneaking out.

"You want to shower first?" she asked, brows raised. "Because I'm kind of in a rush to—"

"Together," he interrupted, and Haddie couldn't hold back

her amusement at this morning-after, caveman version of her roommate-turned-something-more.

"I have a meeting," she lied.

"Go early too," he responded, and then he held out an open palm to reveal a small, square package that looked an awful lot like the others she'd seen in his nightstand drawer.

Her insides turned molten and a deep, needy ache pulsed between her legs.

"Fine," she relented. "But this can't happen every morning." She grabbed his wrist and tugged him toward her.

"Why not?" he asked, his first intelligible sentence of the morning.

And Haddie realized she had no good answer to his question.

"Actually…" she drawled. "You have a point. Consider solo showers a thing of the past."

And then she led him into the bathroom where she let him lift the T-shirt over her head and lead her beneath the steaming spray of hot water.

Levi kissed her neck and nipped at her ear. "Good morning, Birthday Girl."

And for the first time since she was a kid—and despite it being a month since the date had passed—Haddie thought she might let herself celebrate today.

"Can we have cake for dinner?" she asked him as he peppered her skin with feather-soft kisses that made her knees turn to Jell-O.

Levi dropped to his knees and kissed her pelvis. "We can have anything you want, Birthday Girl." And then he buried his face between her legs and gave her a very generous gift.

CHAPTER 23

Levi didn't ask any questions about Haddie's early-morning meeting the day before. After their shower had left him in need of a power nap before heading in for the start of his Monday, he'd happily sent her ahead to tend to her own responsibilities.

But early-morning meetings two days in a row? Didn't she work hard enough for the administration to not call her in before the official day began? He told her he was happy to leave early and drive with her. Haddie and her entire team were coming to support the varsity boys in their home match against rival Middleton that evening. Wouldn't it make sense to drive together?

"It's perfect weather outside. I'll walk, and we can ride home together tonight," she'd told him before distracting him with a kiss and then slipping out the door before he even had his shoes on.

She rushed out without even a sip of coffee, which he knew would catch up with her later. He'd just have to bring her some.

So imagine his surprise when he showed up outside her classroom with an insulated tumbler only to find Sarah Ramirez and Teddy Kostas snagging two steaming to-go cups from a chair parked in front of Haddie's closed door. Through the small window on top of the doorframe, Levi could see Haddie had circle time well underway with her gaggle of tiny humans.

"Wait…" Levi demanded when the two students looked at him with wide, terrified eyes. He motioned for the culprits—because he was sure they'd done something—to follow him a few steps away so they wouldn't disturb Haddie's class.

"Hey, Coach," Teddy replied with a nervous laugh once they were out of earshot from Haddie's door. "How's it going?"

"We were just leaving," Sarah added, then pivoted to walk in the direction opposite Levi, even though that route led to the elementary cafeteria and not to the high school.

"Wrong way, Ramirez," Levi told her, and she halted mid-step, her shoulders slumping.

"Right." She pivoted back to face him and glanced at Teddy, who was frozen where he stood.

"Did Coach Martin buy you two coffee?" he asked, arms crossed over his chest.

Teddy glanced at Sarah, who rolled her eyes.

"Seriously?" she said to her accomplice. "You never shut up, and now you're tongue-tied?"

Teddy clenched his teeth and spoke out of the side of his mouth, as if Levi couldn't hear him. "I can't lie to my coach, Ramirez."

Sarah squared her shoulders and jutted out her chin. "Yeah," she admitted. "Coach bought us coffee. So what?"

Levi narrowed his eyes. "Yesterday too?"

Sarah swallowed. "Mm-maybe?" she sputtered.

"Shit," Teddy whispered. "We're going to get kicked off our teams for blackmail."

"Shut *up*, Teddy!" Sarah hissed.

"Blackmail?" Levi inquired, aware of the anger seeping into his tone. "You two better fess up to whatever is going on here if you don't want to be kicked off your teams."

Sarah groaned. "Fine." But first she spared Teddy one final glance. "You're the worst, by the way. Hotness wasted."

Teddy coughed. "Wait… You think I'm hot?"

Sarah ignored him and turned her attention back to Levi. "As I was saying…it's no big deal, really. It's just…at the car wash I accused Coach Martin of being sweet on you, and she let it slip that the two of you were living together right when this one"— she elbowed Teddy—"showed up. So she's bribing us to keep our mouths shut about it."

Levi's jaw clenched. "Why did she have to bribe you? Did you threaten to make our living situation which is so far from being any of your business—public to the rest of your teammates?"

Sarah threw her free arm in the air and then glared at Teddy. "Look at how fast this guy cracked under pressure."

Teddy shrugged. "She's right, Coach. I am the worst." He sighed.

Levi let out a mirthless laugh. "Yeah, I think you both earned that title today." Levi checked his watch. "And it's barely even eight. Congratulations." He nodded at their coffee cups. "So what's in the cups?"

Teddy protectively hugged his travel cup to his chest. "Hot cocoa with extra whip cream."

Levi groaned. "Cocoa? Come on, man." He turned his attention to Sarah. "What about you?"

She shrugged. "An extra-shot caramel macchiato."

"Extra shot, huh?" Levi asked. "I guess that deserves a little respect."

"Thanks, Coach," Sarah replied with a grin.

Levi shook his head. "Don't thank me. If Haddie or I liked either of those drinks, I'd be directing you to return your ill-gotten beverages. But, since I'm not going to let Haddie waste her money, you can keep them. But appreciate them since this will be your last day collecting anything from Coach Martin."

Teddy blew out a breath. "Does that mean I'm still on the team?"

Levi sighed. "For now. But you both know that respecting your coaches or your teachers should go without saying, right? Coach Martin works her ass off all day with the kids in that classroom"— Levi pointed toward Haddie's door—"and then still gives this soccer program everything she's got. She doesn't get all up in your business when it comes to who you're living with or not living with or dating or whatever."

"Wait…" Sarah interrupted. "Are you and Coach Martin dating?"

This time Teddy had the good sense to lightly elbow Sarah. "He just said we shouldn't be up in their business," Teddy told her, speaking again out of the side of his mouth.

Sarah sighed. "Sorry, Coach." And she had the decency to sound sincerely regretful. "We're not assholes, you know," she continued, and Levi raised a brow. "We like you and Coach and just thought it would be kind of cool if you were a thing." She pressed her lips into a nervous smile. "Also, having you guys be all united and stuff might mean a better fight to keep the soccer program."

Levi's mouth fell open. "You guys aren't supposed to know about that yet."

Teddy sighed. "I wish I didn't. Makes it feel pointless to even try on the field."

Sarah rumpled Teddy's overgrown brown curls. "Aww, is the wasted hotness a little sentimental?"

Teddy's cheeks turned pink, and Levi had to bite back a grin at seeing a guy he knew could be ruthless on the field turn to a pile of goo in front of the girl he was obviously crushing on. Levi knew the feeling.

"And yeah," Sarah added. "We know. Hard to keep a secret in a town like this, especially when you've got blabbermouths like this guy." She nodded toward Teddy who smiled sheepishly.

"My uncle's on the school board. He told me about Principal Crawford's plan to save the budget by getting rid of the program. How could I not tell my teammates…and Ramirez?"

Levi scrubbed a hand over his jaw and blew out a breath. The looks on both of their faces—that doe-eyed loss of hope—ate up his insides. And if all of them knew? Then how could he blame Teddy or any of his team for not giving it their all? Coach Crawford had labeled them as unnecessary, given them a coach who knew barely enough about soccer to play it, let alone coach it, and all they were doing was playing the part.

He looked at his watch. He had a little less than ten minutes before first period began, and he needed to talk to Tommy.

"Get to class, you two," he finally told them. "And apologize to Coach Martin the next time you see her and tell her that she doesn't have to bribe you because you are going to do your best to keep her private life *private*, okay?"

"Okay," they both grumbled together. "But I'm not going to stop shipping you two," Sarah added.

Levi shook his head with laugh. "Just…keep your shipping to yourself, will you? I don't need any rumors getting back to the big guy when our program is already in jeopardy. I gotta run. Teddy, I'll see you out on the field for warm-ups at four, okay? Because we are going to own Middleton tonight and show Coach Crawford what we are made of."

Teddy forced a smile. "Sure, Coach. If you say so."

Uh, yeah. Levi Rourke freaking said so because this was what he did. He took scrappy potential and turned it into a trophy-winning, Bowl-dominating team. This would just be on a slightly smaller scale but—he realized—no less important.

His team was *necessary*. Haddie's team was *necessary*. And they'd figure out how to prove it to Coach Crawford and the rest of the town.

Levi pivoted back to Haddie's door, left the coffee tumbler on the chair, and then booked it to the high school wing and, more specifically, Tommy Crawford's classroom.

"Hey, Commissioner," Levi said, announcing his arrival without even knocking on the door.

Tommy was sitting at his desk grading papers when he looked up at his friend with tired eyes and a forced grin.

"Rough night?" Levi asked with a wince.

His friend sighed. "Just overextended. Enrollment has grown in the past few years, and we could really use another English teacher on staff, but you know what that does...eats into the budget. So, my classes are too big, grading load too high, and with debate and this budget rescue committee, I've kind of given up on sleep."

"Budget rescue committee?" Levi strode toward the front of the classroom and perched himself against the window across from Tommy's desk.

Tommy nodded. "Turns out quite a number of the faculty are not happy with my father's fiscal decision-making, so a group of us are getting together to try to come up with a solution. Not sure if that means extra fundraising or just barging into a school board meeting and airing our grievances. What I do know is that this will totally strengthen my relationship with my father." He let out a bitter laugh and leaned back in his chair, arms crossed over his chest. "Aren't you happy you asked?"

Levi's stomach twisted into a knot.

"Why wasn't I asked to join your committee?" He wasn't sure why he was asking when he already knew the answer. Maybe he needed to hear it straight from Tommy's mouth.

Tommy blew out a breath. "Look, I know how important the football program was to you...*is* to you. I mean, if Thomas Crawford Sr. had offered you head football coach instead of soccer, you'd be singing his praises for how great he's always been in supporting the team that is the heart of Summertown. Guess I figured you weren't going to rock the boat for a team you won't care about anymore come June."

"Ouch," Levi replied with a wince, but he didn't correct his friend. "Maybe that was me a month ago, but that doesn't mean it's me now."

Tommy raised a disbelieving brow. "What's changed? You're still leaving at the end of the year, right? Football is your life, and I don't disrespect that. But I know you see this town and almost everyone in it as part of your past rather than your future. So what does it matter if you're included on some time suck of a committee that so far has no idea how to solve the budget issue?"

Okay. Double ouch. Maybe he had put Summertown in his rearview mirror, but the people he cared about still mattered to him. Tommy mattered to him. But did he really have to remind his best friend that distance didn't change that?

"Billy McMannus," Levi replied, taking the less vulnerable route to start. Because what if Tommy confirmed what he was pretty sure to be true? That he'd been a shitty friend since he left. A shitty brother and a shitty son. That Levi's fear of looking back at all the parts of life that sucked had only paved the way for a future where the people he loved resented him.

Tommy's brows drew together. "I don't follow."

Levi wasn't sure he could explain it in a way that made sense. Yes, he was still leaving when he was reinstated, but also... He cared about the team he was coaching now and cared about what happened to it even after he was gone. Maybe that didn't solve the budget issue, but it was a step in the right direction, right?

"Why is McMannus still ineligible? Hasn't he done anything to make up for whatever assignment he blew off the first week of school?"

Tommy groaned. "I am trying with that kid. I swear I am. But he comes in here every morning, sits in the back row, puts his head down on the desk, and sleeps. I've offered him extensions on every assignment I've given, but this is Honors English III, Rourke. The pace is fast, and the writing load heavy." He held up a stack of papers on his desk. "These kids complain about having to write one eight-page paper and then have the balls to ask if I'm done grading thirty of them a day later, not giving a shit that I have two more sections of the same class."

Levi scratched the back of his neck. "Sleeping?" he asked. "In an honors class? Wait, English III? I thought he was a senior."

Tommy nodded. "Yep. He's a senior repeating his junior English class. He was a straight-A student through his sophomore year, but something changed last year. He failed both semesters of English and bailed on summer school. My father agreed to let him graduate this year if he passed my class and then took his senior credit over the summer."

Levi pushed himself off the windowsill and started pacing.

"Something is up with him. You've got too much on your plate to deal with it outside of school hours, but I don't." Not for the first time, he thought of Haddie's words again about not letting other people tell Billy's story. Maybe it was time Levi found out what that story was, right from the source.

He stopped in front of Tommy's desk, slapping his palms down on top of it.

"Mark McMannus eligible for tonight's game."

Tommy scoffed. "I can't, man. He has a zero percent in my class."

Levi nodded. "I know. But...if I can get you a partial assignment from Tommy by the end of the day—like an act of good faith that there is more to come—can you give him the benefit of the doubt?"

Tommy pinched the bridge of his nose and tilted his head back against the whiteboard behind his desk. He might have also erased part of his class agenda with his hair, but Levi didn't have the heart to tell him.

"Fine," Tommy finally replied. "But I need something I can give him points for. How about a one-paragraph review of *The Poet X* by Elizabeth Acevedo? It was his summer reading assignment."

Levi groaned. "What if he didn't read it?"

Tommy shrugged. "Then we don't have a deal. He's a smart kid, Commissioner. If he wants to be eligible to play tonight, he'll figure out a way to pull it off."

Levi stood, filled with renewed hope as he pointed at his friend with a grin. "You are a scholar and gentleman, and you will not regret this."

Tommy laughed as Levi started to back toward the door. "*You're* an idiot," he replied.

Levi smiled. "Maybe. But if I play my cards right, I'm going to be the idiot who wins his first game tonight and shows your dad how badly he misjudged the Summertown soccer program for being able to put asses in seats." He paused before pivoting through the door. "Can I count you and Juliana in for two of those asses tonight?"

Tommy shook his head and laughed. "Yeah. You can count us in."

Levi tapped the doorframe with his palm. "Excellent. And speaking of asses, spread the word that Summertown is going to hand Middleton theirs."

"Idiot," Tommy mumbled again, and Levi spun out of the room but then pivoted back for one more second.

"And Tommy?" he said, hoping the use of his friend's actual name would get his attention, which—judging by his raised brows—it had. "You're right. You are part of my past. But you're also my present and my future. You can't get rid of me that easily."

Tommy rolled his eyes. "You're embarrassing yourself, Commissioner," he replied and then glanced back down at his pile of papers, a smile tugging at the corners of his mouth.

"You're my hero, Crawford! The wind beneath my wings!" Levi added.

"Get the hell out of here, Rourke!" Tommy called without looking up, unable to hide the laughter in his voice, and Levi did as he was asked and left his friend to his work.

Maybe this was how he turned his guilt of running from his hometown into a way to save the varied parts of it that mattered to so many different people. He needed to do what he did best, which was win.

He just had to get through a day of teaching, find Billy

McMannus during his free period and get him to write that paragraph, and do everything he could to fill the Muskie bleachers for a soccer game on a random Tuesday night.

Piece of cake…if by piece he meant an entire three-tiered monstrosity fit for a wedding. But what did he have to lose other than his team's morale and a program that was beginning to mean more to him, the more time he spent with his players?

And Haddie. Somehow he knew if he couldn't help keep the program in the books, he had no chance of keeping Haddie Martin in his life. And that was a price he wasn't willing to pay.

CHAPTER 24

Haddie stayed late to set up her classroom for the next day's activities. She finally had a moment to sit and collect her thoughts before heading out to the football field that tonight would be host to the varsity boys' soccer game against Middleton. So she collapsed into her desk chair and decided to waste a few minutes scrolling through social media.

The first thing she noticed when she opened Instagram was that she had a new follower. *Muskies Soccer.*

Brows furrowed, she clicked on the handle to check whether it was legit or if it was a student account trying to pose as a school-sanctioned account. She'd seen plenty of those, even in elementary ed. Fourth and fifth graders were social media savvy in some pretty scary ways.

The account was public, had one post and...704 followers? 705. No, 706.

What was happening?

She tapped the post, which was a reel of the Muskies mascot—a giant fish wearing a purple Muskies jersey and baseball cap—dancing to Taylor Swift's "...Ready For It?" But the mascot wasn't alone. On one side of the fish, Sarah Ramirez held out a Muskies tee, dancing awkwardly along with Teddy Kostas on the mascot's opposite side. Below the reel, a caption read, Are you ready to watch #muskiessoccer dominate on the field tonight? Grab your tickets at the #linkinbio. Be one of the first 100 in the stands to grab your free Muskies T-shirt and a coupon for one free item at the concession stand (home team only). #gomuskies #giveaway #muskiessoccer #letsbeatmiddleton #freebies #muskiesspirit #catsruledogsdrool.

Haddie snorted when she read the final hashtag but realized she'd seen that hashtag before. A certain social media marketer she knew loved to sneak *hashcats*, as she liked to call them, into some of her professional posts.

She quickly brought up Emma's contact on her phone and tapped the green button to call.

"Hads!" Emma answered on the first ring, but Haddie could barely hear her amid what sounded like cheering in the background. "Where are you? You're missing all the pregame fun!"

"Did I just hear an air horn?" Haddie asked.

Emma laughed. "Yes! You need to get your ass over here! Levi somehow got his hands on a T-shirt cannon, and the crowd is going wild! It's amazing."

Haddie laughed, trying to reconcile what she was hearing from her friend with what she believed to be true. *No* one showed up to Muskies soccer games other than a few scattered parents to watch their kids. An air horn? A T-shirt cannon? She wasn't even sure the football game had the latter.

"I'm on my way!" Haddie replied, already out of her seat. "But Ems…did you start a Muskies Soccer account?"

"Nope!" Emma replied, further aiding in Haddie's confusion. "I just gave the poster a few marketing and posting tips. You know, like using a reel instead of a post and a few good hashtags. Looks like he was gullible enough to do the hashcat one as well. Pancake made me do it." Pancake…Emma's cat who Emma was deathly allergic to, which forced her to take daily meds in order to be the cat lady she was always meant to be. "Don't you want to know who the poster is and who is in the Muskie suit?"

Haddie didn't need her friend to say it. She just needed to understand what was happening. Everything from the tumbler of coffee that magically appeared outside her door that morning to Levi dancing in a fish costume… What the hell had gotten into him, and why was all of it—fish costume notwithstanding—making her belly perform all sorts of acrobatics?

"I'll be right there," Haddie told her.

"Good!" Emma replied. "Because the bleachers are filling up! I might have also made a call to a couple of local papers, so you know…do what you always do and look pretty."

Haddie laughed and ended the call. Local papers? What the hell was happening on that field, and what did it mean that it was all thanks to Levi?

The bleachers were not full when Haddie arrived, but they were more than half full, which was already an exponential increase from the crowds at previous games. While she had asked her team to be there to support the varsity boys, she wasn't expecting to see them sitting together, in uniform, waving poster-board signs for each player boasting their jersey numbers and well wishes. Though she should probably make Sarah Ramirez change *Ass* to *Butt* on her poster for Teddy Kostas that stated a place he should kick Middleton's team.

Come to think of it, she'd probably have to talk to her team about positive vs. negative school spirit in general, but for now, her heart swelled at the sight of everyone coming out to support Levi's team, not only because she was happy for him but also because he'd done this. And somehow she knew that when she had her next home game, she'd see the same turnout if he had anything to say about it.

Haddie finally found Emma, Matteo, Tommy, and a pretty blond woman with a slicked-back ponytail who she guessed was Tommy's new wife.

"Hads!" Emma called. "Come sit!"

To her credit, rather than one of her quirky tees, Emma was decked out in full Muskie attire—a hoodie and purple Muskie leggings.

Haddie looked down at her own outfit, a plain white T-shirt, floral maxi skirt, and her white Adidas court shoes. She'd been so caught up in slipping out before Levi that morning to grab her bribery coffees that she'd totally forgotten to bring a change of clothes for the game.

She shivered, rubbing the gooseflesh on her arms. As they approached mid-September, the afternoons and evenings were finally starting to feel like autumn.

The air horn blew, startling Haddie so hard that she stumbled, her ass crashing hard into the bleachers next to Emma. Ready to curse whoever chose that moment to sound the alarm and bruise her tailbone, she softened when her eyes met Levi's where he stood on the track with the air horn in one hand and the T-shirt cannon hooked under his other arm.

He mouthed the word *Sorry*, then dropped the horn and aimed the T-shirt launcher in her direction. With a wink and one of his trademark Levi smiles that made her melt a little more every time he threw one her way.

And then he fired a T-shirt directly into her lap. Haddie unfolded the ball to find it wasn't just any free T-shirt. It was a long-sleeved tee she knew was only given to faculty who coached or sponsored a team. Sure enough, the back of the shirt read *Coach Rourke.*

Haddie stared at him, eyes wide. What would students think if she was at a game wearing his shirt? What would Coach Crawford say if he saw? She imagined the over-the-top coffee beverages or pastries she would have to use to sweeten the pot for Ramirez and Kostas to keep their mouths shut.

"Uh-oh," Emma said, pulling Haddie briefly from her spiral. "Someone is overthinking a T-shirt when she is clearly freezing her kittens off."

Haddie laughed. "My kittens? What does that even mean?"

Matteo leaned forward and gave Haddie a conspiratorial grin. "I find it's best not to question the things she says and just chalk it up to Emma being Emma."

"Someone you both love dearly and trust implicitly, no matter what she says," Emma added.

Haddie glanced down at the T-shirt still sitting in her lap. A short burst of wind was enough to make her quickly turn the garment inside out and pull it over her head. As the neckline passed over her face, she breathed in Levi's scent, momentarily intoxicated by the memory of rolling over in bed that morning to bury her face in his neck. To breathe him in.

They'd switched to her bed last night, not only changing up the room but also the side of the bed where both of them finally drifted off to sleep. It was complete and utter chaos for someone whose life had felt very much compartmentalized up until the past month. Yet somehow, chaos with Levi felt like a puzzle piece finally snapping into place.

"I saw that," Emma said, bumping her elbow against Haddie's.

"Saw what?" Haddie replied, fidgeting under her friend's stare.

Emma leaned closer and whispered in Haddie's ear. "The sniff." Then she straightened in her seat.

Haddie's cheeks flamed, and Emma's mouth fell open. "I knew it!" she whispered, albeit loud enough that the people in the row behind them could probably hear. "There is something between you two that is more than just a Haddie Martin fling."

Haddie winced. "It sounds really shitty when you brand my love life like that."

Matteo popped his head back into the conversation. "Are we confirming that I lost the bet?"

"There was a *bet*?" Haddie shouted under her breath, thankful for the already rowdy fans.

Matteo nodded and Emma shrugged, not even bothering to look guilty.

"I said there was no way anyone could live with my brother and actually want to date him when his dirty laundry always made our entire upstairs smell like a locker room."

"And *I* said," Emma interjected, "that the Levi that Matteo lived with was a gross, teenage boy and that he's now a hot grown-ass man living with my hot grown-ass friend and that once you two lived together, there would be no way sparks wouldn't fly." Emma touched Haddie's arm with her index finger and feigned getting shocked. "See? So. Many. Sparks!"

Haddie rolled her eyes. "What happened to you worrying that I would break his heart?"

Emma sighed. "So maybe that was a little harsh, but it's only because I know that you're afraid of relationships. If I said something and you still went through with..." She motioned between Haddie and where Levi now stood facing the field as he coached his players through warm-ups. "Whatever it is you're going through with, then I figured it might actually be the real deal. And judging by the sniff, I think I was right."

Haddie groaned and buried her head in her hands.

"I don't even know who I am anymore," she admitted when she lifted her head again.

"Hey, Haddie..." Tommy was now leaning past Matteo to greet her.

"Hey, Tommy," Haddie replied with a wave.

He put his arm around the blond woman next to him and gave her a gentle squeeze as the woman met Haddie's gaze. "This is Juliana. Jules, this is Levi's roommate, Haddie." Jules's eyes widened, and she stretched a manicured hand across everyone's laps to shake Haddie's hand.

"It's nice to meet you, Haddie. Roommate, huh? Levi had quite the reputation for being a heartbreaker in high school. It's so nice to see him maturing enough to live with someone without trying to get her into bed."

Haddie pulled her hand away, and Tommy blanched at his wife's words. "Jules," he responded. "Not cool."

Jules laughed that mean-girl sort of laugh you knew meant she was judging not just you but everyone else in her orbit. And ugh. Sweet Tommy was orbiting her hard.

"Sorry," Jules called with a smile and then turned her attention back to whatever was going on on the field.

"Don't listen to her," Emma told her. "We ran in different circles in high school, and now we just tolerate her for Tommy."

Haddie forced a laugh. "Did Levi date—?"

"Ohmygod, no!" Emma exclaimed, leaning in close to whisper the next part. "I think she had a crush on him, but Levi never even acknowledged it because he knew Tommy had a thing for her. She only finally acknowledged Tommy after he came back from college with quite the glow up." Emma raised her brows and nodded back toward where Levi's very good-looking, very charming friend sat with his arm around a woman Haddie hoped was deserving of him.

"It's none of my business who Levi was before he and I met," she reasoned. "We already established that my relationship track record is hardly anything to write home about, right? Why else would you have been afraid of me breaking his heart?"

But Haddie didn't like the knot of unfounded jealousy and uncertainty growing in her belly, so she stood, straightened Levi's too-big shirt over her skirt, and let loose a long breath.

"I'm going to go check in with my team, give them some props for showing up for the program."

"Hads," Emma said, grabbing her friend's hand. "I didn't mean—"

"It's okay," Haddie told her. "I'm fine. And I'll be right back, okay?"

Emma nodded with a forced smile and, ugh, Haddie hated making her feel bad for simply reminding Haddie that she was swimming in very unfamiliar waters.

Haddie climbed up the bleachers and slid across the empty row in front of her team.

She was greeted with various versions of "Hey, Coach!" and "What's up, Coach?" But for some reason, Sarah Ramirez stayed quiet, barely even able to look Haddie's way.

"Hey, team!" she called back. "I just wanted to pop by and thank you all not only for showing up but for Showing. Up!" She gestured to their attire and the signs, the purple, black, and white ribbons tied around ponytails and braids. "You really outdid yourselves."

"It was Coach Rourke's suggestion," Sarah told her, finally speaking up. "He said if we did it for his team, then his team would do it for ours."

The belly acrobatics were back. It was one thing to fill the stands—or at least halfway fill the stands—for his own team, but it was something else entirely to promise to do it for Haddie's. He gained nothing by supporting her team. Hell, he'd gotten her to swear off solo showers as well as sleeping alone. She was a sure thing. But this? Everything he'd done today? It made her feel lightheaded.

"Then expect to see our stands looking pretty much the same for our game on Thursday." Haddie held her hand up like a visor against the not-yet-setting sun. "Well, I guess that's it. See you all for practice after school tomorrow. And thanks again for the excellent school spirit."

She turned to head back to her spot in the stand but stopped when she heard, "Coach Martin? Can I talk to you for a second?" Haddie spun to find Sarah Ramirez climbing down the few rows of bleachers to meet her where she stood.

"What's up, Sarah?" Haddie asked.

Sarah looked down as she fidgeted with the hem of her uniform jersey, then back up at Haddie. She groaned. "I'm sorry Teddy and I made you think that if you didn't buy us coffee that we would spill the tea about you and Coach Rourke."

Haddie narrowed her eyes. "Sarah. You two pretty much told me you'd be incapable of minding your own business unless I made it worth your while."

Sarah grimaced. "I know. That was kind of crappy of me." She leaned a little closer to Haddie and lowered her voice. "I kind of have this mad crush on Teddy, and the only way I know how to flirt with him is to be an intimidating bitch in front of him."

Haddie barked out a laugh and leaned back so she could look Sarah square in the eye. "Oh, Sarah," Haddie began, "your crush is so obvious. But guess what I'm not doing."

Sarah's shoulders sagged. "Making me bribe you not to tell everyone that I am out of my mind for a goofball marshmallow like Teddy Kostas?"

"*Ding! Ding! Ding! Ding! Ding!*" Haddie cried. "I think we have a winner!"

Sarah rolled her eyes, which made Haddie smile because that was the Sarah she knew and adored.

Haddie crossed her arms. "We do some stupid shit in the name of love, don't we?" she asked with a conspiratorial grin.

Sarah's eyes brightened. "Coach with the potty mouth. I like it!" Then her mouth fell open. "Wait! You said 'We.' Does that mean you mean me *and* you? Did you just admit that you have a crush on Coach Rourke? I swear I'm just asking for me and not for any sort of extortion purposes."

Haddie laughed. "Goodbye, Sarah. I'll see you at practice tomorrow." She spun back toward the stairs and heard Sarah gasp.

"The...the shirt! You're wearing his shirt! I can see the outline of his name through the fabric!"

Haddie didn't bother to dignify Sarah's accusation with a response. If Levi wasn't worried about how it would look for her to be wearing his shirt in front of both of their teams, then neither was she, even if she had been trying to hide it.

She glanced down to where Emma, Matteo, Tommy, and Jules

were getting poised to watch the kickoff, and then she squared her shoulders and marched down the bleachers and back to her seat.

Who cared what any of them thought when all that mattered was Haddie and Levi's assessment of their situation? It wasn't like Coach Crawford could fire them for their entanglement. She'd reread the policy and procedure handbook twice just to make sure. If their performance in the classroom went unaffected, then Coach Crawford would have no means to enact consequences.

She lowered herself back into her seat and grabbed Emma's hand. "Go, Muskies," she said.

Emma looked at her with a relieved grin. "Go, Muskies," she replied.

And then, when Billy McMannus... *Billy McMannus was on the field?* When Billy McMannus intercepted Middleton's kickoff, Emma and Haddie flew up from their seats.

"Go, Muskies!" they cried in unison.

And for the first time in her life, in a small town she never would have known existed were it not for the woman by her side, Haddie Martin finally felt like she had a home.

CHAPTER 25

Not running into the stands and kissing the hell out of Haddie after that final goal had made Levi feel like he was going to explode. Never before, not even when he was a player on the field, had he wanted to share a victory like this with someone other than his family.

Even now as they pulled out of the school parking lot, he wasn't sure how he was keeping it together, especially when she looked at him like that.

"You need to stop," he told her, unable to contain his grin.

"Stop what?" she asked innocently, pulling his free hand over to her lap and threading her fingers through hers. "Being so freaking proud of you, impressed by you, maybe even awed by you that I might burst? I can't turn it off, Rourke. So you're just going to have to deal."

He groaned. "Yes. That," he confirmed. "Stop smiling at me and making me want to kiss you and do other unspeakable things to you when I have to somehow navigate this tin box on wheels down the road and safely into a parking spot before I can do any of it."

Once on the road, she pulled his hand to her lips and pressed a soft kiss to his knuckles.

His heart was a jackhammer in his chest, his ribs a concrete cage. Tonight would have been amazing on its own, but handing Middleton their asses was nothing compared to Haddie's praise. His team could have shit the bed once again, yet if Haddie would have told him he and the team looked great on the field despite the fictional loss, he'd have believed her.

"You still haven't told me how you got McMannus on the field," she said, lips still resting against his skin.

Levi smiled. "I listened to you and let Billy tell me his story. Turns out his dad skipped town and his mom took on a second job to make ends meet, which left Billy in charge of his little brother, Henry."

Haddie gasped. "Henry's in my class! He's totally thriving, so I didn't even think there'd be a connection between him and Billy's issues with keeping up with his classes."

Levi nodded. "He's doing everything from grocery shopping and cooking for himself and Henry to carting Henry around to his after-school activities when Billy doesn't have soccer practice…and even sometimes when he does." Levi swore under his breath. "I wish he'd just told me why he was late a few times so I didn't chew him out in front of his teammates."

"He's probably embarrassed," Haddie told him. "Think about how hard it was for you to even show up at that group meeting and say something vulnerable about yourself. Now think about having to do it when you were seventeen."

Levi sighed. "Shit. You're right. I'm just glad I know now. He's been burning the candle at both ends, keeping up with some classes but not all, and English is one that kind of fell by the wayside, especially since he already failed the exact same class last year."

"What's the point?" Billy had asked him. "It's not like we have money for me to go to college anyway. I might as well just accept the fact that I'm going to be a wage worker like my mom and let the cycle continue."

Levi knew that there was nobility in doing what you had to in order to support your family. But if Billy could go to college, he might be able to better lessen the load for all of them rather than simply bearing some of the weight. He had never talked to any of his football players about the life he left behind in Summertown. Hell, Haddie was right. He hadn't even made it through the entire hour of his first mandated counseling session, but something made him want to open up to Billy.

"Money was tight with my family too when I was your age," he'd admitted. "Even with health insurance, my mom's medical bills really took a toll on the family. And there is nothing wrong with working for an hourly wage. For some, it's what they want. For others it's a necessity. Football gave me a chance at a future I didn't think I had. One where I could get us out from under the debt we were accumulating." He shrugged. "I'm just saying that if you want to have a choice, it's not too late for that. You are an excellent athlete, Billy. And even if it's not something you want to do for the rest of your life, it can pave the way for you to figure out what the rest of your life might be."

Levi glanced at Haddie as he pulled his truck into a street spot in front of their building.

"I talked to Tommy," he told her, putting the truck in park. "We made a deal to get McMannus on the field tonight, and moving forward, I told Billy that we're going to sit down and map out a schedule for all of his responsibilities. I think that might lessen the anxiety about all he has to do if I can show him that it's manageable." He shrugged. "And I took him grocery shopping for the next two weeks so he can cross that off his list."

Haddie's breath hitched, and her eyes went glassy. But she sniffed back what Levi guessed might have been tears and exhaled a shaky breath.

"I'm sorry," she said.

Levi let out a nervous laugh. "Not exactly the reaction I was expecting to getting my star player back on the team and pushing him toward a scholarship."

Haddie laughed too, her voice thick. "I'm sorry I ever for a second accused you of not caring about the program or your team. I was wrong." She pulled the cuffs of her sleeves over the heels of her hands, and even though Levi knew it was a fidget, he warmed at the thought of Haddie finding comfort in his clothes. "About a lot of things."

He unbuckled his seat belt and leaned over the center console, cupping her cheek with his palm.

"Not us, though, right? You're not having second thoughts, are you?"

She cupped a palm over his and pressed her cheek into his hand.

"No, Mr. Tux. I am not having second thoughts about us. It's more like…first thoughts? Like, I've never thought the things I'm thinking about anyone else before."

A smile bloomed across his face, and Levi let out a relieved breath. He leaned forward, his lips a breath away from hers, but then paused. "Wait…the things you're thinking are good things to think, right?"

Haddie snorted. "Just kiss me already!"

So he did.

Levi kissed her as they barreled through the front door to their apartment. He kissed her as they kicked off their shoes. Then he kissed her as she removed his shorts and undid his belt. As she reluctantly pulled off her Coach Rourke T-shirt, telling him how much better the game was, being wrapped in his scent.

"How did I live for weeks without doing this?" he asked as they stumbled trying to decide whose bed would be their destination tonight.

"Yours," Haddie insisted, breathless. "I want to be surrounded by everything that smells like you."

They made their way, hungrily kissing and touching, teasing and tasting, until finally she was splayed out beneath him.

He slipped a hand between her legs, but Haddie shook her head.

"You. Inside me. Now."

Levi didn't have to be told twice.

He pulled open his nightstand drawer, and Haddie reached around his hand and pulled out a condom. In seconds she had him sheathed and ready, guiding him with her hand to where she opened for him.

When he sank inside her, everything that had transpired that day hit him all at once. The coffee bribe and his unbridled need to protect her even when he knew she was perfectly capable of protecting herself. Tommy and the budget committee. Billy McMannus. Pulling off a half-filled stadium and whopping Middleton's ass. And the part that seemed to overshadow all the rest—Haddie Martin being proud of him.

As he kissed her again, the words just slipped out without any conscious thought.

"I love you," he told her.

She said nothing in return, just kissed him harder. And although it wasn't the response he'd have hoped for, he also didn't see a Haddie-shaped cutout in any walls or doors.

So there it was. Levi loved Haddie. But he also loved the job he'd been forced to leave. Hopefully, with several months ahead, he'd be able to figure out how to keep both.

———

Levi woke to a cold, empty spot beside him where Haddie's body used to be.

Shit.

He'd spooked her. What kind of an asshole drops a bomb like *I love you* right in the middle of sex? Apparently, the kind who had never spoken those words to anyone else before in his life other than immediate family and guessed the best time to do it was preclimax so she'd think twice about bolting.

Shit. Shit. Shit. He was in way over his head, and they still had months to go living in the wake of his royal, emotionally stunted stupidity.

He scrambled out of bed and was padding toward the bathroom to rinse away his humiliation under the hot spray of the shower when he smelled coffee.

"Birthday Girl?" he asked, his voice still thick with the remnants of sleep.

Haddie popped up from below the sink wearing her robe, her hair damp from having already showered.

Okay, so she hadn't bolted, but she also hadn't waited for him to shower. He figured they weren't in crisis mode yet.

"Hi!" she exclaimed in a tone way too perky for how tired Levi still felt. "I was just grabbing one of those tablet thingies for the dishwasher." She followed his gaze as it roamed over her attire. "Right," she replied, reading his thoughts. "I woke up early and couldn't fall back asleep, so I went for a run. When you still weren't up, I figured I'd just shower and get the coffee going, and from the looks of it, you could really use a cup or seven." She spun toward the gurgling coffeepot and reached for a mug in the cabinet overhead.

Levi took a chance and strode into the kitchen, settling behind her and wrapping his arms around her waist.

She sucked in a sharp inhale and froze.

"Breathe, Birthday Girl," he whispered softly, and Haddie exhaled, lowering her hands to set two mugs down on the counter.

"It's too soon," he admitted, then kissed her cheek. "What I said last night. I was just overwhelmed by the game and having you to celebrate with. I got carried away. So how about we go back to how amazing things have been this week and not get all weird about my brain short-circuiting during some pretty fantastic sex?"

Haddie let out another long breath and finally spun to face him.

"Yeah," she replied, clasping her hands around his neck and rising up on her toes. "I'd like that."

Except when she kissed him, Levi's brain short-circuited again, and he had to fist his hands in the cotton of her robe to keep from blurting out the words again. What the hell was wrong with him? And even worse, why was he bent out of shape at her responding exactly how he hoped she would?

"I should shower," he told her, pulling away because… Hello? Asshole who has no idea what he's doing.

"Oh," Haddie replied. "Okay. Well, there will be coffee waiting for you when you get out. Also, good news. No more early meetings this week, so we can ride together if you want."

Something inside him sank like an anchor. He was happy that Ramirez and Kostas had done their part in simply being good humans and respecting Haddie's privacy. But part of him thought that maybe she'd tell him about it once it was all over. *Hey, you'll never guess this stupid thing that happened at the car wash…* But she hadn't.

"Really?" he asked, giving her another opening to tell him something real. "No more meetings? That's great. What changed?"

She gave him a noncommittal shrug. "I guess admin took pity on us and decided to give us our mornings back. Lucky us, right?"

Levi nodded. "Yeah. Lucky us."

When they got to school, Haddie stealthily gave him a quick peck on the cheek. "See you after practice?" she asked, perky as ever.

Levi might have been lacking in experience when it came to having big feelings for someone and admitting those big feelings, but he was pretty sure it wasn't a great sign that she was so relieved he was *not* actually in love with her.

You know, except for the part where he was.

"Yeah," he said absently. "See you after practice."

She hopped out of the truck and slammed the door, giving Levi the privacy to throw his head back against his seat and swear.

"Nice going, asshole," he mumbled to himself. "What's your next rock-star move?"

Sadly, for the success he'd had in the casual dating arena, when it came to shit getting real, Levi had no moves at all. Zero. Zip. Nada. All he had was a woman who'd gotten under his skin, flustered him, and made him forget how to human.

He laughed to himself, wondering what Haddie would say if the tables were turned. The only French he knew was Voulez vous coucher avec moi? Yet somehow he didn't think sex was the answer to his problem despite how fun it would be to try to solve it that way.

His phone buzzed in the cup holder beside him, and since

he hadn't yet turned off the car, the caller's ID popped up on his Bluetooth screen.

He answered it immediately.

"Chancellor Barnes," Levi said upon answering. "I'm surprised to hear from you, sir."

"Coach Rourke," the chancellor replied. "There's been an interesting development in your…situation."

Levi swallowed and braced himself for the blow. "Okaaay…" he replied, drawing out the word. "Whatever it is, I can take it."

Chancellor Barnes groaned. "Your temporary replacement is an abomination to the title of coach. I know we paid good money for your talents, but I was always a little skeptical about how much a coach could really do if the team already had some star athletes that knew what they were doing. But it is abundantly clear that the answer is *a lot*. This abomination on top of the news hitting about what you've done with a high school soccer team in the matter of a month? Well, I daresay your talents are invaluable to our university."

Levi's heart leaped into his throat. "Sir, are you saying that I'm going to be reinstated early?"

The chancellor barked out a laugh. "Oh, goodness no. I may be a powerful man on campus, but there is not a whole lot I can do against the word of the law, especially after you've been sentenced. But, if you can have Principal Crawford write a letter of recommendation and get your court-approved therapist to agree to some telehealth sessions, I think I can get you back on campus as a consultant to the…" He sighed.

"Abomination?" Levi added, aiming to finish the chancellor's sentence.

"Yes. Yes. That's the one," the other man replied.

"Um…" Levi continued, unable to form cohesive words.

"Um?" Chancellor Barnes asked. "I was expecting something closer to *Yes, sir. I'll get right on that, sir.*"

"Yes, sir," Levi parroted. "I will get right on that, sir. Do you have a time frame you're looking at to get me back in the saddle behind the scenes? Because my brother's wedding is in a few weeks, and I'd like to stay at least through that."

After a long pause, the chancellor replied. "How about the second Monday of October, then? I've also already sent a short contract via the USPS that should be arriving any day now. Sign it and send it back ahead of your arrival to help expedite getting you on the payroll again."

"Yes, sir!" Levi exclaimed, forgetting for the moment why he was sulking in his car to begin with. "Thank you, sir!"

The chancellor ended the call, and Levi threw open his door. His first instinct was to rush to Haddie's classroom and try to catch her before her day began, but he stopped halfway through the parking lot.

Haddie.

They were supposed to have months to figure this out, and now they had weeks. What was he going to say to her now? *Remember how I said I loved you but didn't mean it? Well, funny thing. I did mean it, and I'm also leaving in four weeks.*

Yeah, no. That was not a bomb he was going to drop on her

minutes before her students arrived, and it certainly wasn't one to drop before her team's big game tomorrow.

So he'd wait one night. After her game, he'd simply put everything out in the open, and they'd figure it out together. Maybe it wasn't a rock-star move, but it was the only move he could make.

CHAPTER 26

Haddie was still on cloud nine after yet another win, this time with the home bleachers almost three-quarters of the way full. True to his word, Levi—with Emma's help, she guessed—crafted another viral reel. And by viral, she meant locally viral, but still. It got both the boys' and girls' soccer teams to turn a high school hallway into a flash mob during one of yesterday's passing periods, with Muskie—a.k.a. Levi—dancing along as the teams lip-synched Whitney's "I Wanna Dance with Somebody." It also go butts in seats for the game.

But the short ride home was filled with stilted stops and starts, just like yesterday.

"Super proud of you and the teams for another great effort at social media marketing," she told Levi as he drove with both his hands on the wheel at a steady ten and two.

"Thanks," he replied, pressing his lips into a smile that didn't reach his eyes.

After several seconds of silence, Haddie added, "Should we celebrate the same way we did after your winning game?" She nudged him with her elbow. "I was thinking that the couch might be feeling left out. Maybe instead of the dreaded decision between my bed and your bed," she teased.

Levi shrugged. "Sure. Couch sex. Sounds good."

The truck rolled to a stop in front of the hardware shop, and Haddie unfastened her seat belt so she could turn to face him.

"Hey...what is up with you this week?" she asked. "I thought things were going so well. Didn't you?"

He sighed. "Can we talk upstairs? I really don't feel like doing this in my truck."

"Doing what?" she asked.

Levi groaned and finally turned to face her.

"Jesus, Haddie. I know my timing was shit, but I told you I loved you, and you bailed. Maybe not physically because I get that you are still here, and we are still us to a degree. But I can't unsay what I said or unfeel what I feel, and I kind of get the feeling that you're happier believing what is so obviously a lie."

Haddie's brows drew together and she shook her head, trying to make meaning out of what he was saying.

"I didn't bail, Levi." But her words came out more defensively than she'd intended.

"You disappeared from the bed the first chance you got and literally froze when I touched you until I told you to forget what I said."

Haddie laughed, not that anything about this was funny. "There is no way you love me after knowing me for a month."

"Why not?" Levi threw his head against the back of his seat.

"I've spent more time with women I don't love even after knowing a week in that I wasn't committed for the long haul. Why can't I know with you that I am?"

Haddie held her hands up in surrender. "This is the dumbest argument. Let's just go upstairs, maybe have a drink to celebrate, and then I can remind you why we work so well with things the way they were before you said what you think is true but actually isn't."

She hopped out of the truck and through the doorway that led up to their apartment before he had a chance to respond.

They weren't in love. Haddie had only agreed to try an actual relationship. If she let the L word into the picture, then it was only a matter of time before someone got hurt, and she was starting to think that Emma had it all wrong, that the someone in question wasn't Levi…but her.

Haddie heard Levi jogging up the stairs behind her. She stopped only to grab the mail from in front of their door and then strode inside.

"Haddie…" Levi called from behind her, following her into the kitchen where she was sorting the mail into piles on the counter.

She stopped when she got to a thick envelope made of strong paper stock. She was staring at a hand-written message on the back above an embossed university seal.

Welcome back, Coach Rourke.

She flipped the envelope over to see the front, already knowing that she'd find the letter or whatever was inside addressed to Levi.

"What is this?" she asked, looking up at him, hating the tremor in her voice.

"Haddie…" he said again, softer this time. "It's not what it looks like."

"Really?" She brandished the envelope at him. "Because it looks like you've been reinstated, and you didn't tell me."

He shook his head, holding up his hands as he took a step forward, treating her like a feral animal that could be easily spooked.

"I wasn't reinstated. I can't be until a year is up. But Chancellor Barnes found a loophole. I can't have direct contact with the team or attend the games, but he wants me around to consult with my replacement because he's apparently tanking the team."

Haddie rolled her eyes, still holding the envelope out like a shield. "Semantics, Levi. You're not reinstated, but you're still leaving before next summer. Am I right?" She should have stormed off when he didn't answer, but she needed him to say it. She needed him to prove she was right, had always been right. "Am. I. Right?" she asked again.

He let out a defeated breath. "As long as Coach Crawford signs off on it and Hope agrees to see me on a telehealth basis, then I head back the Monday after the wedding."

"Oh," she replied with an incredulous laugh. "You haven't even been back to the grief group for a second meeting, but you're already setting up telehealth? How long have you known?"

He pulled off his stupid coaching visor and ran a hand through his already tousled hair. "Two days," he admitted. "Chancellor Barnes called me two days ago and said a contract was already on its way." He nodded toward the envelope. "I was going to tell you tonight, Haddie. I swear I was."

She slapped the envelope against his chest. "Well, I guess now you don't have to." She brushed past him and bolted toward her room.

"Come on, Haddie," she heard from over her shoulder as Levi followed in her wake. "Can't we talk about this?"

She whirled on him just inside her room. "What is there to talk about, Levi? You are doing exactly what I knew you'd do. Don't you think I know how this works by now? If I love, I get left. Do you know that my mom didn't just die when I was a kid? She left me with my grandmonster *before* the end so I didn't have to see her at her sickest. Did she ask me if that was what I wanted, to lose her before I lost her? And my grandmonster?" She huffed out a bitter laugh. "She taught me the art of keeping people at a distance so they couldn't hurt you. But guess what? It still hurts like hell that she's gone, and I can't, Levi. I can't hurt like that again, which means you *can't* love me, and I certainly can't love you." She was crying now, but she didn't care.

He took a step back, but he didn't walk away like she had. God, she was good at walking away. But what else did she know? You love, you lose. That was how it worked in Haddie's world. But she didn't have to be the victim of circumstance this time. She had the power to choose how it ended.

"Haddie..." he said gently. "I am so sorry for the losses you've had to endure. But how is shutting me out going to make this hurt any less? I told you I loved you, which means you were always going to be a part of the conversation about me going back to Indiana. I was just waiting for the right time. Don't you get that those words don't just fall out of my mouth because the sex is good or because I'm just trying them on for size. You can be scared of this…" He motioned between them. "But you don't get to tell me it's not real."

Haddie pulled a suitcase out of her closet and tossed it onto her bed. Then she began pulling random items off of hangers and throwing them sloppily into the case.

"You're leaving?" he asked, and the way his voice broke on *leave* gutted her.

Her movements slowed and her shoulders sagged, and Haddie was just so damned tired of being right about what the universe had in store for her. Just this once she wanted to be wrong.

She took a few steadying breaths and then turned to face Levi.

"Maybe I am leaving," she admitted. "But only for a night or two so I can get my head on straight. The difference is that even if I leave this apartment, Summertown is my home now. When you leave, you'll be gone for good."

Levi took a step closer to her, and although she flinched, Haddie didn't push him away.

"We'll figure it out," he pleaded, hands sliding over her cheeks and his fingertips burying themselves in her hair. "That was always the plan."

Was there even a conversation to have? Maybe…when they'd had months to get over the honeymoon phase of whatever they were and could part ways with level heads and clear hearts. But she was tangled up in feelings she didn't know how to navigate. They'd done exactly what Principal Crawford had warned them not to do, and now Levi's team would suffer, and Haddie... Haddie would leave before she went the way of Humpty-Dumpty and couldn't put herself back together again.

He dipped his head, and Haddie was powerless against the nearness of him, against the way his scent filled her with an ache she wasn't sure she'd ever be able to ignore, even if she never saw him again.

"Tell me it's not over," he whispered. "Not when we've barely gotten started."

He didn't wait for her to answer. Instead, he brushed his lips over hers, and they kissed like it was the last time they ever would.

Because both of them knew that it was.

CHAPTER 27

TWO DAYS LATER

Levi: Trying to give you the space you need, but I went back to grief group today, and you weren't there. Just tell me you're okay.

ONE WEEK LATER

Levi: Come on, Haddie. We have to talk about this. Are you at least seeing Hope privately? Should I? I get that you don't want to see me, but I know group is important to you. Are you staying with Emma? Text me something. Anything. Plz.

TWO WEEKS LATER

Levi: Went to your game last night. Just to see that you were okay. You looked happy when your team won. My team lost our last one, but no one was offside. Silver lining, right?

Levi: It's supposed to storm tonight. I hope you're with Emma so you don't have to wait it out alone.

Levi: So I guess this is it, huh? Message received. I wanted to fight for us, but I can't do it alone. I'll stop texting. You know where to find me for at least the next couple of weeks.

During one particularly violent crash of thunder that night, he flung himself out of his bed like a slingshot, rushing to Haddie's room only to be reminded that she wasn't there. So, being wildly inexperienced with love and heartache and everything in between, he crawled into *her* bed rather than go back to his alone. He could still smell her shampoo on her pillow, could still imagine his legs tangled with hers like tree roots planted so deep and for so long that they couldn't possibly be unwound.

His chest felt like it had been carved out, leaving him with nothing but a raw, hollow ache.

He'd been running ever since college, trying to outrun any and all pain. And here he was in Haddie's bed alone, effectively proving his theory that home equaled hurt. Yet more than a decade later, the running hadn't solved a single thing.

Levi had finally gotten used to talking about his mom with a bunch of people who weren't exactly strangers but also weren't exactly friends. He'd even noticed the painful feelings of loss giving way to the unexpected joy of keeping her memory alive. But when he walked in for his final session before the wedding, he stopped in his tracks when he saw his father and Matteo already sitting in Hope's circle. Wait, was this why she'd asked him to pop in ten minutes before the group actually started?

"Levi!" Denny Rourke called to his oldest son, then patted the metal chair beside him. "Come on over!"

Levi made it there in a series of halting steps. He knew, according to Tilly, that his dad and Matteo showed up to the grief sessions every now and then. But when they hadn't come the past couple of weeks when he'd finally started showing up again, he thought he was in the clear.

"Dad!" Levi replied with something mixed between enthusiasm and dread. "Teo," he added, parking himself in the chair next to his brother rather than his father who he suddenly didn't trust.

"Is this an ambush?" he asked sarcastically.

Denny laughed. "Not exactly," he replied, but it still felt like an admission.

Matteo held up his hands. "I have no idea what he's talking about. He just texted me and said, 'We're going to group.' So I came to group."

Hope appeared in the meeting space from a side door Levi hadn't noticed before and nodded toward the three Rourke men. "Okay, Denny," she began. "Only for you would I arrive ten minutes early. What did you want to talk about?"

Both Levi and Matteo spun to face their father, who had the decency to look chagrined.

"Busted!" Denny said. Then he produced a blue velvet box from his pocket, opening it to reveal a pretty sizable diamond.

"Aww, Dad. You shouldn't have!" Matteo held out his hand as if their father was about to slide the ring up his finger.

He swatted his son's hand away. "Knock it off, jackass. I'm asking Tilly to marry me, but I wanted to run it by you guys first. I wanted to make sure…you know…"

Levi knew. His father wasn't alone anymore. He'd been given a second chance at having love in his life, and he still wanted to put his sons' needs before his own. How could he possibly have any problem with that? He did, however, question the venue.

"Here?" Levi asked, eyes wide. "You're going to ask her to marry you in the same place you've been coming to work on your grief for your last wife?"

Denny stared at his two sons, shaking his head with a laugh. "Tilly loved your mom too, boys. And she knows that I don't need to stop loving what your mom and I had to be able to love her today." He scratched the back of his neck. "Is that all you guys are worried about? Where I'm going to propose?"

Matteo shrugged. "She makes you happy."

"Yeah, Dad," Levi chimed in. "Little Teo and I have grown up a bit recently. And seeing as how you're not *that* old yet, we'd be selfish a-holes if we expected you to be alone for the rest of your life. If, according to young Teo, Tilly does make you happy, then

I think *we* are more than happy for you." He laughed. "Man, that was a lot of happy in one sentence from a guy who is anything but." He playfully backhanded his brother on the arm.

Hope cleared her throat. "Remember me? The woman who apparently only showed up to unlock the door?"

Denny Rourke offered her the same apologetic smile he'd given his sons. "Tilly is always one of the first ones to arrive to any gathering, so we needed to beat her to it. I also wanted you to be here when it happened," he told her. "You're part of the reason Tilly and I work like we do, Hope. And I can't thank you enough."

Hope blinked and then swiped a finger under her eye. "Wow," she said with a loud sniff. "Bad day for allergies, am I right?"

Levi watched his father wink at his group grief therapist, and he couldn't help but laugh to himself. Only in Summertown did a man plan a proposal to the second love of his life at a group grief meeting.

There was so much he'd forgotten that he loved about this place, having been away for so long.

"And Levi…?" Hope added. "You can talk about more than just your mom here too. Grief comes in all shapes and sizes, and people experience different kinds of losses every day."

Levi swallowed. Had he really lost her? He had tried to fight for her, for them. But Haddie bailed without giving him a chance to make things right.

"Does that mean you've talked to Haddie?" he asked.

"I can't talk about other patients I may or may not see privately," she explained. "I'm just saying that I'm here to help with all kinds of loss."

"Doesn't talking about it mean it's real?" he asked.

"It does," Levi's father chimed in, clapping his son on the shoulder. "But it also helps you let go."

Levi turned to face both his father and his brother.

"I'm sorry," he told them, his voice thick with years of being so afraid of those two little words.

"For what?" Denny Rourke asked, his brows furrowing.

"For running back to school the second I finished PT for my knee and never looking back." He turned to Matteo. "*I'm* the big brother, Teo. But I let you shoulder the burden of holding things together when Mom died. I should have been there for you."

Their father let out a shaky breath and blinked away what looked like the threat of tears. "There is no rule book for how we deal with this kind of loss or for how long it takes to heal."

"Yeah, man," Matteo added, bumping his shoulder against Levi's. "You weren't able to be there for me then, but I don't fault you for it. You're here now, aren't you?"

Levi's eyes burned, and he tilted his head toward the ceiling in a feeble attempt to collect himself. But when he met their eyes again, his lashes were damp.

"All these years, I've been so sure you resented how fucking afraid I was to be...to be...*here*." He motioned around the empty room but hoped they understood he meant *home*.

"If I might interject..." Hope suggested, and the three men nodded in unison. "Maybe *here* won't be so scary anymore if you forgive yourself, Levi."

He pressed the heels of his hands against the dam that was his tear ducts and cleared his throat. "For what?"

"For waiting until you were ready to come home." She nodded toward his father and brother. "*They're* happy you're here. You're the only one who has ever thought you don't deserve to come home."

He swallowed, but before he could agree or disagree with her assessment, they were all interrupted by Tilly Higginson strolling through the door and Levi's nervous father immediately dropping to his knee.

Tilly yelped and then slowly approached the center of the circle.

"Denny...what are you doing? What if you tweak your back trying to get up again?"

Levi bit back a laugh, grateful for the immediate mood shift, and he could see his brother trying to do the same.

"Then say *yes*," Denny told her. "Say you'll marry me, and I'll get off the floor before I do some real damage here."

She let out a tearful laugh and nodded her head. "Of course I'll marry you!" She held out a hand, not for the ring yet but to help her new fiancé off the floor, and Levi knew from this moment forward that his father would be loved and cared for unconditionally for the rest of his life, and there was no way he couldn't be happy about that.

The thing was, though their mom had been sick for a long time before she passed, she never lost her youthfulness. Because of that, Levi couldn't imagine her as an almost sixty-year-old warning her husband about tweaking his back. He couldn't imagine a lot of things about her anymore now that she'd been gone so long. What he did remember was his parents' love and the hope that one day he might have what they had. And now, because the universe had the good thought to smile on his father twice, Levi found himself wanting this too—someone who worried about processing his grief ten years after the fact or who patched him up after cutting himself on a broken window. And maybe, if he could find it in his heart to forgive himself for still not knowing how to fully process that grief, he might want those things in a town where he could plant roots. And focus on a new team. And maybe even earn a spot on a favorite things poster one day.

But Haddie had to want him too. And she either didn't or wouldn't let herself want what could possibly cause her pain. Because it already had. *Levi* had.

Despite his promise to leave her be, he fired off one final text before they had to come face-to-face at the wedding tomorrow.

Levi: Last text. Promise. But I need to say what I should have said that night. I'm sorry I hurt you, Haddie. But it's not because I don't love you. I do...love you. I messed up, and I own that. Just thought you should know.

He held his breath, allowing himself to hope. He counted the seconds, the time it took before he had no choice but to exhale and fill his lungs again. He made it more than a minute, staring at his screen and willing those three dots to appear.

But they never did.

CHAPTER 28

Haddie pushed through Posh's shop door and out onto the sun-soaked sidewalk, breathing a sigh of relief that she would, in fact, be able to continue breathing even once in the dress she now held in a garment bag draped over her forearm along with the slightly poofier bag containing Emma's wedding dress.

Despite there not being a cloud in the sky, the brisk October air sent a shiver from her neck down to her toes, and she was grateful Emma and Matteo had rented heat lamps for the ceremony in the square that evening.

"It was traipsing through Summertown trying to solve the mystery of the Gardener's art installations where we fell in love again. Only made sense for us to get married in the center of it all."

Because if you were born and raised in a place like Summertown, you could shut the place down for a night, especially if the venue *was* the town, which meant everyone was invited.

"Coach Martin!" someone called, and Haddie had to crane her neck to see over the pile of formal wear in her arms.

"Oh!" she replied. "Sarah. What are you doing out so early on a Sunday morning?"

Sarah stood on her toes to meet Haddie's eyes above the dresses.

"Yours is the only signature missing," Sarah told her, and Haddie's brows furrowed. Also, her shoulders ached. Did Emma's dress double as a weighted blanket?

"What?" Haddie asked. Then added, "Hang on a second..." She stumbled to the general vicinity where she remembered there being a park bench just outside the shop. When she plowed into it with her hip, she swore under her breath but then carefully laid the dresses over the back of the bench. "Okay," she told Sarah, rubbing her soon-to-be bruised hip. "What about my signature?"

Sarah held out a clipboard she'd been hugging against her chest. "It's a petition. Well, two, really. One to keep the soccer program...and one to keep Coach Rourke. The first one is for Principal Crawford, and the second... Well, we just want Coach Rourke to know how much we appreciate everything he's done for the program so far this year. We got every player to sign, every teacher from kindergarten to senior year, and all of our parents. Mr. Crawford—junior, not senior—got his budget committee to come up with the idea to charge a registration fee for activities and sports, football included. The idea is for those fees to go toward supporting all programs, like a communal account, and we will continue fundraising efforts to try and make up for any deficit." She pointed to the pages-long petition. "Even the football players signed. They're even willing to stage a sit-in for their next game and every game thereafter, where they'll basically let their opponents crush them if Coach Crawford doesn't place equal importance on every other sport or activity Summertown offers. We're going to present both petitions to the school board at Thursday night's meeting, but we really wanted to get your signature before calling it complete."

Haddie's throat tightened and her eyes burned.

"Wait...you all know about the budget cuts? And the program cuts?" Sarah nodded, and Haddie's heart sank. "Also, Coach Rourke is leaving tomorrow," she reminded Sarah, her voice thick.

Sarah shrugged. "Maybe he'll change his mind if he sees your name on the lists. He's the one who got the whole football program to sign about the communal fund, you know. I think he might have also had something to do with the sit-in idea." She leaned in close, a conspiratorial gleam in her eye. "Did you know that Billy McMannus has a C- in English now? I don't want to spill any tea, but I heard Coach Rourke has been babysitting Billy's brother after school so Billy can catch up on his homework. Does that sound like a guy who wants to leave?"

Haddie's knees buckled, and she had to grab the top of the bench to steady herself. "How...?" she asked. "How do you know all this? And how did these petitions materialize without me hearing anything about them?"

Sarah grinned. "You'll have to ask the head of the faculty's budget rescue committee. He's the one who proposed the idea for the registration fees in the first place. The one for Coach Rourke was Teddy's idea." She blushed. "Turns out his hotness isn't so wasted after all."

A knot of guilt sank deep in her gut. Haddie remembered an

email from Tommy she'd flagged for later about joining a group of faculty members who wanted to rethink the budget, something about overturning Coach Crawford's cuts. But her inbox had grown exponentially since school started, and then there had been the whole losing Levi thing that had preoccupied her thoughts for what felt like more minutes than actually existed in a day.

Haddie motioned for Sarah's clipboard and the attached pen. "I'll sign the budget petition, but I don't think it would be right if I signed the other one." She swallowed the knot in her throat. It wasn't as if putting her name on a piece of paper was going to make Levi stay. And why was she even considering what it might mean if her signature did matter? He broke her trust...and her heart, which was maddening because Haddie knew better than to fall for any of it.

Sarah sighed and handed Haddie the clipboard. "I know I'm breaking the rule by even butting in to your private business, Coach Martin, but you have been such a downer the past few weeks. You should just admit how you feel about him so we can stop watching you torture yourself."

Haddie had finished signing her name to the budget petition when her head shot up, her wide eyes meeting Sarah's.

"What do you mean 'breaking the rule,' Sarah? *What* rule?"

Sarah clamped her hand over her gaping mouth. "Nothing!" She shook her head. "I mean...no one! *Shit.* I'm not supposed to crack under pressure. That's Teddy's job!" She grimaced and grabbed the clipboard back from Haddie before Haddie could officially decide not to sign the *Beg Coach Rourke to Stay* petition.

"Sarah…" Haddie began, taking a slow step toward her student. "You can tell me. It's okay. What rule?"

"I am too young for this type of stress," Sarah groaned. "Look… Coach Rourke caught me and Teddy outside your classroom grabbing our coffees after the whole roommates thing. And he sort of ripped us a new one and told us to respect your privacy if we wanted to stay on our teams." She grimaced. "Teddy and I felt pretty bad about what we'd done, and I swear we didn't apologize just to stay on the team."

Haddie's breath caught in her throat. "He knew?" Levi *knew*. And he hadn't judged her for mishandling the ridiculous situation, nor had he even let on that he'd figured out what was going on, most likely because he knew she'd be humiliated.

"Give me back that clipboard," Haddie demanded.

Sarah beamed and handed it over.

She knew it was too little, too late. Levi wasn't going to stay because of some list of signatures, not when he had his career to go back to. But maybe with this tiny gesture, if he ever even saw the list, he'd at least know that Haddie thought he belonged here in Summertown, just like everyone else did.

"I was right the whole time, wasn't I?" Sarah asked, a knowing smile on her face.

Haddie relinquished the clipboard a final time, scooped the dresses into her arm, and said goodbye to her student.

She marched through the square and back toward the inn.

"Yes, Ramirez," she whispered under her breath. "You were right the whole time." She still was.

If there was one thing Haddie had never imagined on her best friend bingo card, it was holding the skirt of Emma's dress above both of their heads while the bride relieved herself in the tiny bathroom inside Mrs. Pinkney's sweet shop.

"Oh. My. *God*. That felt so good!" Emma exclaimed as Haddie struggled under the weight of the skirt. "I should probably cool it on the sparkling grape juice." Emma stood and flushed, then reached past Haddie to open the stall door so Haddie could back out and carefully lower the dress back to the floor.

Haddie stared at the wedding band now stacked with Emma's engagement ring and sniffled.

"You and Matteo are *married*, Ems."

Emma finished washing and drying her hands before meeting Haddie's gaze.

"Hads? Oh my god, are you crying?"

Haddie swiped a finger under her eye, and it came away wet. She let loose a tear-soaked laugh. "I feel like I don't do anything else these days!" She laughed...or maybe cried...some more and then attempted to clean herself up before heading back out to what was officially the best block party she'd ever been to.

"Hads...?" Emma asked, more tentative this time. "Are you okay?"

Haddie nodded with a sad smile. "Thanks for having me and Levi walk down the aisle solo tonight instead of...you know..." She sighed. "Can I tell you something?"

"Anything," Emma replied.

"Do you know why I refer to my grandmother as my grandmonster?"

Emma shook her head, and Haddie sniffled.

"Because if I thought of her as this horrible monster incapable of love instead of a woman who just didn't know how to grieve her own daughter while taking care of her spitting image, then I wouldn't feel so…impossible to love."

Emma cupped Haddie's cheeks in her palms. "Oh, honey." Tears pooled in her friend's eyes. "You are, without a doubt, the most lovable human I know. I am willing to bet the deed to this entire town that your grandma loved you so much and died hoping that even if she failed to show it, that you somehow knew."

Haddie hiccupped. "It hurts so much to be left," she admitted. "God…it's the fucking worst."

Emma nodded. "You get that even though I moved away, I didn't leave you, right? No matter where we are physically, I'm never *leaving* you."

Haddie blew out a long breath and nodded. "I'm starting to get that, I think. But Levi is *leaving* leaving. Like in all senses of the word."

Emma nodded, and even though her friend was stunning in her dress with that unmistakable wedding glow, Haddie couldn't help but smile when she gazed up to the bride's crystal-beaded tiara that boasted two tiny, pointy cat ears.

"You are so unabashedly yourself, Ems. I love that about you."

"Why, thank you," she replied with a small curtsy. "You know, I was thinking… You could ask Levi to stay." She shrugged like she'd just suggested that Haddie grab a carton of milk on the way home.

Haddie shrugged. "I signed the petition."

Emma narrowed her eyes.

"What?" Haddie asked. "Am I supposed to ask him to give up his career after he told me he loved me, and I walked out the door and ghosted him for weeks?"

Emma raised her brows. "What if that was all he wanted, Hads? To be asked? For you to chase him a little? He sure as hell tried to chase you with all those unanswered texts."

Haddie flinched. "I don't chase, Ems. That's how I stay safe."

Emma laughed and grabbed her friend's hands, giving them a reassuring squeeze. "Oh, honey. You chased *me*. And I don't mean to Summertown, though I'm super happy that's how it all played out. But even back in Chicago when I would have been content with the little hermit life I'd built for myself, *you* wouldn't let me. And your grandmother? You went to her assisted living facility for every FIFA Women's International game that was broadcast in the United States because *she* loved the game. She's the reason you fell in love with soccer in the first place. You chased her love or her connection or *something*, Hads. And it's okay to admit that, even if your relationship was strained."

Haddie squeezed Emma's hands back. "I thought it would hurt less if I didn't admit that I loved her." If she didn't admit that she loved Levi. But it still hurt. *So* much.

Emma sniffled, then blinked wildly. "You're going to make my mascara run, but you know what? I really like this new, vulnerable Haddie."

Haddie laughed. "I'll remind you of that a week from now after calling you each night of your honeymoon as I sob through all my new feelings."

"I'd answer every time," Emma replied without missing a beat, and Haddie believed that she would.

"Should we go back out there?" Haddie asked. "I think I'm supposed to give a speech or something."

Emma's face lit up with the all-consuming type of joy reserved only for someone who just realized she was about to go greet her new husband again. Then she nodded, and Haddie squared her shoulders and led her friend back outside.

She'd felt her feelings, and her heart still ached. But she would also be okay. Eventually. Because the more she let Emma in, the less she'd be alone. And maybe the same would be true for other people who entered her life, if she could just be brave enough to let them in too.

CHAPTER 29

Um…excuse me, everyone. I know you'd rather continue dancing in the middle of the square or enjoying the delicious food prepared by the Woods Family Inn, but you're going to have to pause for just a few minutes to let me steal the spotlight from the bride. My name is Haddie Martin. I'm the maid of honor, and I'd like to say a few things to Emma and Matteo."

Levi dropped the meatball on a toothpick he'd been twirling around his plate, his head jerking in the direction of the square. There, standing in the parklike area of the town's main square, beneath fairy lights that had been strung from the branches of last summer's newly planted trees, stood the woman who'd eluded him all night—and for the past four weeks.

He abandoned his plate on top of a trash can where many others were piled and weaved between various high- and low-top tables peppered along the sidewalks and barricaded streets until he was standing on the perimeter of the square, close enough to see that the whites of Haddie's eyes were tinted pink as if she'd just been crying.

"As many of you know…" she continued, "Emma and Matteo's story began long before I met either of them, but I like to think that I'm the reason for them finding love a second time around. I say this because I was present when it happened, and therefore it must have something to do with me."

She grinned, and Levi found himself laughing along with many others around him.

"Actually," she continued, "I have always been quite the skeptic when it comes to matters of the heart. But Emma and Matteo, and many other wonderful people I've met since moving to this town, have made me question my beliefs…and quite possibly all my life choices."

More laughter burbled through the crowd, but Levi's chest grew tight. Was Haddie being self-deprecating for the purpose of the speech, or did he dare to hope there might be an admission hiding between the lines?

"Happily ever afters are alive and well in Summertown, everyone. And nothing makes me happier than being able to raise a glass to two people who deserve the overflowing joy they're experiencing tonight." She lifted her champagne flute, and everybody else did the same. "Ems…Matteo…may the rest of your life continue to overflow. I love you."

Applause, cheers, and several *Awes* rang out. Then silverware chimed against crystal as wedding guests insisted the bride and groom kiss, which they were more than happy to do.

"And now…the best man….brother of the groom…Levi Rourke." Haddie set the microphone down on a stool that had been next to her, but before she walked away, she looked directly at Levi as if she'd known exactly where he was for the entirety of her speech. She gave him a soft smile, and everything inside him lit up like a thousand fireflies illuminating a summer sky.

He wanted to follow wherever she went, wanting anything other than taking his eyes off of her and losing her once more in the crowd. But he was next at the mic, and the one thing he would not do tonight or ever again was disappoint his brother.

So Levi made his way to the center of the square, swiping his own flute of champagne from where several were lined up for the taking along the outdoor bar and lifting the microphone that had just been in Haddie's hand. He shivered from the inside out, imagining—remembering—her touch. Then he cleared his throat and pulled out his phone, not wanting to forget a single word.

"Good evening, everyone. I'm Levi, the groom's older brother. You might know me from such things as growing up in this town, playing ball for the Muskies, and quite recently from a little mishap that was lucky enough to make it onto national television." Unlike Haddie, Levi's attempt at levity only earned him a few uncomfortable laughs. "I'd say you were a tough crowd, but you're right. I shouldn't make light of the things I've done that I'm not proud of. None of us should. But here's the thing. I'm not the guy I was ten, fifteen years ago. Hell, I'm not the guy I was ten, fifteen weeks ago.

"Truth is, I look at the second chances at love bestowed upon my brother and Emma…" He glanced to where his brother and sister-in-law stood hand in hand on the opposite end of the square. "Upon my father and his new fiancée." He gave his dad and Tilly a nod. "And I think about how much their stories have changed in the span of the years we've all been stumbling around this town or country or planet. None of us are the people we've always been. We aren't the mistakes we've made or the losses we've endured. Those things are a part of all of us, but they aren't the whole story."

He scanned the crowd for Haddie but of course couldn't find her. "Someone once told me," he continued, "not to let others tell you someone else's story. So I'm not going to tell you Emma and Matteo's or my father's—or anyone's story, for that matter. What I will say is that we cannot rewrite the chapters we've already lived. But the ones not yet written are so full of possibility, and I cannot wait to see what my brother and Emma—now my sister—write next." He held his glass high. "To Emma and Matteo and the best parts of the story yet to come. Cheers."

He saw Emma swipe a tear from under her eye and caught his brother mouthing the words *Thank you*, and Levi knew that his whole family's story still had so many more good chapters to come, even if he had to live them without Haddie.

When an hour had passed and Levi swore he'd scanned every face in the crowd, had peered into every possible nook and cranny of the closed-down square, he finally gave up and made his way to the pop-up bar in front of the town hall.

He was opening his mouth to order something strong when a voice from behind interrupted before he could.

"I'll have whatever he's having," she said, and for a moment,

Levi lost the ability to speak or move or pretty much anything. Because if he turned to face her and it *wasn't* Haddie, he was pretty sure his heart would turn to dust and he'd basically disintegrate along with it. If he turned and it *was* Haddie, then what? He got his hopes up and she got scared and bailed again?

"He hasn't ordered yet," the bartender said.

"Then I'll order for both of us," she told him. "Two old-fashioneds."

"An extra cherry in hers," Levi added, finally finding his voice.

The bartender nodded and got to work mixing their drinks.

When she didn't say anything else, Levi decided he couldn't take the silence any longer, so he turned slowly until he caught the familiar shade of green in the corner of his eye. And then, there she was...holding at least ten Toblerones.

He barked out an unexpected laugh.

"I never paid you back," Haddie told him, her voice wobbling.

Levi shook his head. "I only gave you two."

She bit her bottom lip like she was trying not to smile, like she was as terrified as he was to take the next step in whatever this reconnecting was.

"Two old-fashioneds," the bartender announced. "With an extra cherry for the lady." Levi grabbed both of the tumblers and nodded for Haddie to follow him to an empty table several feet away.

He set their drinks down and then reached for the Toblerones. "You look ridiculous holding all of those. And there is a whole table full of Mrs. Pinkney's homemade sweets. I don't want to insult her."

But Haddie hugged them closer to her chest. "Not until I say something first," she told him.

Levi gave her a slight bow. "The floor is yours, Birthday Girl."

She jutted out her chin. "Thank you, Mr. Tux." Then she took a steadying breath. "You might be good at petitions, but I'm good at lists. So this is my list of ten reasons why…um…you should stay. In Summertown."

Levi's heart leaped into his throat, and it took everything in him not to just blurt out what he'd been trying to tell her all night. Not when Haddie was finally letting him in.

She blew out a breath and set the first candy bar on the table. "One… Your family is here." She deposited bar number two. "Two… Rumor has it you are kind of a local football legend, which means you'd probably get the all-star treatment if you moved back home."

The corner of his mouth twitched.

"Three…" she continued. "You look really good in Muskie purple." She paused to look him up and down. "And also tuxedos. You should wear them more often."

Levi laughed, and Haddie continued.

"Four… Your best friend is here, and he calls you Five-Oh-One, and you should never be too far from someone who gives you a great nickname." She paused, swallowed, and blinked a few times before setting down Toblerone number five. "Your students and colleagues care about you so much that they signed a petition for you to stay, and while I haven't had the privilege of seeing you in the classroom yet, that's all I need to know that you're a great teacher." Bar number six. "Six, you are also an amazing coach, no matter the sport, and those students don't want you to leave either.

"Seven… You have put so much work into your team, which I think means you love them as much as they love you, and so I'm guessing you'll probably miss them if you leave. And I know you probably also miss the team you were forced to leave, but I can't help thinking that your connection with your students here hits different. But… I digress."

She dropped the eighth Toblerone. "Eight… I asked Tommy about the budget proposal for the school board, and he told me it was all your idea." She sniffled. "You went against Coach Crawford for these kids, which kind of piggybacks on number seven, so… See the footnotes for that one." She tossed the last two bars onto the table, but tears were suddenly streaming down her face. "Nine and…" She hiccupped. "Nine and…" But she couldn't get the words out. She fished her phone from some secret compartment in her dress and started hammering away at the screen while simultaneously swiping at her falling tears.

Levi wanted to reach for her, but before he could, his own phone vibrated in his pocket.

She looked up at him with a teary smile and nodded toward the phone now in his hand.

Birthday Girl: 9. I love you, and I would really, really miss you if you left. But also, 10. If getting your football coaching job back is really your dream, then I will support you 100 percent. And I will fight for us even if it scares the hell out of me that I could one day lose you because it turns out that being without you is just as scary.

He dropped his phone on the table and stepped toward her, his hands cradling her tear-streaked cheeks. "Haddie, I sent Chancellor Barnes my resignation two weeks ago." He swallowed. "And letters to every player on my team thanking them for their hard work, apologizing for my reckless behavior, and promising to do better with my new team."

Her breath hitched in her throat. "Your new team? You're... you're staying?"

He nodded. "I'm staying." His hands were shaking. "You... love me?"

She let out something between a laugh and a sob but nodded her head too. "I love you."

He brushed his thumbs softly over her cheeks, catching the falling tears he still couldn't believe she was shedding for him. "I'm going to kiss you now. Okay, Birthday Girl?"

Her teeth skimmed over her bottom lip, and she finally, *finally* smiled. "Okay, Mr. Tux," she told him. "You can kiss me."

And then, with a light, tentative, careful brush of his lips over hers, he did.

Despite their many starts and stops, kissing Haddie now felt like kissing someone brand-new and also like they'd fit together like this for years.

"Come home, Haddie," he whispered against her, and he felt her lips part into a smile.

She clasped her hands around his neck and pulled him closer. "I'm already there," she told him.

Yeah. Come to think of it, Levi was too.

EPILOGUE

It's winter break," Haddie told him. "Why do we have to do it now?"

Levi held the main door to Summertown Elementary open, shooing her inside before anyone saw them.

"Because I want it to be the first thing your students see when they get back from the holidays, and I kind of need you to see it too." He kissed her on the cheek and the shooed her again, this time toward her hallway. "Come on… If Coach Crawford finds out I swiped his key ring at the Crawford Christmas party, it's not going to matter if he finds out about us. I will be toast."

Haddie snorted, then covered her mouth with one hand while holding tight to the rolled-up piece of poster board under her other arm. "He and the board agreed to the activity fees and communal fund. I think it's safe to say you're his golden child again."

Levi shrugged but a smile spread across his beautiful face. "I'm just happy he named Tommy the director of athletics and activities. There is no one better to make sure the new way of doing things runs smoothly."

In the months since the wedding, Haddie had never seen Levi so happy as he was at—of all places—a school board meeting where Principal Crawford not only let a petition change his mind about running his ship the way he'd always run it, but also gave his son the much deserved honor of helping him navigate new waters.

They reached Haddie's classroom door, and she retrieved her own key ring from her coat pocket to unlock it. But her hands were still cold from the crisp December evening, and she fumbled the retrieval, dropping the keys to the floor with a metallic clang that sounded so much louder in the silent, vacant school.

A light flicked on across the hall in the main office, and Haddie and Levi froze when Principal Crawford appeared in the doorway.

"How did you two get in here?" he asked, striding toward them with his arms crossed over a Muskies hoodie that he wore with matching sweatpants.

Haddie picked her keys up while stammering, "We were just... I mean, Levi wanted to... See, I have this poster..."

Levi, on the other hand, still stood like an ice sculpture. Haddie wasn't even sure he was blinking.

"He can see you," she stage-whispered. "You're not fooling anyone."

To her surprise—and she hoped Levi's too—the older man laughed.

"Do you kids think I don't know you've been swiping my keys for the past fifteen years or more?" He clapped Levi on the shoulder. "And I see you've gone and gotten yourselves entangled even after I warned you against it."

Levi swallowed and finally showed signs of life by nodding.

"We're not entangled, sir. Just...um...in love," Levi told him, and Haddie swore she fell for him again in that very moment.

"And you're breaking into school because...?"

"Not breaking, sir," Levi continued. "We used your keys."

Haddie winced. "Oh, Babe, you are just digging us deeper."

Coach Crawford held out his hand. "Keys, Rourke."

Levi produced the school's master key ring.

"How long has this been going on?" he asked them both, and Haddie tried to beat Levi to the punch, but he couldn't *stop* talking now.

"Since the beginning, sir. I fell for her the night I met her at the same hotel where Tommy had his wedding."

Haddie's heart both leaped and sank as she realized how utterly romantic that was but also—sadly and adorably—stupid to admit because it sealed their fates.

Coach Crawford gave them both a self-satisfied grin. "I don't think I'd ever see you smile as much as you did when you met her at the bar, Rourke. Happiest I'd seen you in more than ten years." He jingled the keys in his hand and then tucked them away in the kangaroo pocket of his hoodie. "Took you long enough to get your acts together, though, and take the plunge, right?" He nodded toward Haddie's classroom while they both stared at the man, speechless. "Ten minutes. After that, I'm giving Deputy Hayes the go-ahead to drive by and see if the lights are still on. If they are, you might get to spend the night in closer quarters than that little apartment of yours."

He spun on his heel and strode back toward his office, but he passed right by it and kept on strolling out the main entrance.

"What the hell just happened?" Haddie asked.

"Did Coach Crawford just admit to playing matchmaker when I thought the guy was going to fire me?"

"But…" Haddie blurted out. "I don't get… I mean, did he really…?"

Levi shrugged. "Let's not waste time trying to figure out anyone in this town, least of all Thomas Crawford the First. We've only got about nine minutes unless you want to call his bluff on whether or not we're sleeping in the town jail."

Haddie shook her head. "I want our bed."

"I want you naked in our bed," Levi added.

"Is there any other way?" she teased and then finally opened her classroom door.

"Would you like to do the honors?" Haddie asked, pointing to her first-day-of-school All About Me poster.

"With pleasure," he told her, then strode right toward the piece of posterboard that did *not* have a picture of him on it and tore it off the wall in one strategic yank.

"Wow," Haddie remarked. "You really hated that poster, huh?"

He rolled it up and dropped it into the nearest trash can. "I really did. But your new one is the best piece of art I've ever seen."

Haddie shook her head and laughed as she unrolled and hung the *art* in question, which was still populated by stick figures representing Haddie's students, her team, Matteo and Emma, but with a few additions. Every one of her favorite people in Summertown now stood under a giant rainbow. Above the rainbow she'd drawn two birds to represent her mom and grandmother. And in the center of it all, between her students and her team, right beside Emma and Matteo, she'd drawn a giant heart, inside of which she'd placed a large decal of the Summertown mascot, Muskie. Except she'd taken a silver Sharpie and added a number to Muskie's jersey. Twenty-three.

"The fish is me, right?" Levi asked, for like the fiftieth time that day.

"The fish is you," she confirmed with only a slight eye roll because Haddie would never truly tire of Levi wanting to hear that he was loved, nor would she ever tire of letting him know how much he was.

He slid his arms around her waist and pulled her close. "Because I'm one of your favorite people," he added.

Haddie nodded. "One of my most favorite," she admitted. "And you're right. This is much more appropriate than the coaches calendar."

Levi groaned and let his forehead fall against hers. "Does it have to hang in the bathroom?"

Haddie laughed and kissed his nose. "Not if you let me put it on the ceiling so waxed and oiled-up Levi is the last thing I see before I close my eyes at night and the first thing I see when I wake up in the morning."

He tilted his head back and narrowed his eyes at her. "Sometimes I think you love waxed and oiled-up Levi more than me."

She clapped her hands gently on his cheeks and brushed her lips over his. "I love every single version of you, Mr. Tux." She felt his cheeks warm beneath her touch. "But this one right here…" She kissed him again. "Is my favoritest of all the favorites." This time she kissed him longer, slower, her lips lingering on his even when she paused to add, "You always were, even before you officially made it onto the poster."

"I knew it," he whispered.

"You did not," she teased.

He ran his hands up her back, and even through her coat she could feel her skin prickle with goose bumps at his touch. Then he slowly dipped her back so far she had to clasp her hands around his neck to hang on.

"I knew it," he said again, then kissed her with so much love that Haddie felt the final, trickiest, most stubborn lock inside her chest open to finally set her heart free.

"Okay," she relented. "You knew it."

And what did Haddie know? She knew that loving this man was as wonderful as it was terrifying and as beautiful as it would be—at times—disastrous. But she also knew that for every down there would be an up, and for every fear there was also the security in knowing that they would fight for each other time and again and that neither of them would run.

"Oh my god," Haddie whispered, and Levi smiled against her.

"I know, right? I am, like, rom-com-level swoon right now, aren't I?"

"No!" She tapped his shoulder and pointed out her window toward the front of the school where flashing red and blue lights illuminated the circle drive.

"How many minutes have we been here?" Levi asked.

"More than ten, I'm guessing." Haddie grabbed his hand and gave it a sharp tug. "Run!"

Okay. Fine. Maybe just this once…

ACKNOWLEDGMENTS

First, if you got this far and you're still reading, thank you! That means you made it all the way to the happily ever after and thought, "I'd like to know more!" Writing a book, for much of the time, is such a solitary endeavor. Even now as I'm working on copyedits (thank you Diane, India, and Jocelyn for all your hard work!), I'm doing it alone, on my couch, fighting off a cat who thinks a lap is a lap regardless of whether a laptop is on said lap. This is all just to say that while it sometimes feels like a lonesome path getting a book from idea to shelf, I couldn't do it without such a wonderful team of people supporting me every step of the way.

Thank you to my editor, Deb Werksman, for championing me and this book even when it got tough, and boy did it! Same goes for my agent, Emily, who—despite all the wild ideas I come up with—is always in my corner.

Thank you, readers, for continuing to let me do this thing I love. Thanks to my friends who put up with my "I can't be social until after deadline" antics. Thanks to my daughter for putting my books face out every time you walk into a bookstore and to my son for getting pumped about book releases even if HEAs aren't your thing...yet.

And to Ted Lasso—that's right, I'm thanking a fictional character—for inspiring Levi and for teaching us that joy is possible even when life makes it seem otherwise. Believe.

ABOUT THE AUTHOR

A corporate trainer by day and *USA Today* bestselling author by night, A. J. Pine can't seem to escape the world of fiction, and she wouldn't have it any other way. When she finds that twenty-fifth hour in the day, she might indulge in a tiny bit of TV to nourish her undying love of K-dramas, superheroes, and everything romance. She hails from the far-off galaxy of the Chicago suburbs.

Website: ajpine.com
Facebook: AJPineAuthor
Instagram: @aj_pine
TikTok: @aj_pine

ALSO BY A. J. PINE

THE MURPHYS OF MEADOW VALLEY

Holding Out for a Cowboy

Finally Found My Cowboy

The Cowboy of My Dreams

HEART OF SUMMERTOWN

The Second Chance Garden